#NERD

The Hashtag Series #1

by Cambria Hebert

Published by: Cambria Hebert Books, LLC

http://www.cambriahebert.com

Interior design and typesetting by Sharon Kay
Cover design by MAE I DESIGN
Edited by Cassie McCown

Paperback ISBN: 978-1-938857-62-1

DEDICATION

To all the #Nerds out there.

And for anyone who's ever loved one.

#NERD

CHAPTER ONE

Football season is in full swing here at ALPHA U. Buckle Up, ladies, #24 is about to take this season for a ride.

...Alpha BuzzFeed

RIMMEL

Being nervous was stupid.

I wasn't a stupid person; even still, I couldn't shake the nerves coiling in the pit of my stomach like a cornered poisonous snake. The paper clutched in my hand trembled like the coloring leaves that dotted the trees outside in the cool autumn air.

I didn't want to be here. I'd probably rather be anywhere else. But the choice wasn't mine today. In fact, it wasn't going to be between the hours of five and seven p.m. on Monday, Wednesday, and Friday for the foreseeable future.

Saying no wasn't an option. This "job" was presented to me as something I had to do to keep my scholarship. Considering none of the other scholarship recipients (that I knew) were practically ordered to tutor struggling students, I wondered if this really was a requirement.

Not like I would say anything, though. I hated confrontation; it made my stomach hurt. And I certainly wasn't going to argue with the dean over what I needed to do to keep my free ride. So I agreed. It was only a few hours a week, right? And I'd get points for doing a good deed.

Inwardly, I cringed.

Everyone knows the nice guy always finishes last.

Once I was good and committed to the tutoring, I was given a sheet of paper—the same sheet I was now crushing in my nervous hand—with a list of the subjects the student needed help with. Math, English, and history.

Geez, it was like half this person's schedule. Did they do no studying on their own?

Then I saw the name.

* * *

There it was, typed neatly at the top of the paper, right there in black and white. It appeared so simple, just letters arranged in a row. I remember being slightly shocked the second I read his name that fireworks didn't appear overhead and the marching band didn't storm through the hall, playing the university's fight song.

"You want me to tutor Roman Anderson?" I'd squeaked, and the pathetic sound reminded me of the nickname my nervously high voice had earned me in high school.

Mouse.

But this wasn't high school, and I didn't squeak anymore. Okay, not much.

"Is there a problem with that?" the dean had asked, choosing to ignore my shock.

Yes! He's like way out of my league. I cleared my throat again just to be sure my voice was normal when I spoke. "I guess I'm just surprised he needs a tutor." There was no reason to even pretend I didn't know exactly who he was.

Everyone knew Romeo.

"Being the incredible athlete that he is, football takes up a great deal of his time. We thought it would be best if he had some additional help with his academics," the dean replied.

"We?" I asked.

"Myself and the coach."

Ahhh.

So basically, Mr. Perfect was failing, and the school was freaking out because it was football season and they needed their best player and crowd drawer on the field. And who better to stick with the job? The scholarship girl with the perfect average. The girl with no life.

And so here I was sitting at a table in the university library, waiting on Mr. Perfect. I glanced at the watch fastened around my wrist. Then I checked the time against the large clock hanging on the wall. The times matched up.

Romeo was late.

Romeo, Romeo, wherefore art thou, Romeo…

I snorted. It was so loud it startled a girl at a nearby table. She jerked back in her seat, causing her chair to teeter dangerously backward and hover over the ground. I watched as she grappled for the table ledge, her hands grasping instead to the thick book open before her.

The book wasn't a good anchor.

She yanked it right off the table as her chair barreled toward the ground. The chair, the girl, and the book made quite the clatter when they hit the ground. Everyone in the general area turned to stare.

You know you're a clumsy person when you cause *other* people to fall down.

I started to get up, to help her, but the daggers she shot out of her eyes froze me in my tracks. I sat back down. Her face was flaming red as she huffed to her feet and packed up her stuff. Before storming off, she picked up the large book, and I had a sudden vision of her swinging it at my head.

Instead, she wrapped her arms around it and glared at me again.

"Sorry," I whispered.

If her stomps to the other side of the library were any indication, I was pretty sure I wasn't forgiven.

Well, that was eventful.

And a waste of time. I glanced at my watch again and wondered if I would get out of tutoring if he didn't bother showing up.

Since I was already here, I figured I could at least do some of my work, so I bent down to retrieve my notebook out of my bag. When I sat up, I saw him.

He was standing just inside the glass doors that led outside. His shaggy blond hair was darker than usual because it looked damp. The ends of his hair curled up at the base of his neck, above the collar of his jacket. A navy-blue backpack was slung over one of his shoulders and his insanely large hand was curled around the strap, holding it in place.

Romeo was tall, well over six feet, with broad shoulders that tapered into a narrow waist. He wasn't a bulky guy; he played too many sports for that. But even so, it was obvious his body was all muscle.

He was looking around, his blue eyes sweeping the room, likely looking for his tutor. I felt my cheeks heat when he glanced my way, and I ducked my head. But then I realized this wasn't the time to be shy. I needed to tell him I was his tutor.

Holy hell, I was going to get to talk to him! Embarrassment burned the back of my throat. Talking to guys wasn't something I did very often.

I looked back up to wave at him, but Romeo had already looked away. I wasn't surprised. I wasn't very noticeable. I wasn't the kind of girl that drew eyes and held a stare.

I watched him another minute as he looked over his shoulder at the tables on the other side of the room. The girl who fell out of her chair was watching him, her eyes eating up his face.

Could she be any more obvious?

Romeo caught her looking and his mouth pulled into a slow smile. I bit the inside of my lip as little butterflies fluttered around my stomach. He wasn't even looking at me with that charming half smile and I was affected.

Ugh.

I didn't have time for this.

I snatched the paper with his name and information off the table and marched toward him. Halfway there, I collided with the corner of an empty table and the unforgiving edge jammed into my hipbone. In the center of the table was a cup filled with pens and pencils and the force of impact knocked it over.

Writing utensils rolled across the wooden surface and some rained down onto the floor.

Sharp pain burned through my hip and I drew back, fighting the urge to double over as I rubbed the sore spot.

That was going to leave a bruise.

Doing my best to ignore the pain, I walked around the table to where the pencils were scattered on the floor. Bending down, I began scooping them up with my hand.

One pencil had rolled farther away than the others, and I had to stretch my arm all the way out to reach for it. Just as I was about to snatch it up, two overly large feet wearing a pair of Nikes appeared right beside it.

I pushed my glasses up on my nose and followed a pair of jean-clad legs all the way up, past the familiar jacket, to full lips and a chiseled face.

"Need a hand?" he said, tipping up the corner of his lips. Amusement sparked in his jewel-like blue eyes.

I opened my mouth to reply, but no sound came out. I tried again.

A little squeak escaped instead of actual words. I slapped my lips together and went back to collecting pencils.

And this was why I preferred animals to people. So much easier to talk to.

A rich chuckle floated over my head and my cheeks heated even more. At this point, I wouldn't be surprised if my hair caught on fire from the force of my embarrassment.

He crouched down and reached for the rogue pencil the same time I did. Our fingers collided.

Electricity jolted through my hand and bolted up my arm. Shocked, I gasped and fell back. All the pencils in my hand clattered on the floor around me.

Romeo gave me an odd look and then picked up everything in like three seconds flat.

I guess having large hands like that is useful.

When I realized I was just sitting on the floor like a complete weirdo, I scrambled to my feet and looked at him. He was already turning away.

"Wait," I said.

He glanced at me again.

I held up the severely wrinkled paper. “I’m your tutor.”

The doubt in his eyes kind of made me mad. Did he think I wasn’t smart enough to tutor him?

“See,” I demanded, shoving the paper in the space between us.

That half-smile thing he did resurfaced, and he took the paper out of my grasp. “What’d this paper ever do to you?” he said, taking in its crumpled appearance.

I scowled. For starters, it was forcing me to talk to him.

He sighed and I thought he muttered something beneath his breath, but I couldn’t hear what it was. “All right, then, Teach,” he said, motioning for me to take the lead. “Let’s get this over with.”

Obviously, he didn’t want to be here.

That made two of us.

CHAPTER TWO

The elite are picking new members! Get ready for rush! #FratParties #GetReadyForRush

... Alpha BuzzFeed

ROMEO

The sounds of the locker room were always the same. Laughter, catcalls, and men ribbing each other rose above the sound of the showers running in the back. The air was humid from the constant running water, and the scent of sweaty jerseys permeated the room.

Basically, it was home.

I was one of the last ones off the field tonight and most everyone else was already out of their uniform as I walked through the room toward my locker. A couple damp towels snapped me on the ass as I went by, and I promised revenge later.

Laughing, I swung open my locker door and turned just in time to see something fall out and land near my feet.

What the hell?

The sounds of the room faded to the background as I picked up the cream-colored envelope with a black wax seal on the back. My pulse picked up when I recognized the crest in the seal.

Inside was a matching cream-colored card, completely blank on the outside. I lifted the bottom to reveal the inside.

TONIGHT.

That's all it said. No signature. No other writing. Just one word.

But I knew what it meant.

I grinned and gave a loud whoop. A couple of the guys echoed the sound. Beside me, my teammate and friend Braeden leaned in to look at the card.

"Aww, shit," he said and slapped me on the back. "You're in, dude."

I held up my fist so we could pound it out. "Hells yeah," I said.

"You know Alpha Omega is like the most exclusive frat on this campus," he said, reaching into his locker to pull out a T-shirt.

Everybody knew that. It's one of the reasons I wanted in so bad. I didn't think it would happen, because last year—my freshman year—I didn't get in. That had been a bitter pill to swallow because my father and grandfather had both been members.

I never did find out why they never let me in, but obviously, whatever it was didn't matter now.

This was the opening I needed. From here I knew I could make it in.

"Congrats, man," Braeden said, slamming his locker door closed.

"Anderson!" Coach yelled from the door of his office. "Get your pansy ass in here!"

The usual *oohs* and *awws* followed me as I walked into the office and Coach slammed the door. "There a problem, Coach?" I asked.

"Your grades suck, Anderson," he said, blunt.

"It's only the first month of the semester," I argued, even though yeah, my grades sucked.

"Last year you were points away from getting kicked off the team." He leveled me with a harsh stare. "I've already spoken to your professors. You're already headed down the same path this semester."

I sat in the chair near his desk. "It's hard to find time to study with all the practicing I do," I hedged. It wasn't exactly a lie. I got up early to work out, then fueled up, went to classes, and then had football practice for several hours each day. And some days we had more than one practice.

"I hear you're rushing Alpha Omega."

How the hell did he find that out so fast? I'd only just gotten the note.

He looked as if he'd smelled a bad fart. "You're my star player. I know exactly what you're up to."

"I—" I started to make some excuse, but he held up his hand and sighed.

"I get it, Anderson. School sucks. You're here to play football and chase women."

I grinned.

"I was your age once. But the hard truth is you can't play if your grades don't come up."

That wiped the smile right off my face. "But, Coach." I sat forward in my chair, ready to beg. Football was my life.

"Relax," he intoned. "You're still on the team. You're still starting, and I intend to keep it that way."

I didn't like the sound of that.

"You now have a personal tutor. You'll meet in the library every Monday, Wednesday, and Friday for two hours after practice."

"Two hours!" Holy shit, that was brutal.

"I mean it, Anderson. The team needs you. You're the best player we have, and the dean wants a championship this year."

I wanted a championship too. It would draw in the NFL scouts. The NFL was my endgame. Hell, it was my *only* game.

"Fine," I muttered. This was going to suck.

"You start tonight," Coach added, then pointed at his door for me to get out.

The locker room was emptying out when I opened up my locker again. Braeden sat there with his duffle at his feet, waiting for me. "What'd Coach say?" he asked.

"I have to get a tutor," I muttered.

Braeden laughed. "Have fun with that," he said and stood. His laughter drifted behind him as he left.

Fun? Yeah right. Not bloody likely.

By the time I was showered and changed, everyone else was gone. I threw all my gear into my locker and grabbed my backpack, heading for the library. I was starving, and as I walked, I scarfed down a protein bar.

The library wasn't a place I visited very often, and when I stepped inside, I realized Coach hadn't even told me the name of my tutor. I looked around for someone who looked like they might be meeting someone else, and my eyes landed on a hot chick sitting near the back. Her blond hair brushed the low cut collar of her top. When she saw me looking, she leaned over a little more and gave me the perfect view of her cleavage.

Nice.

Maybe she was my tutor. Maybe two hours in the library wouldn't be that bad. I was just about to head over there and ask her if she was waiting for me when I heard some commotion behind me.

A cup of pens and pencils had fallen off a nearby table and some girl was rushing around to pick them up. I couldn't even see her face because of the mess of dark hair falling around it. She didn't look very big and was dressed in a baggy sweater that made checking out her body impossible. The way she scrambled around and kept her head down told me she probably spent a lot of time in this place.

I glanced back at the girl with the awesome tits, and she smiled. But when my feet moved, it wasn't in her direction. Instead, I found myself towering over the pencil girl.

When she saw me, her entire body stilled. I watched as she took in my legs and tilted her head all the way back to stare up at my face.

Tangles of dark hair hid most of her features and covered her shoulders. I wondered if she'd combed it at all this week. Her skin was pale and she was wearing a pair of black-framed glasses that could have been my grandma's. Her face was clearly makeup free and her pink lips didn't shimmer with any kind of gloss.

"You need a hand?" I asked. All she was missing was some of that white tape in the center of her glasses.

Her cheeks turned bright pink and sound erupted from between her lips. Poor girl. She was so incredibly awkward. I couldn't help but laugh at the look on her face. It was almost like she'd never had a conversation with anyone before.

We reached for the pencil by my feet at the same time. Our fingers bumped together, and she jerked back like she'd been shot. She fell backwards onto her butt, and the pencils she'd been gathering spread across the floor again.

Geez, this girl was a disaster.

I picked up everything I could find and straightened to dump them all in the cup. I thought about bending down to help her up, but judging by her reaction when we'd accidentally touched, I figured it wasn't a good idea. Besides, I had a hot tutor waiting for me.

"Wait." Her voice was small when she called out behind me. Something about it speared my chest, and I turned.

"I'm your tutor," she said.

What? No. There was no way in hell Coach would hire this meek little… *nerd* to tutor me.

Oh yes, he would, a voice in the back of my head taunted.

"See," the girl demanded and shoved a crumpled paper at me. It was my schedule and the courses I needed help with. At the top was my name.

"What'd this paper ever do to you?" I teased her.

She scowled. I guess nerds didn't like to joke around. This was going to be worse than I thought. "Thanks a helluva lot, Coach," I muttered.

I glanced back at the girl. She was short, didn't even come to my shoulder. Her hair hid most of her, and what it didn't, the god-awful sweater she was wearing did. It hung all the way to her knees and was brown, making it look like a sack. She pushed up the glasses on her nose again, her slight fingers poking out from her too-long sleeves.

I guess it could be worse.

She could smell.

"All right, then, Teach," I said, resolved to my tutoring future, and pointed for her to lead me to her table. "Let's get this over with."

If being tutored by her was what I had to do to stay on the team, then that's exactly what I was going to do.

CHAPTER THREE

Rally Up! Friday night when darkness falls. See and be seen. #BYOB

... Alpha BuzzFeed

RIMMEL

Romeo had the attention span of a slice of bread.

Which is none at all.

Every time I started to explain something, it's like not only his eyes glazed over, but his entire body. At one point, I wondered if it were possible for him to be asleep with his eyes open.

And God, he smelled good.

It was a clean scent, like soap, the kind of soap that probably costs five dollars a bar. It was a thick scent, but it wasn't heavy. Every time he fidgeted in the chair, a cloud of it would waft over me and I would inhale just a little deeper.

The way the ends of his damp hair curled up around the collar of his jacket made it hard to keep my eyes trained on the paper. Clearly, he had just showered. He probably didn't always smell this good. Most guys were stinky… weren't they?

Truth was I had no idea. This was the closest I had gotten to a guy since high school, and even then that was limited mostly to the guys who sat around me in class and Nick, my childhood friend.

Nick never smelled like this.

Focus, Rimmel. I scolded myself. I couldn't very well criticize him for his lack of attention when I was sitting over here sniffing the air.

"Hey," I said, tapping my pencil on the notebook in front of us. "You're supposed to be paying attention."

Romeo was doing some kind of trick or something with the pen in his right hand, somehow passing it through all his fingers. Back and forth, back and forth.

I snatched it and slapped it on the table. "I think that little trick is using up all your concentration."

He laughed, his straight white teeth flashing at me. "Sorry." His tone was sheepish and he leaned forward, placing both his elbows on the table, and looked at the notebook. "I'm listening."

When he moved, his arm brushed against mine, and I jerked back, feeling my cheeks heat. He gave me an odd look, but I ignored him and focused back on the paper.

"Okay, so for this assignment…" I began.

He interrupted, sliding his chair back from the table. "Hang on a second," he said, not really looking to see if I was indeed going to hang on.

Romeo started across the room where the girl who fell out of her chair earlier was standing at the exit, her bag slung over her shoulder. She was twirling the end of her long blond hair around her finger and smiling at him coyly.

I rolled my eyes and pushed up my glasses.

Romeo stopped in front of her and slid both hands into the front pockets of his jeans. The action pulled the material tighter across his butt—which was very toned.

I glanced away, embarrassed.

I heard the girl laughing and then a deeper chuckle followed. I sneaked a glance back in their direction in time to see them both walking away, his hand on the small of her back, guiding her around the corner.

Annoyance slammed into me. I thought that girl was leaving. Where were they going anyway? He was supposed to be over here learning!

I thought about packing up my stuff and leaving right then. I could leave him a note on the table with one word on it: **LOSER**.

I snorted slightly because the idea was totally amusing. Even so, I wouldn't do it. He'd get mad and tell his coach. The coach would call the dean, and then my funny revenge note would get me in trouble.

No thank you.

But I wasn't just going to sit here like a goof and wait.

I'd do my homework. I'd get it all done and then maybe I could stop by the shelter after tutoring for just a few minutes before they locked up for the night. Just the idea of that short visit made this day seem a little less crappy.

Quickly, I pulled out my notebooks and texts. I had an open-book quiz the professor in my history class gave us, so I decided to start with it. After that, I could check out a couple reference books for an English paper I had due in two weeks.

I was halfway done with the quiz when I glanced at Romeo's books and notebook beside me. His chair was still empty and he had yet to return. I glanced up, blowing some stray hair out of my vision.

What in the world was he doing? We were in a library for crying out loud.

I pushed away from my books and notes to walk around the corner, where Romeo and the girl headed. The row disappeared into the back of the library, deep among the shelves. I trailed through the racks slowly, partially looking for him and eyeing the books at the same time. The deeper into the shelves I went, the more the air was permeated with the scent of old books—a cross between paper and dust.

I liked the fragrance. It smelled liked comfort to me. There was something soothing about being surrounded by books. It also reminded me of my mom and of the fairytales she used to read me when I was a little girl.

I didn't read fairytales anymore.

I read non-fiction.

A deep, throaty gasp pulled my attention back to the present and halted my steps. I cocked my head to the side and listened, but it didn't happen again. It came from the right, so I turned the corner to step into another row of books. Clearly, this section of the library wasn't visited very often.

Even the lighting back here was dimmer than everywhere else in the place.

I heard another low moan followed by a lighter, more feminine sound. My stomach tightened. Those kind of noises didn't come from reading. Well, at least nothing I ever read made me do that.

I knew I should turn around and go back the way I came, but I didn't.

The moans came from just on the other side of the aisle I was in. Slowly and carefully, I reached up and pulled a really thick book off the shelf in front of me, right at eye level. My fingers tightened painfully around the spine of the hardback when my eyes landed on them.

It was definitely Romeo and the girl.

He was leaning up against a rack, facing me, but I knew he wouldn't see me because his head was tilted back and his eyes were closed. One of his hands was splayed out along the shelf beside him. And his other hand…

It was tangled in the blonde's hair, at the back of her head. She was on her knees before him, and by the rocking motion of her head and the way his hand gripped her scalp, I knew exactly what she was doing.

The bottom fell out of my stomach, and I bit back a gasp.

Oh my gosh! Romeo was totally getting a blow job in the library!

What if someone saw? What if someone heard? Wouldn't they be embarrassed?

Unable to look away, I peered a little closer. His jaw muscles were clenched tight and his eyes remained closed. His hips jutted out away from the shelf, giving the girl all the access she needed.

She blocked the most intimate part of him, thank goodness, but I could see the ends of his belt and the open portion of his jeans around her.

My face heated as I brazenly watched them. I'd never given anyone a blow job before. He sure looked like he was enjoying it. And the girl, she seemed like she liked it too because she kept making these soft purring sounds.

Romeo groaned and muttered, "Faster…"

The girl did what he wanted and her head started bobbing much faster than before. Romeo brought his other hand to the back of her head and thrust his hips closer. I jerked back, feeling like a complete pervert for watching.

I shoved the book back onto the shelf and turned to flee. I must have miscalculated where the book belonged because I heard it fall to the floor behind me with a thump. I didn't stop. I kept going.

"What was that?" The girl gasped.

"Nothing." Romeo's voice was hoarse. "Don't stop."

I barreled out of the rows of books and into the main room of the library like I was being chased by a demon. My heart was beating furiously when I sat down in my chair and stared down at the unfinished work.

I couldn't make out any of the words. My vision was blurry and I was completely flustered and embarrassed. I took a deep breath.

What kind of guy shows up for his first night of tutoring and then disappears in the back for a blow job?

I couldn't stay here. I couldn't tutor him. I'd just have to pray I didn't get in trouble with the dean.

I packed up my stuff as fast as I could, not taking the time to organize it neatly in order of subject. When that was done, I zipped up the bag and bolted out of the chair. I got maybe three steps when I slammed into something hard and bounced back.

"Whoaa," Romeo said, reaching out to steady me. His hands were so big they completely covered my shoulders.

Just moments ago, they were holding some girls face to his… *his crotch.*

"Where you off to in such a hurry?" he asked.

I jerked away from him and stepped back. "I'm leaving," I said and lifted my chin.

Why did God have to make all the good-looking guys complete asses?

He frowned, a little crease appearing on his forehead. "We're done?"

Irritation made me forget about what I just saw. I laughed, sounding like a moose getting hit by a car. "You made it pretty clear you aren't really into studying."

He brought his thumb up and swiped at his full lower lip. I wondered if that girl got to kiss him too.

"Hey, I'm sorry." He actually sounded sincere. "I was just…" He glanced at me, and I raised my eyebrows, waiting for his explanation.

He sighed. "I didn't ask for a tutor. It was sort of pushed on me."

I crossed my arms over my chest, the movement making the strap of my book bag fall down my arm, and the bottom of the bag hit me in the leg. I ignored it. "Well, I didn't sign up for this either."

His eyebrows shot up to his hairline. "Seriously?"

"You think I don't have better things to do than sit around this place?"

His face turned sheepish. "Well, no."

I growled a little because his answer was idiotic.

He laughed and reached for my bag, which was starting to cut off the circulation on my lower arm. Before I could tell him no, he slipped his hand under the strap and lifted it off my arm. The relief from the pressure was really nice, so I didn't stop him from swinging it up over his shoulder.

"So what do they got on you?" he asked, taking my bag back to the table.

"What?" I replied, spinning around to glare at him.

"You know… Why do you have to tutor me?" He sat down and placed my bag right between his legs on the floor.

"The dean said it was a requirement of my scholarship."

"You have a scholarship?"

Duh. "Didn't I just say that?" I snapped. I was immediately contrite, but Romeo grinned.

"Yeah."

Damn if I didn't notice the way his blue eyes sparkled when he looked at me.

"Maybe we could try this again?" he asked, turning on the charm.

"You didn't even ask for my name," I blurted out.

So much for thinking I was impervious to his charm. Clearly, it made me gullible.

"I guess I didn't." He agreed and pulled out the chair beside him for me to sit in. "What's your name?"

"Rimmel." I sat. But only because it got me one step closer to my bag.

"Hey, Rimmel." He started, speaking my name like he'd said it a hundred times before. "I'm—"

"I know who you are, Romeo."

His lips curved up. "My schedule says Roman." He pointed at the paper I was given.

"No one calls you that." *And now I know why,* I silently added. I mean, sure, he was like super popular and great at football, but I hadn't realized just how far his charm extended until I followed him deep into the bookshelves.

He leaned forward, bringing his face close to mine. "My mother does."

"Does your mother know what you do in libraries?" I countered. My lips snapped closed, and I ducked my head. *Oh my God, what if he knows I saw?*

His warm laugh dusted the air around us. "You mean study?"

He knew damn well I wasn't talking about studying.

"I have to go." I started to rise.

He placed a hand on my shoulder and pushed me back into the seat. "Stay. I really do need help or I'm going to get thrown off the team."

"Why should I care?" I asked nonchalantly.

He tugged on the long ends of my hair. "Because if I do, you'll be known as the tutor who couldn't help the star player stay on the team."

"What makes you think I care what people think of me?"

"Everyone cares."

I looked at him from underneath the black rims of my glasses. "Well, I don't. But I want to keep my scholarship."

He grinned like he won.

"We should probably set some ground rules." I continued.

He slumped back against the chair, crossing his arms over his chest. "You want to make rules for tutoring."

I nodded. "And if you don't follow them, I'll quit."

He studied me for long moments. It made me squirm in my seat. Romeo had a very intense and level stare. "Okay, Rimmel," he drawled. "Let's hear these rules."

I swallowed. Every time he said my name, the spit in my mouth seemed to thicken. "Okay." I agreed. My shoulders straightened and I held up my hand to count the rules as I went. "One: do not be late. It's rude. If you're late again, I won't wait."

His lips twitched, which brought me to the next rule. "Two: Don't bother trying to charm me into doing your work for you. I won't."

He pressed a hand to his chest like he was offended. "You think so low of me." He gasped.

I rolled my eyes. "Three: No girls during tutoring. No disappearing."

"But you're a girl," he said, sitting forward swiftly and tucking a bunch of hair behind my ear. The back of my neck broke out in goose bumps and they scattered down my spine, and my toes curled in the Converse I was wearing.

"Rule four," I said, ignoring the funny way he made me feel. "No charm at all."

"I can't help it, Rimmie." His intensely azure eyes roamed over my face like he was looking at me for the first time. "It's so easy to make you blush."

I hit away his hand. "Rule five: Do *not* call me Rimmie." Ugh, he was irritating!

He chuckled and sat back. "Fine. Now, can we get to work?" he asked, pointing at his paper.

"No," I snapped. "Tutoring is over for today."

"But what about this assignment?" he whined.

"Here's a thought," I said as I snatched my bag and stood. "Sit here and do it."

I started to stalk away, nearly tripping over my half-untied shoelace.

He laughed beneath his breath, and I thought about kicking him.

"Rimmel," he said. I stopped and turned. "See you day after tomorrow."

I rushed outside into the cold autumn air and dragged in great gulps of the crisp atmosphere. He was absolutely infuriating! Full of himself. Arrogant. Far too pretty.

He was terrible!

This was going to be torture!

So then why was I already anticipating our next study session?

CHAPTER FOUR

#SexOnAStick
Thanks for the show last night Romeo. We didn't see your face, but we'd know those muscles anywhere.

... Alpha BuzzFeed

ROMEO

The disruptive gleam of a too bright light broke into my deep sleep. Annoyed, I grabbed a pillow and pulled it over my head.

"Get up," someone said from above and poked me in the ribs.

I jack-knifed up; the pillow flung off the bed. The intense beam from a flashlight glared in my sleep-heavy eyes and I threw up my hand to shield my face.

"What the hell?" I muttered.

The covers tangled around my legs were ripped free and cool air rushed over my bare skin. Before I knew what was happening, a bag of some kind was tossed over my head and hands pulled me up out of the bed.

Adrenaline surged through my body, making my heart rate accelerate tenfold. All my muscles tensed and the person still grabbing my arm paused.

"You got the note, right?" he whispered.

A couple other voices broke out behind the guy who spoke, telling him to shut up and no talking was allowed.

Relief poured through my system. This was the frat. I should have known right away.

I nodded, and the hand on my arm jerked me forward. "I need clothes!" I hollered when we passed through the door of my place and out into the cold night air.

Everyone was snickering. "Not where you're going," someone said.

I was dressed in nothing but a pair of boxer briefs. Sometimes I slept naked. Thank God I hadn't last night. The last thing I needed was my boys flapping in this chilly-ass air on the way to some undisclosed location.

"Nice digs," someone said from behind me as I was led through the backyard of my parent's place and toward wherever they were parked.

It was nice, better than nice in fact, and it was also the exact reason I lived at home and not on campus. Well, technically, I lived at home, but not with my parents. I lived in the pool house behind the main house. It was a one-story building that my mother designed to look like a cottage on the outside. The siding was white, the shutters black, and the front door red with a gold knocker on the front.

The pool house was basically a spacious one-bedroom apartment. It had a full eat-in kitchen, a big living room, and a gym so I could train.

There were shrubs and rose bushes planted along the front and several windows that looked out onto the huge pool. The pool house might have been my mother's project, but the pool was my father's.

It was huge and looked like a lagoon. He had large rocks imported from who the hell knew where and underwater lighting to make the aqua-colored water light up. It was the kind of pool you could walk right into; the water was as shallow as your ankles but gradually declined all the way to eight feet deep. There was also a small waterfall at the deep end.

We only lived about fifteen minutes from campus and they didn't make me pay rent. It was a sweet deal.

I heard the creak of the gate on the fence and then my bare feet sank into the cold, damp grass. My skin broke out with goose bumps and inside the burlap bag, I grinned because at least I wouldn't have to be worried about sporting a morning wood.

I wondered what time it was when they shoved me into the back of a car and took off down the street. I couldn't see anything beyond the bag, but it still seemed dark. The brown fabric would look lighter if the sun was up.

And of course, they wouldn't have needed a flashlight in my room.

The car went over a huge bump in the road and I was tossed to the side, my bare arm slapping against someone whose arm was also bare. I jerked upright as the person beside me stiffened and everyone around us laughed. I assumed then it was another pledge.

It didn't take long to get to wherever they were taking us and we were being herded out of the car and led through more cold, damp grass.

It sounded like another gate was banging open, and then I was being shoved in my back.

"Better watch your step," a guy said with clear amusement.

My feet left the grass and met with something hard, like concrete, and the guy who sort of helped me out earlier by telling me who they were leaned in to whisper low, "Steps."

I didn't acknowledge that he said anything because I figured he wasn't supposed to tell me.

My suspicions were proven when I heard what sounded like someone falling and a bunch of guys laughing. "We got a clumsy one on our hands!"

My steps slowed and I cautiously moved forward, anticipating the first step. A finger poked me in the back just as my foot met air. I stepped down and concentrated on getting down the stairs, which seemed really steep.

As I went, I counted them. There were seven. The air down here was cold, maybe colder than outside, and the floor was still made of some hard material that was rough like concrete.

About thirty steps into the room, we were ordered by a new voice to halt. I stopped and turned toward where I heard the sound.

"The past is just that," the voice intoned. "It's in the past; it's now irrelevant. You're reborn tonight, starting a whole new chapter in your life!"

Some of the guys whooped their agreement. I remained silent.

"And so you will begin this new life the way you were brought into it!" he said.

What the hell did that mean?

After a few beats of silence, he yelled, "Strip! Come on, get nekid!"

Grumbling from both sides of me filled the air, but I grinned and reached for the waistband of my boxers. Once they were off, I held them in front of my junk, almost like a shield, but stood casually.

Seconds later, the bag on my head was ripped off and I blinked, focusing on the room.

The only lighting came from what had to be at least fifty large candles lit around the room. There were about ten pledges to my right and left, all of us naked.

I looked the best.

Of course.

In front of us was the president of the Alpha Omega fraternity, and of course he was fully clothed. Some of the other frat members all stood behind us in a row, and I glanced around to see who was behind me. My eyes connected with one of the running backs on the team, and he gave me a very subtle *what up* gesture.

I knew it was him who had helped me with the stairs. We were teammates. Brothers. We looked out for each other. And me falling and getting injured would seriously piss off the coach.

"For some of you losers…" The guy who ordered us to get naked spoke. He was the frat president, Zach Bettinger. He was a senior here. Some said he was going to make it to the White House one day. "This is as close as you'll get to this frat. Some of you just won't make the cut. Don't let it get you down, boys. Some of you just aren't good enough."

What a douche.

"Being here doesn't mean you're in." He went on, his eyes colliding with mine. Even in the low lighting of the candles, I saw the emotion that flared when he looked at me. This guy didn't like me.

Noted.

"It means you've been given a chance. A prayer, if you will." He spread his hands. "To join the most exclusive, most epic fraternity ever."

Cheers went up behind me. I grinned.

"What you do next will determine if you have what it takes to get in."

"What do we have to do?" the guy next to me asked.

Zach stopped and stared at him. "You think you can hack it?"

"I know I can." He smirked.

"All right." Zach motioned at the line of pledges. "Take a good look, boys. This here is your competition for the next month."

A month of pledging? That was insane.

We all looked around. I noticed a couple of the lingering stares sent in my direction. I was used to it. My football background, my parents' connections, and my looks earned me a sort of campus celebrity status. It was one of the reasons I was surprised I hadn't been allowed to pledge last year.

"During the next few weeks, you will be sent tasks either by note or text that you will need to complete. You don't need to tell us you completed them. We'll know." Zach glanced at me again. "We're always watching."

I stared back at him. He didn't intimidate me, and I was pretty sure he was trying to.

He glanced away, pacing in front of the flickering candles. I glimpsed around. It seemed like we were in a cave of some sort. But it wasn't a place that was unused. The walls were unfinished, but there were throw rugs on the floor, leather club chairs and furniture around. Behind the candles, I could make out what looked like a pool table. Maybe this was some sort of club or hangout for the frat.

"You have twenty-four hours to complete a task once it is given. If you don't, you're out. No exceptions."

That didn't seem so bad. I could handle it, no problem.

"There's one other thing," Zach called, drawing back our attention. "You'll have the entire month, just up until you're inducted into the frat."

The guys behind us snickered.

"Get a girl into bed—have sex with her."

I felt myself smirk. He thought I needed a month for that?

I guess some of the other guys thought it was going to be easy because Zach grinned and held up his hand to silence all the boasting going around. "But not just any girl. We'll be choosing for you."

Ah, well, wasn't this interesting?

Still, I wasn't worried. I hadn't yet met a girl I couldn't charm.

From down the line, someone said, "It seems like some of us might have an unfair advantage."

All eyes turned to me.

I grinned and shrugged.

I felt Zach's stare so I looked his way. "Not to worry. This will be a challenge for everyone."

I grinned wider. *Bring it on.*

"One other thing. Get proof once it's done. A photo. You'll be texted a number where you will text the picture."

The bag I was wearing when I entered the room was shoved back over my head.

"Get the hell out of here," Zach said like the sight of us underlings was making him sick.

We all shuffled back up the steep stairs and into the chilly air. So for the next month, I was to complete random challenges, sleep with a woman they selected, and take a picture as proof.

I thought rushing a frat was supposed to be hard.

The guys brought me back to my place and guided me into the backyard. I was pretty sure this wasn't the same guy as before (my teammate) because he was a lot rougher and silent.

A few steps past the gate into the back he grabbed me roughly, making me stumble before I righted myself. He grabbed the bag over my head and yanked it away. I had two seconds to notice the spray-painted symbol of the frat on my front door before I was shoved forward.

The ground beneath my feet fell away and I felt my eyes widen as the crystal clear water of the pool rushed closer.

Fuck!

My body plunged into the depths and shock rendered my lungs frozen. My entire body jolted from the low temperature. The pool heater was currently not on, so I was left with the icy fingers of the water scraping me all the way to my bones.

My foot hit the bottom of the pool and I shoved up, rushing toward the dark surface. My head cleared the water and I dragged in a heavy breath. It was so cold it hurt to breathe.

I spun around to cuss out whoever shoved me in here, but the yard was empty.

I pulled myself out of the pool and quickly rushed inside, past the crudely painted symbol on the door, and into the bathroom where I turned the shower on as hot as it would go.

I looked in the mirror as I waited for the water to heat. My skin was red and splotchy from the cold and my lips were almost colorless, just like my fingers.

Let the initiation begin.

CHAPTER FIVE

#SnoozeAlert
Mid-term grades post next week. If your already failing, now is a good time to beg.
... Alpha BuzzFeed

RIMMEL

I showed up early and stayed late.

There was just something about this place that I needed extra of today.

Well, I knew what it was. The consistency, the fact that I knew what to expect here. I knew what I was getting when I walked in the door.

Animals were so much better than people. They didn't expect anything, they didn't judge, and they were real all the time. I loved the honesty animals lived by.

Nothing about them was fake. They showed how they were feeling without apology.

It was why I wanted to become a veterinarian. I wanted to give back everything I'd been given. I wanted to be their voice when they couldn't speak. I wanted to be the friend they always were. I wanted the ability to make them feel better when they were sick.

I wasn't good with people… but animals… animals were my passion.

Once I was finished mopping the back room, I emptied out the bucket and set everything in place to dry. I flicked off the lights and wandered into the room where we kept all the cats.

Metal crates lined the walls, some stacked together. The floors were made of white tile and the walls were painted white as well. Posters of animals lined the walls along with some other images of celebrities that supported animal rescue. Against the far wall were a bunch of cabinets that held food and supplies for the cats.

Cats weren't quite as open with their affection as dogs, but it was something I understood. Cats remained aloof and reserved; they were very independent. They liked to study people; they liked to really know who they were dealing with before they got too close. Some cats never bothered to get too close to anyone.

Life taught me to be the same way.

In the corner of the room, on the bottom of the stack of cages, was Murphy. He was curled up in the corner of his home with his face tucked into the curve of his body. I sank down onto the floor in front of the door, unlatching it and swinging it open.

He perked up his head and stared at me, the light green of his eye was always the focus against his midnight fur.

It was even more a focal point because there was only one.

Murphy came to the shelter badly injured and malnourished. He lost his left eye shortly after. No one was ever sure what happened to him. That was over a year ago. He was no longer too thin and frail. His fur wasn't dull and matte, but sleek and shiny. The left side of his face was intact, but where there should be a large green eye, there wasn't. The skin and fur had been stitched together where it healed. And in place of his eye was a curved sort of line, a scar, but it was covered with hair.

"Hey, Murphy," I said softly, holding out my hand for him to smell.

He touched the tip of his cool nose to my finger and I smiled. Keeping my actions deliberate, I slid my fingers up onto his head and scratched behind his ear. The sound of deep purring filled the space around us, and I smiled.

"Sorry I didn't come by yesterday," I told him. "I have to tutor someone at school. He's going to be a real pain in the butt."

Murphy yawned and pulled away from my scratches.

I smiled. He was as bored by Romeo as I was. 'Course, if I were honest, Romeo didn't really bore me. That was one of the reasons I dreaded going there so much.

The cage above Murphy was empty. "Looks like your neighbor got adopted," I said.

Michelle, one of the shelter employees, came in behind me. "Yep, earlier today."

"That's great," I said. It was the primary goal of this shelter to care for animals but ultimately find them permanent and loving homes.

But no one ever wanted Murphy.

Maybe it was why I loved him so much. I felt sort of an odd connection with the cat no one wanted. He didn't fit the image of a good family cat. He was blackest of black, which made it harder for him in the first place. Black pets were always the last to get adopted. Maybe because they didn't appear as friendly and cuddly as the others. Maybe because they looked a little dangerous… and maybe it was because of the stigma that black cats brought bad luck.

But even when someone got past the color of his fur, they would notice the scar and missing eye. He appeared damaged. He appeared to have had a rough life (which, yeah, maybe he had), and no one wanted to deal with damaged. It made them uncomfortable.

So Murphy was continuously bypassed. He was ignored. He'd lived in that cage for the last year as all the other cats came and went.

If I didn't live in a dorm, I would have already taken him home with me.

"What are you still doing here?" Michelle asked as she bustled around the room.

I gave Murphy one last stroke and then latched the door and stood. "I wanted to spend some extra time cleaning in the back. It was a mess."

Michelle smiled. "You're the only college student I know who would rather clean than hang out with her friends."

That's because I didn't have any friends.

"Did Sarah tell you that I wouldn't be here on Mondays, Wednesdays, and Fridays for a while?" I asked, ignoring her statement and the hollow feeling it gave me inside.

Michelle turned from what she was doing and gave me a smile. "Are you tutoring a guy?"

I smiled slightly at the gossipy tone in her voice. "Yes."

"Tell me he's super hot."

I laughed but shrugged. "He's okay."

Michelle groaned. "*That* good?"

I felt my forehead wrinkle with her response.

She shook her head. "I know you, Rimmel. You downplay everything. So if you're saying he's okay, then I know you're drooling on the inside."

I laughed. "I don't drool."

Michelle turned serious. "Have fun. Get to know him. Maybe—"

I held up my hand and halted her words. "It's just tutoring."

"It doesn't have to be."

"Yes, it does." If she only knew I was tutoring the campus celebrity, then she would understand.

Michelle sighed. "Rimmel," she said and came to stand before me. "You don't give yourself enough credit."

"Huh?" I pushed the glasses up on my nose.

"You are such a good person. You have so much to offer. Let him get to know you."

A lump formed in my throat. She was just talking, just words. She was just trying to be nice. Michelle didn't know what I did.

Or maybe she did realize. Maybe she was just trying to make me feel good.

It only made me feel worse.

I glanced back at Murphy. My kindred spirit. Underneath, he was a good cat. Loyal and loving. But no one ever bothered to look past his rough exterior, because in reality, looks meant more than everyone wanted to admit.

Romeo was just like everyone else. My exterior would keep him at arm's length, exactly as it should. I didn't belong in Romeo's world. I was like a round peg to his square hole.

"I should be going," I said, grabbing my bag from the table. "I'll see you Saturday morning."

I hurried out of the shelter before she could say anything else.

The air was cold and crisp. I stood out on the sidewalk, stared up at the inky night sky, and shivered. I still wasn't used to all these seasonal changes. In Florida, it was always warm. I really needed to remember a jacket.

My scooter was parked outside the shelter. I didn't have a car and driving this made getting around sometimes a little easier, but it wasn't a very warm way to travel. As I climbed onto the seat and strapped on my helmet, I knew soon I was going to have to park this thing for the winter.

My dorm was on the second floor of the building, and I had to use my ID to let myself in. Girls milled around, the hallways filled with giggling and the scent of perfume. I could hear a few TVs behind doors and a few more with music playing.

My dorm was one of the ones with music. I let myself in and the sounds of Bruno Mars grew louder. I dumped my bag on the end of my neatly made bed as Ivy, my roommate, turned from her mirror.

"Ugh!" she burst out. "I have nothing to wear!"

Her bed was covered in rumpled tops and jeans. The floor was littered with boots and flats. It wasn't anything new. She was always searching for the perfect outfit, and it was rare her side of the room was ever neat.

"What's wrong with what you have on?" I asked, sinking down onto the bed.

"This!" she demanded, motioning toward a pair of yoga pants and a loose top. "This is loungewear!"

I didn't care about clothes. They seemed like a waste of energy… and also something that got you noticed. Sometimes being invisible was better.

"I'm sure whatever you pick will be fabulous," I replied and scooped up my shower tote with everything I needed to shower before bed.

"Hey, so how'd tutoring go?" she asked.

Ivy and I weren't really friends, but we were roommates who lived in very close quarters. She wasn't the silent type; she was bubbly and talkative and she asked a lot of questions. It was easier to answer her than try to evade.

Besides, I kinda liked talking to her.

I rolled my eyes. "He's a complete douche."

"Is he at least hot?"

My lips curved into a smile. I wondered what she would say if I told her it was Romeo. She'd probably pee her pants.

Before I could say anything, Ivy turned back to the mirror. "Never mind. Of course he isn't hot. What hottie goes and sits in the library three days a week to get tutored? Lame."

I swallowed Romeo's name on my tongue. I knew she didn't mean it as an insult, but it still stung. I went to the library all the time.

I let myself out of the room and went down the hall to the bathroom. Suddenly, I was very tired.

CHAPTER SIX

Looking 4 Romeo?
Follow the trail of bodies. Ladies were dropping behind him like flies.
#LadyKiller #Swagger
... Alpha BuzzFeed

ROMEO

I woke up to the sight of my mother standing over me, wearing a disapproving frown on her lips and holding a mug of coffee in her hands.

With a groan, I rolled over and clutched the blankets up around my waist. The last thing I wanted was to give my mother an eyeful of my morning wood. "What?" I half growled.

"Do not speak to me like that," she intoned, not even stepping back an inch. Valerie Anderson was not easily intimidated. If anything, she was the intimidator. I knew by the way her perfectly arched brows drew together that she was trying to intimidate me.

It wouldn't work.

It never did.

I got the same kind of *never back down* attitude passed into my genes.

"Why are you glowering at me?" I paused to glance at the clock and cringed. It was the freaking butt-crack of dawn. "The sun isn't even up." I finished with a groan. I got no sleep thanks to my little kidnapping and swim last night, and now this.

"I'd like an explanation for the graffiti on your front door," she said coolly.

Fuck.

My mother might be an intimidator, but she was even more of a perfectionist. On top of that, the "mess" was on the front door, where—*gasp*—the neighbors could see.

"It was a prank, Mom." I scrubbed a hand over my face.

"Yes. Well, you know how I feel about the appearance of our home. Clean it."

"Can't the gardener do that?" I whined.

"It is not his job to clean up after your friends."

"Fine," I muttered and sat up as my father walked into my bedroom behind her. What the hell was this? They never came over here, yet here they both were.

"Valerie, give the boy a break. Can't you see it was the Omegas?"

Her eyes turned sharp and she looked over her shoulder. "You mean the exclusive fraternity that you and your father were both members of, Anthony?"

"One and the same." he replied, then looked around her at me. "Congratulations, son. I knew they'd rush you."

"Dad." I sighed as my gut tightened. "Did you have something to do with this?"

He might be acting like this was an expected occurrence now, but last year, he was sorely bitter that I hadn't been rushed by Alpha Omega. He might not have said as much, but he thought it was my fault. For weeks, he looked at me like I was lacking something.

I felt my gaze flatten as I stared at him, waiting for his answer.

"Are you asking me if I had to make a call?"

As in call your old buddy the dean to complain so I would get a spot? "Yes."

"Of course not. You have a spot because you earned it."

I watched his face as he spoke. I learned a long time ago how to read him and read between his words to hear the lie. My stomach unclenched when I saw he was telling the truth.

I blew out a breath, relieved. Truth was I wanted that spot in Omega. But I only wanted it if it was real—if I truly earned it. I didn't want something my father had to buy.

"C'mon, Valerie, give him some space. I'm sure Roman has training to do before classes," my father said.

"Of course," she said, glancing back at me.

I got my blond hair from her and my blue eyes from my father. Even though it was barely morning, she was already dressed in a tailored pair of jeans and a cashmere sweater. Her hair was sleek and cut to her chin. Her makeup was perfect. In fact, there wasn't a time I could remember seeing her without makeup.

My father wrapped his arm around her shoulders and guided her toward the bedroom door. He was dressed in a black three-piece suit with a designer label. He had short, dark hair that was graying at the temples. He was a large man, over six feet tall with a broad build. Over the years, he'd lost some of his muscle mass, but he was still big enough to not look skinny.

My father had the kind of smile that could make people eat shit right out of his hand and think it was caviar. He was a natural born leader, but never had to use force to get what he wanted. Charm was a much better weapon.

It made him a wildly successful lawyer.

"Roman," Mom said, turning back. "No hurry in cleaning off the door. Just focus on training and tomorrow's game."

"Thanks," I said. In other words, now that she knew it was the *exclusive* symbol of the Alpha Omegas, she wanted everyone to see. I didn't bother to remind her that it didn't matter if it was there or not, the main house was so big it hid this one from view. Not to mention, there was a giant privacy fence around the entire property.

I pulled on a loose pair of sweats and ignored the cool morning air against my bare chest. Inside my home gym, I turned on some music, the kind that would hopefully pump me full of energy, and then hit the weights.

After about an hour and a half of training, my muscles were quivering and my legs felt like Jell-O. I showered and blended up a fast protein shake to go. I had a full morning of classes, one this afternoon, then practice until early evening.

Then I had to go to tutoring.

I chuckled to myself as I walked across the property toward the driveway and my car. My tutor was a mess. I kind of felt sorry for her. I thought about all the rules she'd given me and I laughed again.

Her and my mother would get along famously.

All thoughts of my uptight tutor fled when I approached my sweet-ass ride and admired the body. When I graduated high school, my parents bought me a Dodge Challenger Hellcat.

It was lime green with black rims, a black stripe on the roof, and a black hood scoop. The interior was black leather with a lime-green pinstripe on the steering wheel. The engine was a supercharged V8 (that's what made her a hellcat), and it had a stereo system that rattled the windows.

It was a chick magnet.

If there was a girl that was sort of wavering on giving it up that night, all I had to do was put her hand on the gearshift between the seats, wrap my hand over hers, and "show her" how to shift.

It sealed the deal.

Every. Single. Time.

I slid into the buttery leather and turned the key, letting the engine purr to life.

Tonight was the pregame bonfire. Couldn't really call it a pep rally because it was just a bunch of students getting drunk in the name of football.

A few minutes later, I pulled into a large parking lot and drove to my regular spot. No one ever parked here but me. By some unspoken rule, this was my place.

Braeden's jacked truck was parked next to me. The lifted tires made my Challenger look tiny beside it. As I got out, he came around his hood, grinning, and held out his fist. I pounded mine against his as he asked, "How was it?"

I grinned. "Initiation is on."

"So," he pressed as we began walking.

I lifted my single strap book bag over my shoulders and settled it into place.

"What kind of shit do you have to do? How rough is it gonna be?"

"Nothing I can't handle, man."

We passed a group of giggling girls standing off to the side of a coffee cart. Braeden slapped me in the chest. "You got some admirers."

I grinned and gave them the *what up* gesture with my chin. "Ladies," I said. "You coming to the bonfire tonight? Gonna support the Wolves?"

Several of the girls ducked their heads shyly, but a couple of the bolder girls lifted their chins and looked right at us. One of them I was pretty sure I had sex with last weekend broke away and walked toward us.

I slowed my steps and let my eyes sweep over her skintight jeans and low-cut top. "Pretty chilly out here this morning," she said. Her gaze dropped to my blue-and-gold varsity jacket.

I ignored the hint and draped an arm across her shoulders. "Looking pretty hot to me," I drawled.

She wiggled a little closer. "I'll be cheering from the stands tomorrow night."

"I like to see team spirit."

Braeden laughed.

"Oh, I've got spirit," she purred and fingered the edge of my jacket.

I pulled away. She was desperate. I took in her face and committed it to memory so I knew to stay away from this one. If I slept with her again, she'd probably think we were in a relationship.

She gave my wrist a little tug and I let her pull me back and gave her one of my charm-dripping smiles. "You better get that sexy ass of yours out of the cold and to class." As I spoke, I deftly disengaged myself from her and put some distance between us before she even realized what was happening.

By the time she noticed, I was already turning around and walking away.

"Dude," Braeden said and bit down on his knuckle. "You've gotta tap that."

I laughed. "Been there, done that."

"Then I gotta tap that."

We both laughed and turned the corner around the building. Something slammed into me. I reached out automatically and grabbed onto the person bouncing back as a book flew to the side and landed on the pavement. A strangled sound cut through the commotion, and I tightened my grip and looked down.

Dark, tangled hair was everywhere. My hand completely overtook her shoulder, and she wobbled on her feet for balance.

"Whoa," I said as a grin curved my lips. "Watch where you're going there."

The girl glanced up quickly from beneath black-framed glasses. Recognition lit up inside me.

"Hey, Teach," I said.

"Hey," she squeaked, breathless. She pulled back to bend down and get her book. As she bowed, her oversized messenger bag slid around and hit her in the back of the knees and she stumbled.

I caught her around the waist and righted her, then bent and picked up her book. It was a textbook.

Geez, did this girl ever stop studying?

I handed it back to her and she quickly wrapped her arms around it, hugging it to her chest. "Thanks." She glanced at Braeden and then away. "I have to go."

She rushed away, but I couldn't help calling her name. "Rimmel."

She halted. Her body almost froze like she was shocked I'd remembered her name. She peeked around her curtain of hair and gazed at me.

I grinned. "I'll see you tonight."

Braeden straightened beside me and I felt his gaze turn to interest.

Rimmel flushed a deep pink as her eyes widened.

"And don't worry," I added, just because I knew she'd hate it. "I won't be late. I know how you hate that."

"Dude," Braeden said from beside me.

Rimmel made a little squeaking sound and then rushed away without looking back.

If I didn't have such a good self-esteem, I'd be offended.

"She don't look like your type," Braeden said.

I laughed. "She isn't. That's the tutor coach assigned me."

Braeden laughed. "Shit, man. That's just mean."

"What do you mean?" I asked, glancing at him as we walked.

"You playing with her emotions like that. That poor girl doesn't have a chance in hell with you."

Something inside me recoiled. "I was just teasing her. I wasn't hitting on her." He was right. Rimmel wasn't my type. Far from it. I wasn't even flirting with her. I just liked to see her flustered.

"You better be careful, man. A girl like that, she don't understand the difference."

I grunted in reply. He was wrong. I didn't know Rimmel very well at all. But I did know she wasn't stupid. It kind of irked me that he implied she was.

But then someone from across the lawn shouted my name, and I shouted back. Several people started chanting my name and I laughed.

Just like that, thoughts of my tutor faded away.

CHAPTER SEVEN

Your daily #411

From the sounds that can be heard from many bathrooms... might be best to get your chow OFF campus today.

... Alpha BuzzFeed

RIMMEL

I knew when he walked into the library. I didn't even have to look. I felt the change. I felt people actually turn and glance his way. How did he do it?

How did he command so much attention… so much energy just by walking into a room?

I kept my eyes down on the paper in front of me. The guy didn't need any more attention. I was surprised he could even walk upright with his big fat head.

I heard his deep chuckle. His low voice filled the room as he spoke to others as he walked through the library. I sat in the back tonight. I figured the less people around us, the less chance of him wandering off into the back of the aisles with some random girl.

Just the memory of how I found him the last time we were here was enough to make me squirm in my seat. I could still see the look of pleasure on his face, the way his lashes fanned out across his cheeks. I remember the way the girl moved, the sounds she made in the back of her throat. She seemed to enjoy it.

I wondered if that was something I would enjoy.

His dark-colored bag hit the top of the table, and I jerked in surprise. "Are you daydreaming?" he teased as I looked up.

I glanced at my watch. "You're on time."

"Told ya I would be." Romeo used one large hand to spin the bag toward him so he could pull out his books and notebook.

Seconds later, a girl with long dark hair and a big chest sidled up to the table. If she knew I was sitting here, she gave no indication. "Hey, Romeo."

"Hey," he said, offering an easy smile.

"Are you going to the bonfire tonight?"

"Wouldn't miss it," he said. "How about you?"

I watched her tug a strand of hair away from her shoulder and twirl it around her finger. I rolled my eyes and pulled a paper out of his book with his assignments written on it. He had a history paper due on Tuesday.

"Where's your outline for your paper?" I said, interrupting his flirting. She wasn't too happy about the interruption and glanced over and gave me a dirty look. I looked away.

"Maybe I'll see ya tonight," he said, turning away.

She muttered some silly reply and left.

"Your outline?" I asked again.

He gave me a sheepish look.

"Oh my God." I groaned. "Please tell me you have an outline."

He shrugged.

"A topic? Resources?" I tried.

"I've been really busy at practice. Coach has been running us into the ground."

"Those excuses might work on everyone else in this building, but not me," I snapped.

His sinfully blue eyes narrowed. "Excuse me?"

"I told you I wasn't going to do your assignments."

"I didn't ask you to," he bit out.

I blew out a breath. “No, you didn’t. Sorry.” I turned away to get a pen out of my bag. I really didn’t want to get into some kind of argument with him. He was already garnering enough attention for doing nothing at all.

Romeo had gone silent. He was staring at me, and my stomach did a little flip. “Did you just apologize?” He seemed surprised.

“Umm…”

“Girls never apologize.”

I snorted. When I realized what I’d done, I slapped a hand over my mouth and nose. When I peeked up through my hair, I saw the broad grin stretched across Romeo’s face. He was laughing at me.

I turned away. “Do you have a list of approved topics?”

The paper appeared beneath my nose. I scanned it quickly and found a topic I was familiar with. “Do this one,” I said, pointing it out.

I didn’t wait for him to reply. I pushed back my chair and stood. “Let’s get some reference books. Then we’ll start the outline.”

I wandered down an aisle I knew had what we would need and didn't bother to see if he was following. Truth was I probably *would* do his assignment if it got me out of here quicker.

I spotted a row of books that looked to be useful and stared up at them, pondering the titles. Romeo moved up beside me with quiet grace. I figured that was a benefit of being so athletic. Most guys his size weren't as graceful. He moved so close I could feel the heat radiating off his frame.

His warmth was delicious, and I fought the urge to lean closer. Being a Florida girl made it really hard to get used to the seasonal changes here in Maryland. Every time I stepped outside my dorm and the crisp fall air met my skin, I was shocked. But standing here in this narrow, silent row with Romeo's body heat threatening to wrap around me to keep out the chill, I wasn't shocked.

I was something else entirely.

I cleared my throat and blindly reached for one of the books. At this point, any book would do. Of course, the books I wanted were above my head, mocking my short stature. The tips of my fingers brushed the front of the shelf and I rose up on my very tiptoes to try and get a little higher.

In my desperation, I lost my balance and teetered over. I probably would have landed in a heap on the floor, but a solid arm wrapped around my waist and tugged me back. Romeo anchored me against his chest, holding me there while he reached up with his other arm and brought down a book.

He didn't let go.

Leaving his arm wrapped around my middle, he lowered the book in front of my eyes. "Is this the one you wanted?"

His voice was just above my ear, the question a mere whisper against my hair.

I shivered.

His arm tightened around me.

My eyes tried to droop closed. He smelled good again today. Clean, deep, and my eyes popped back open.

What the hell was I doing!

I straightened and took the book. "Yes, thanks."

He dropped his arm but didn't move back. I took a breath and pointed at another book on the high shelf. "Grab that one too."

He did and I moved off, down the aisle and around to the other side. He followed, but this time he didn't crowd me.

After we chose a few more books and articles, we settled back at the table and got to work. It was easy to forget about the effect he seemed to have on even me when we slipped into the assignment. Time flew by as we worked.

Romeo was surprisingly intelligent, and he didn't just sit there and make me give him all the answers. Before I knew it, we had an entire outline and his introduction. My back felt stiff from sitting on the unforgiving library chair, and I pushed back from the papers and stretched a little.

The clock hanging above the exit had me blinking. We'd been sitting here for a little over two hours. Time was up.

"If you follow the outline and write a couple sentences on each bullet point, your paper should be no problem to finish over the weekend," I said.

"Do you ever do anything other than study and homework?" he asked. His voice wasn't condescending or even sarcastic, so I tried not to bristle.

"What makes you think all I do is homework?"

The corner of his lips tilted up. "Because you knew where the reference books we needed were. Because you're really good at homework."

"I did an assignment on your topic last year. I used those books." I defended myself, bending down to snag my bag off the floor. "And yes, I have a life outside of schoolwork."

"Are you going to the bonfire tonight?" he asked, shoving his papers in his bag. He had no organization at all.

"No."

He glanced up in surprise. "No?" Then he smiled. "Is fun not your thing?"

I stuck out my tongue.

"I didn't realize a fire in the middle of a field was considered fun."

He was already standing, towering over me, but once I spoke, he dropped back into his chair and rotated so his body faced me. "It's not necessarily what you're doing. It's who you're doing it with."

He flashed me one of his smiles that lit up the entire room.

It was hard not to be affected by him. Especially when that smile was directed at you and so were his incredibly clear blue eyes. Suddenly, I understood why so many girls fell at his feet. He had an uncanny ability to make whoever he was focused on his entire universe.

I'd never been the center of anyone's universe before. Okay, maybe I had, but it was different and it had been very long ago.

And then there was the other time I felt like this…

I jerked away from his attention, my elbow sliding across the table and knocking into my water bottle. It fell over on its side and the cap popped off. Water gushed out over the surface of the wood, and I shrieked. My chair clattered against the floor as I jumped to my feet and pulled my books out of the way.

Romeo also stood, but it was a fluid, silent movement. As I fumbled around looking desperately for something to stop the water from covering everything, Romeo reacted.

In one smooth motion, he reached behind him, palming the back of his cotton shirt, and slid it up over his back until it was free of his head. He tossed the shirt onto the water, and as it soaked it up, he picked up my now empty bottle and recapped it.

Excited murmurs filled the once silent room around us.

Giggling and loud sighs floated in our direction.

The book in my hand felt like it weighed a million tons as my gaze latched onto Romeo. He was standing there without a shirt.

Completely bare-chested.

His body was incredibly honed and sculpted. If he wasn't standing there breathing right in front of me, I would have thought he was a sculpture. Every single muscle in his torso and chest was precisely defined. The corded muscles in his arms were sleek and long, stretching out across his broad shoulders and meeting with his wide, solid chest. His waist tapered down into a V and he had these muscles…

I swallowed.

These muscles that stood out just above his low-slung jeans. It was like indentations on either side of his hips.

My mouth felt dry as I stared at those hollow dents.

"How much of your stuff got wet?" he asked, his calm tone breaking into my muscle-induced trance.

"Umm, what?" I said, snapping my eyes to his face.

He chuckled and I felt my face flame. He totally knew I was checking him out.

"Is your stuff ruined?"

"Oh," I said, tearing my eyes from his golden skin and down to my things. "No, it's fine," I mumbled. I glanced at the table where his shirt was completely saturated. His wide hand palmed the fabric and mopped up what was left of the liquid.

The way his back muscles moved as he leaned over the table to swipe it stole my attention. I forced my eyes away. Not only should I be embarrassed about the mess, but also for staring this way.

"I'm sorry," I said, reaching out to help him.

He tossed a grin over his shoulder. "I got it. No worries."

The librarian cut through the small crowd gathered around our table (all girls) and gave us a glare. "What's going on here?"

Romeo straightened from the table, clutching his drenched shirt. "We had a spill," he explained. "But it's taken care of."

"Oh," she said. The irritation in her eyes quickly changed into something else… something like admiration.

Oh, gross. The librarian was totally checking him out.

"Sorry for the disruption," he said and gave her a lopsided smile.

He totally knew what kind of effect he had and he was eating it up.

"Well," she said, still looking at him. "As long as everything is cleaned up."

"It is," I said, suddenly irritated.

The librarian transferred her gaze to me and it hardened. "Rimmel." She sighed. "I should have known the commotion was caused by you."

Embarrassment speared me as people snickered. I began packing up as Romeo entertained his audience.

I turned to leave, ready to disappear in the crowd, but I didn't get very far. Romeo wrapped his hand around my wrist and tugged me around. He was wearing his varsity jacket over his bare chest. The front was open and showed the indent of his abs all the way down to his jeans.

"See you Monday?" he asked.

"Sure," I mumbled.

The crowd parted and let me through, swallowing me up as I went. Romeo's rich laugh filled the back of the library as I moved toward the door.

"That's my tutor. Coach's orders," I heard him saying.

Something inside me shriveled just a little. Yeah, I was his tutor and yeah, I wasn't any happier about this arrangement than he was. But to hear him explain away his association with me like it had been forced on him hurt my feelings.

I realized I wasn't in his circle. I was so far removed that we were in different zip codes.

It still hurt anyway.

CHAPTER EIGHT

What happens at the bonfire...
stays at the bonfire.
Ur #BuzzBoss will have a
full report tomorrow!
...Alpha BuzzFeed

ROMEO

I could hear the music and see the orange glow of a massively large bonfire already raging in the distance. I glanced at Braeden in the passenger seat and he grinned.

Bonfires during football season were a tradition here at Alpha U. They happened almost every single weekend. There was this perfect spot on campus—away from all the buildings, out of the watchful eye of the staff.

Although, everyone knew we partied here. It was sort of an unspoken rule that as long as no one caused any serious trouble, the adults would pretend to not know.

I slowed the Hellcat as I turned onto the narrow dirt road that wound through trees with leaves and limbs that reached across the sky to create a tunnel-like effect. The windows were down so our loud music competed with the music blaring at the party. It pumped through my system and vibrated the steering wheel beneath my hands.

I could already feel the energy of the night swirling around and a little jolt of adrenaline released itself into my bloodstream. We curved around the final bend in the dirt and tons of cars parked haphazardly in long grass came into view. Beyond them a large field opened up, a clearing in the center of all the trees.

There was an empty spot just off the dirt path and I slid the Hellcat into it with ease. I shut off the engine and pocketed the keys.

Braeden was looking at me, shaking his head. "You're the only guy I've ever met who gets his own personal parking spot at parties in a field."

I rolled my head toward him and grinned. When I opened the door, the music pumped even louder, and I threw my arms up in the air and let out a loud whoop. "Wolves!" I hollered.

Everyone joined in, and soon everyone was howling at the moon.

I laughed as a full beer was passed into my hand in less than a minute. The team was in a prime spot near the fire. Braeden and I took up position with them. Everything out here was cast in a red-orange glow that stretched out across the ground until it gave way to darkness. The trees loomed in the near distance, their coloring leaves shaking lightly in the night air.

I took a swig of beer and watched some of the girls who were dancing on open tailgates. One of the girls had long blond hair, cut-off shorts, a cropped top, and a pair of cowboy boots. She was shaking her ass like it was a fine art. Beside her were several other girls, all doing an impressive job of showcasing their dancing skills.

Hells yeah. The view from here was good.

It was a good party. The beer was flowing, the team was in high spirits, and the ladies were ripe for the picking. I was into my third beer of the night when my cell went off in my pocket. After another swift chug, I fished it out and lit up the screen.

KISS A DUDE

"What the fuck?" I muttered and looked around for anyone pranking me.

No one seemed to be amused by the text I just read.

I hit the button and sent the screen dark so I could shove it back in my pocket. Over the rim of my SOLO cup, Trent caught my eye.

Our gazes locked for one second and he gave me a knowing look.

Shit.

That text wasn't a joke. It was fucking for real.

It was part of rush for the Omegas. They had said the other night I would be texted certain tasks that I had to complete.

What the hell kind of pervert wanted to watch me kiss a dude? I downed the rest of my beer and tried to think of a way out of it.

I glanced back at Trent. He was on the team with me. He was also an Omega and the guy who helped me out with the stairs during the night I was taken to the rush meeting.

He must have known I would get texted tonight. I wondered if he knew what they asked me to do. Shit, they would want me to do this at a huge party where everyone would see. I thought about Zach and the way he stared at me that first night.

I wasn't going to let him win. No way in hell. If they wanted me to kiss a dude, then I would.

But first I was getting another beer. I wasn't drunk enough for this shit yet.

I went to the keg and filled up my cup and chugged half of it right there. As I was chugging, a slim hand wound around me from behind and flattened against my chest. I looked down, my lips curling up in a smile.

I covered her hand with mine and spun to see who was there. It was the girl with the shorts and boots. Her eyes were heavy lidded and she licked her lips when I caught her gaze. "I'm thirsty," she purred, stroking my chest.

I was taller than her so when I looked down, I was afforded a first-class view down the front of her top.

"We can't have that," I said and handed her my beer. "Hold this."

I turned and pumped another cup full of the amber-colored liquid and turned back. She was drinking out of my cup.

I shrugged and started drinking out of the one I got for her. She wasn't quite as hot up close as she looked from across the field, but those boots were doing it for me and she had a nice ass. I slung my arm across her shoulders. "Hang with me."

She giggled and leaned into my side.

When we made it back to the team, I was feeling the buzz. I usually drank slower, paced myself, but given the text I received, I had extra motivation to get smashed.

Trent was watching me and I knew he probably would until it was done. I glanced around at all the crowds of people but didn't see anyone else watching. 'Course, that didn't mean they weren't. There was a ton of people here, and I knew a lot—if not all—of the Omegas were here.

"Yo!" I hollered. "I got something to say!"

The roar of the crowd around us lowered to a soft buzz and a couple of my fellow Wolves yelled, "Speech!"

I grinned and held up my beer. "A toast!" I yelled, swaying a little to make myself appear even drunker than I was.

"To the Wolves, all our supporters, and to those poor losers that have to get pounded by us tomorrow night!"

Shouts of agreement and cheers lifted up over the fire and floated through the sky. Everyone drank to the toast and then quieted back down, looking at me expectantly again.

"One last shout out to my brothers, my teammates, the defensive linemen, like my buddy Braeden here." I released the girl with the boots and flung my arm around Braeden's shoulders and pulled him in. Some of my beer sloshed over the rim of my cup and onto him. "Who keep the assholes at bay so I can throw some sah-weet passes!"

Everyone cheered again and started drinking.

I swayed, pretending to be super drunk, and glanced at Braeden. He was probably gonna deck me for this.

"I love you, man," I roared and then pressed my lips to his.

It was over in two seconds flat. Long enough for me to press our lips together and then jerk back. Everyone around us roared with laughter and whistles cut through the music.

I lifted my beer and howled at the moon. "Wolves!" Then I downed the rest of the cup.

Braeden was looking a little shocked, and I gave him a short, clear-eyed gaze, hoping he'd let me explain later.

A heartbeat passed and then he lifted his beer and followed my actions.

I found Trent in the boozy crowd. He gave me a slight nod with a half-smile on his lips.

Done.

I threw my arm back around Boots and pulled her in. "I just kissed a dude," I said loudly. People around us snickered. "I'm gonna need you to erase that from my memory."

She arched her back into my side and pressed her ample breasts against me. "With pleasure," she purred.

She had a dark-haired friend standing just behind her. I glanced up and gave her my charming smile. She stepped forward.

"Go make out with my buddy Braeden," I told her. "He needs some good luck for tomorrow night's game."

She giggled and rushed over to where Braeden was standing and threw her arms around his neck. He barely had time to look down before she was locking onto his lips.

"C'mon," I said and led Boots over to the truck she'd been dancing on. I lifted her up onto the tailgate, then hopped in beside her. Several other couples were up there already, making out, and I leaned back against the side as she straddled my lap and sat down.

Her lips tasted like beer and she was a little too eager. Three seconds into the kiss and she started grinding herself against me. I grabbed onto her hips and let her go for a ride. I barely had to make an effort because she was doing enough for both of us.

Her fingers went through my hair and her hands roamed everywhere she could reach. It wasn't the worst kiss I'd ever had, but it sure as hell wasn't the best. Some girls were just too eager to turn me on and it worked against them.

I don't know how long we made out, but I was starting to get bored when a deep voice spoke beside us.

"You gonna come up for air, man?"

I pulled the girl away and looked at Trent. Without any effort, I lifted Boots off my lap and sat her aside. "Thanks for the fun," I said and hopped down out of the truck.

I heard her irritated huff as I walked away with Trent, but I didn't bother looking back. "Dude, thanks for the save. She kissed like a dead fish."

Trent grinned and handed me his beer.

I took it gladly.

"Hey, I never did get to say thanks for the other night," I said quietly.

"We're Wolves," he said with a shrug. It was that simple. It always would be.

"You get in trouble?" I asked him.

"Nah." He shoved his hands into his front pockets and stared out over the fire.

I knew he had something to say so I waited for him to say it.

"I normally wouldn't do this." He began, still not looking my way. I sipped the beer. "But…"

"We're Wolves," I repeated.

"Yeah, we are. And you're a decent guy. But you didn't hear this from me."

"Hear what?" I echoed.

A ghost of a smile played on his lips before we both turned back to look out over the crowd.

"Zach doesn't like you, Romeo. In fact, I think he might hate you."

"I kind of got that the other night."

"He doesn't want you in Omega. He managed to keep you out last year, but he couldn't this year, not without getting backlash."

So that was why I didn't get rushed last year.

Son of a bitch.

"I can handle him," I said, my voice dropping because I was angry.

Trent glanced at me. "He's gonna make it hard on you. He wants you to fail. He's taken to selecting your challenges personally, and I can guarantee they aren't gonna be easy."

My spine stiffened and my jaw hardened with resolve. "Bring it."

Trent nodded. "Figured you say that."

"You know I can't run," I said. I wasn't built that way.

"Yeah, I know. You made a name for yourself freshman year. No one does that. Zach knows it too. He wants to knock you down a couple pegs."

"Thanks for the heads-up, man." I held out my fist and he pounded his to mine.

"I'll help you as much as I can…" His voice trailed away.

"Don't get yourself on Zach's bad side. I got this."

"Yo, Barnes!" Trent hollered, and the team running back turned from the keg and looked our way. "Pour me one!"

Trent looked back at me before walking away. "I've never seen a guy get off so easy for kissing another dude like that."

I grinned and held up the SOLO cup. "Don't ya know? Too much beer always brings out the brotherly love."

Trent laughed. "Nice play," he commented and then went to get his beer.

Braeden was still getting hot and heavy with the dark-headed girl, so I went back to the crowd to party.

I wondered what else Zach was gonna pull on me during rush. What he didn't know was I might smile and charm everyone, but I didn't get my rep by being pushed around. I didn't back down. Not ever.

And I sure as hell wasn't about to start now.

CHAPTER NINE

Brotherly drunken love...
or rush initiation?
#ThingsThatMakeYouGoHmm
... Alpha BuzzFeed

RIMMEL

I was dead asleep when my phone rang. It cut into my bliss like a chainsaw through a Christmas tree farm. I didn't bother to lift my head; instead, I flung out my arm and moved my hand around until it landed on the cell.

"Hello?" I said drowsily into the line.

I got another loud ring as response.

I winced and pulled it away from my ear and looked at the screen, making sure to hit the answer button this time.

"Yeah?" I said and collapsed back onto my pillow.

"Rimmel?" A familiar voice cut into my half sleep. It was Ivy.

"Please tell me you aren't drunk." I groaned.

She giggled, and I rolled my eyes. "Would you mind coming to get us? Our ride is passed out beneath a tree."

I should tell her to walk back to the dorm. Maybe next time she'd think twice about getting so drunk. I glanced at the clock on the table near the bed. It was after two a.m. "Fine," I muttered and threw off the covers.

Chilly night air brushed against my legs and I shivered. "You owe me," I muttered.

"See you in a few!" she slurred, and then the line went dead.

I pulled on a pair of sweats, the first pair my hand closed around in the drawer. They were too long and too big, but I didn't bother changing. I just tied the drawstring a little tighter. I rummaged around and found a hoodie and pulled it over the tank top I'd gone to bed in. Once I jammed my feet in some shoes, I fished around Ivy's desk for her car keys.

I didn't have a car, just my scooter, and I didn't think Ivy would appreciate being picked up on it. This wasn't the first time I'd had to go retrieve her from a party. She didn't call very often, but when she did, I always went and got her. We weren't exactly friends, but she was the closest thing I had to one. Besides, I couldn't let her wander around out in the dark, drunk. If something happened to her, I'd never forgive myself for not going.

Her Corolla was parked outside the dorm, and I climbed in and pulled out of the lot. I knew where to go. Even though I'd never been to one of the bonfire's, I'd picked Ivy up there before.

It was only like a five minute drive and then the car dipped onto the dirt road that led to the field. I could hear the loud music and the rumble of the people. I wondered if Romeo was there.

Of course he is. He practically is the party.

Behind my glasses my eyes watered from sleep, and I blinked to clear my vision. Once the cars came into view, I didn't bother to find a place to park. I just stopped right in the center of the lot and threw open the door.

I looked around for Ivy but didn't see her anywhere nearby. I muttered to myself because the least she could do was wait by the road for me.

With a sigh, I reached in and pulled the keys out of the ignition. I weaved through the cars and listened to the laughter and off-key singing. My stomach twisted a little; this really wasn't my scene. I could feel a few stray stares as people noticed me. The girls laughed as I passed, but I held my chin up high and kept moving.

I stopped and scanned the crowd for Ivy. It took a minute to find her, but then I did. She was in the back of some truck, dancing. Her butt was practically hanging out of her shorts, and I wondered how the hell she wasn't freezing out here with so little clothing on. Of course, maybe that's why she added the boots.

At two a.m., the sun was long set and the chill of an autumn night was in full effect. My fingers were almost numb as they tightened around the keys.

I walked a little ways toward her, watching her fling her hair and shake her junk as she moved. I finally managed to catch her eye and wave. She gave me a bright smile and hopped down off the truck, falling a little and laughing at her own drunkenness.

"Rimmel," she said enthusiastically, linking her arm through mine. "You came to party!"

"You called me." I reminded her. "For a ride."

She laughed. "I gotta get Missy."

She pulled me along through the field, stumbling as we went in search of her friend Missy.

A few minutes later, the heat of the fire was close and the feeling in my fingers came tingling back. It was a huge fire. Easily ten feet tall and probably just as wide.

Ivy spotted her friend, shrieked her name, and rushed off to get her. I knew Missy from when she hung out at the dorm, so I recognized the back of her dark head. She was plastered all over some guy and things looked like they were on the verge of going from heated to indecent right out here in the open.

Ivy pulled her back just a little, but the guy kept his arm around her. Ivy pointed at me and three sets of eyes swiveled around to stare. I lifted my fingers in a wave as my cheeks heated.

All three of them started my way. I bit back a groan.

"It's you," the guy said, coming up beside me.

My eyes snapped up to his and I realized I knew him. Well, sort of. He'd been with Romeo when I ran into him on campus. People never recognized me, so of course this guy did. Here. Now.

"You know him?" Ivy asked, turning to look at me.

"He's drunk and confused," I said. "Can we go now?"

"I'm not ready to leave," Missy said, draping herself across Romeo's friend.

"Let's stay!" Ivy shouted.

"Oh no you don't," I said, grabbing her arm. "You called me to come get you."

"I changed my mind." She pouted.

"Too bad," I said and started pulling her away. She dug in her heels.

I sighed. "I have cookies in the car," I lied.

Her face brightened.

Drunk girls were idiots. I was never going to act like this.

I turned back to bribe Missy. Braeden wrapped his arms around her from behind and looked at me over her shoulder. For some reason, his actions made my stomach tighten. I wondered what it would feel like to have someone wrap around me like that.

"I'll make sure she gets home," he said.

I didn't argue. I wanted to get the hell out of here.

Ivy linked her arm through mine again and I led her toward where I left the car. As we walked, some shrieking and yelling broke over the sounds of the party, and I glanced around for what was going on. Over on the other side of the fire, two girls were on the verge of what looked like a fight. I couldn't help but stare because I was so surprised. One of the girls reached out and yanked a handful of the other's hair. It was all downhill from there.

Beside me, Ivy laughed. "That's what she gets for trying to steal someone's man."

I tore my eyes off the fight and glanced at Ivy. "Seriously?"

"Them bitches be cray-cray," she slurred.

I didn't understand what that meant, but I laughed because it sounded ridiculous.

Ivy giggled beside me and we started walking again.

That's when I saw him.

Romeo wasn't more than thirty feet away.

The smolder of the fire only enhanced his already superior good looks. He seemed sharper, more toned. The heavy shadows cast by the flames gave his cheekbones a more carved-out appearance. His lips seemed more defined and his body appeared larger against the black backdrop of night.

He was wearing a baseball hat turned around backward on his head. The edge of the material seemed to slash across his forehead, just above his naturally arched brows, and draw even more attention to his unbelievably blue eyes.

In his hand was a SOLO cup, and people crowded around him, laughing and slapping each other on the shoulders. There was a girl with long curly hair hanging halfway down her back who had affixed herself to his side, and he didn't seem to mind one bit.

Our gazes locked.

Recognition flared through his body. I knew by the way he stiffened slightly even as his body turned toward us.

Please don't come over here, I prayed to myself. The last thing I wanted was to hear him remind everyone that I was someone he was forced to know.

I turned away abruptly, breaking eye contact and tightening my grip on Ivy. "Come on," I told her, my tone harder than usual.

"I wondered where he went," she said, dragging her feet and craning her neck to look behind us. "Let go. I'm going to stay."

"We're leaving," I said, trying to hold on to my patience.

She dug in the heel of her boot and rooted herself into the dirt. "No."

With a frustrated sigh, I turned to face her, making sure my eyes stayed averted from where Romeo was standing. "You called me for a ride. I came. We're leaving."

"You're not my mother!" she snapped and yanked her arm away forcefully.

I stumbled and stepped to steady myself, but the stupid too big, too long pants I was wearing got in my way. My foot got tangled in the fabric and I fell over.

I lay there stunned a few seconds as people around me laughed. Ivy stood over me, staring down with her mouth in a little O shape. I don't know why she looked so surprised. This was her fault.

My wrist was stinging because I'd stupidly tried to catch myself when I fell. All that resulted in was me jamming it into the hard ground beneath all my weight. I sat up and pulled my hand into my chest, rubbing the sore area a little.

"Are you okay?" Ivy asked, reaching out to help me.

I pulled back and climbed to my feet alone. "I'm fine."

I felt the stares of a thousand eyes. I hated it. "Look…" I began. "If you want to stay, fine. But don't call me in an hour to come back."

She didn't reply. She didn't even look at me.

Her gaze was fixed off to the side, her attention solely focused on someone else.

"Ladies," Romeo said. The people standing around watching our little scene parted and he stepped through.

Ivy stuck out her chest a little and tossed her hair over her shoulder. "I've been looking for you," she said.

"You found me," Romeo replied, holding out his arms.

Oh. So he'd come over here for her. Well, that made sense. I really shouldn't have thought he would come over here to see me.

"I needed a ride." She went on, shimmying up to his side.

"I'll walk you to your car," he said, dropping an arm over her shoulders and steering her toward me.

Our eyes met briefly before I turned and led the way to where I left the Corolla. Ivy didn't fight him one time.

Jerk.

At the car, I opened the back door and motioned for him to dump Ivy in the backseat. She'd likely pass out before we even got back to the dorm.

When she was in the car with the door shut behind her, I breathed out in relief and turned to climb into the driver's seat.

"Hey." His voice brushed over me. It was incredibly close. So close I could smell the beer on his breath.

I paused in opening the door and turned my head just slightly to look at him out of the corner of my eye.

Romeo was standing just behind me, just like earlier at the library. "Yes?" I asked, my voice a little raspy.

"You okay?" The concern in his voice had me spinning around. He took a slight step forward and I backed up. My back hit the side of the car and I was effectively trapped.

"W-what?" I asked.

Romeo reached between us and lifted my wrist. "You were holding this like it hurt."

My breath caught when he pushed the too long sleeve back to reveal my slender wrist. His fingers brushed over the skin on the inside and I shivered. My eyes shot up to see if he noticed. He said nothing, but the soft smile on his lips spoke louder than words.

I tried to pull my arm back, but he encircled my forearm with his thumb and pointer finger. "Looks okay, but maybe you should ice it just in case."

He released me and I hurried to let the sleeve fall back in place like it was some kind of armor. "I will." I lied.

He didn't move. He didn't say anything. He just stood there.

"You better not be ready to pass out," I told him. "You're way too big for me to pick up."

He cocked his head to the side and regarded me. "And what would you do, Rimmel?" The way he said my name brushed over me like a fine caress. "If I passed out right here?"

He bent at the knees as he spoke so he could get closer to my eye level.

I saw the playfulness in his depths. I knew he was probably drunk and wouldn't remember this tomorrow. I told myself beer made people do crazy things.

I lifted my chin and returned his gaze. "Well," I said, wetting my lips with the tip of my tongue. "I'd just have to run over you on my way out."

The whites of his eyes grew bigger when his they widened in surprise. Then he threw back his head and laughed.

I used the opportunity to wrench open the door. I slid in and moved to pull the door closed, but Romeo was faster. He caught the doorframe and held it open. His broad shoulders filled the opening as he leaned in. "I'd tell you to watch out for crazy drivers, but I have a feeling you're one of them."

"Where ever did you get that idea?" I asked, batting my eyes innocently.

He chuckled and moved back so I could shut the door. Behind me, Ivy was already snoring in the backseat. At least the ride home would be quiet.

Romeo stood there and watched as I performed a three-point turn and drove back the way I came. Before I disappeared around the bend, I glanced in the rearview mirror. He was still standing in the same spot, but he wasn't alone. People already crowded around him.

For once, I kind of wished Ivy wasn't passed out and was in the back giggling like an idiot. The quiet was a little too loud.

I had too many opportunities to replay the short conversation I'd just had with Romeo.

He hadn't really said anything all that unusual, but I had.

There for a moment, I had actually been flirting.

CHAPTER TEN

#BuzzBoss words of wisdom
Shake what your momma gave ya. But not for someone else's man. Look for the bruises from the catfight friday night. Beer and claws are a dangerous thing.

... Alpha BuzzFeed

ROMEO

Guys were streaking naked through campus.

Eating challenges commenced in the eating hall.

Girls were running around taking selfies of themselves kissing every guy they saw.

Rush was in full swing. It was entertaining as hell.

I was given a couple tasks throughout the week, but they were almost lame. After the bonfire and Trent's warning, I was expecting a lot worse.

Part of me thought it was the calm before the shit storm.

That's okay. I was ready.

I was also getting kind of irked. Most the Omega pledges had their assignments of who they needed to sleep with. But not me.

Not one word, not one name had been sent to me. I was beginning to think Zach was waiting, letting the clock run down so I had less time to close the deal with whoever he chose.

Maybe it was his way of trying to level the playing field. But it didn't matter. This was a game I knew how to play and I was going to win no matter how long he gave me.

Coach put us through the ringer at practice tonight, and I was dog tired. My muscles were shredded, and I really wanted to slip into an ice bath and let the frigid cold work out some of the worst.

But I couldn't.

I had to be at the library. On top of it, I was late. Rimmel said she wouldn't wait if I ever showed up late. Part of me was glad because I wanted to go home. Dark clouds crowded the sky and the air smelled like rain as I walked into the library.

Where the hell was the rain an hour ago when we were killing ourselves on the field?

I loved football, it was my life, but sometimes even I wanted a break.

As soon as I stepped through the glass doors, I looked toward the back where Rimmel always sat. She chose back there because she thought people wouldn't see us; she thought we would blend into the books and stuffy atmosphere.

It never worked and it was always fun watching her get flustered when people would stop by the table to shoot the shit. I don't know why it bothered her so much. No one ever talked to her. It wasn't like she was forced to have a conversation.

She looked up and frowned at me as I made my way toward the table. I grinned because she was still here. Her hair was wild as always. We'd been meeting for tutoring almost two weeks now, and I still had yet to see her full face. Her glasses were perched on her nose and she looked small sitting in the wooden chair with an oversized shirt concealing her upper half.

"You're late," she said when I sat down.

I leaned across the table and spoke into her ear. “You waited.”

She ducked her head and I pulled away. I loved getting a reaction out of her. It was so damn easy. She reached out and slid a tall Styrofoam cup with a plastic lid toward me. “I got you a coffee.”

There was an identical cup still sitting in front of her.

I groaned a little and reached for it. “How’d you know I needed this?”

She gave me a sidelong glance as I sipped at the sweet brew. “I didn’t. But I thought it would be rude to bring one for me and not you.”

“Well, thanks. Practice today was a bitch.”

She swung her full gaze at me. It wasn’t the first time I noticed how wide her eyes were beneath her glasses. They were brown, but there was a ring of hazel around her irises. Some days the center looked more green and some days it was gold. Today they were deep green, like a freshly mowed football field.

“You’re welcome.”

I set aside the coffee and pulled out my laptop and powered it on. I might not feel like being here, but my grades were better and Coach wasn't breathing down my neck every day about teetering on the edge of being suspended from the team.

"I have this assignment due in science. It's a one-page paper on hypothesis vs. theory. Would you mind taking a look at what I have so far?"

The document flashed onto the screen and I tilted it toward her. Rimmel pushed up her glasses and leaned in to read. Her hair fell forward and brushed my arm, but I didn't bother to move away.

She smelled good.

A combination of vanilla and apple. Usually she stuck to her side of the table like glue. This was the first time she'd leaned over into my personal space. I lounged back in the chair and kicked out my foot and sipped the coffee while she read.

She seemed intent on the computer, so I took a minute to study her without her knowing. Her skin was pale and smooth. Her eyes were framed with thick, dark lashes and her full lips were a pale shade of pink. The urge to reach out and push back some of her hair so I could study the rest of her came over me, and my hand flexed around the cup.

She must have felt the shift in the air because her body tensed. She glanced at me and her eyes widened when she realized just how close she was.

I didn't bother moving. I smiled lazily. "What do you think?"

"A-about what?" she fumbled.

Without thinking, I reached up and fingered a strand of her hair. It was silky soft. "The paper."

She jerked back like I'd tried to strike her. "It's good. You don't need to change it. Just finish the conclusion and it'll be fine."

I wasn't used to girls trying to get away from my touch. "Are you a lesbian?" I shot out, sitting up.

She made a little squeaking sound and her mouth fell open. "What?"

"Are you?" I demanded.

"No!"

I grunted. "Then why do you dress like that?"

Her mouth snapped shut, then opened again. Hurt flashed into her eyes but quickly disappeared. What the fuck was I saying? What did it matter how she dressed?

"You know what?" she said. "I've had enough tutoring for today."

"I just got here."

"And I've already had enough of you," she snapped and packed up her things. The way she slapped them into her bag drew some stares.

When she was done, she pushed away from the table and stalked toward a row of books and disappeared between them.

My cell went off.

I picked it up and looked at the message.

SHE'S YOUR GIRL

I really wasn't in the mood for this cryptic shit.

WHAT?

A second ticked by and then I got a response.

YOUR CHALLENGE. IT'S THE NERD

I sucked in a breath and looked around for watchful eyes. I didn't see anyone. Zach sure knew how to pick them. And at the perfect moment too. It's like he knew she was a complete disaster and she was pissed at me.

She was the only girl on campus who didn't seem to be affected by my charm. And I'd just insulted her.

Shit.

I wouldn't give Zach the satisfaction of my defeat.

I pulled out my phone and texted back.

GAME ON.

CHAPTER ELEVEN

The traffic in the library has tripled because Romeo hangs there now. Sources tell the #BuzzBoss even the librarians enjoy the view.

... Alpha BuzzFeed

RIMMEL

My phone beeped with yet another notification from the #BuzzBoss. I winced and put the ringer to vibrate. Didn't that guy have anything better to do than send out texts every five minutes?

Still, I looked to see what he posted. I regretted it immediately. *Of course* it had to be about Romeo. I sank back against a row of books and took a deep breath. Usually people didn't get to me. Usually I never gave them much thought.

But not with him.

Romeo got to me.

It didn't matter that I pushed him away, that I kept my distance. He was just a student I was tutoring. That's all.

But he wasn't.

Sometimes… sometimes just sitting beside him made my stomach do funny little flips. Sometimes when I caught the curve of his lopsided smile, I wanted to smile back. When I walked to class in the mornings, my eyes sometimes looked for him. At night when I lay in bed, I thought about the night of the bonfire and the way he gently stroked my sore wrist.

I didn't want it. I didn't want any of it.

But it's like I couldn't stop the softening of my insides. It was like driving way too fast and knowing you were going to crash, but your foot stayed on the gas.

I brought him coffee.

He insulted me.

I leaned my head against a shelf and looked up at the ugly lights on the ceiling. Guys like him were dangerous. I knew it firsthand. They took what they wanted, wrecked your insides, and walked away while you stood in the center of chaos without anyone to pull you back.

This was why I preferred animals. Since I ended tutoring early, I still had some time. Seeing Murphy was exactly what I needed right now. His unconditional love could heal anything, including a stupid insult from Romeo.

When I got to the end of the row I peeked out toward the table to see if he was still there. He wasn't, and I let out a breath. A loud roar of thunder shook the building, and I grimaced. Of course it would be raining right now. I'd left my umbrella and my scooter at the dorm and walked here.

I debated just running back to my room and staying there, but the urge to see Murphy was pulling at me. I decided to just go grab my umbrella and a raincoat, then walk the few blocks to the shelter. Riding on a scooter was kind of pointless in the rain.

Through the glass doors I could see the rain spattering against the sidewalk, and I prepared myself for the cold drops as I stepped outside. Romeo was parked at the curb, in a no-parking zone, leaning up against a lime-green car.

He had a baseball hat pulled low over his face and his arms were crossed over his chest.

Why in the world was he standing out here in the rain?

"Come on," he called to me and motioned at his car.

I glanced behind me to see if he was talking to someone else.

His chuckle floated through the rain. "Yes. You. Come on."

He wanted to give me a ride? "No thanks!" I called out.

He moved fast. Of course that wasn't a surprise. But the way he sank low and wrapped his arms around me was. I shrieked as he lifted me off the ground and carried me over to his car. When I was on my feet again, he opened up the passenger side and looked at me from beneath the rim of his hat. "You aren't walking home in the rain."

His glare was steady, and since I was getting wetter by the minute, I gave up and slid into the warm leather seat. I settled my bag between my feet as he dashed around the front of the car and got in. The seats were bucket style, so I could barely see over the dashboard, but he fit behind the wheel just fine.

He tossed the hat into the backseat and ran a hand through his hair. "What dorm you in?"

"Why are you doing this?" I asked.

He glanced at me. "Because I was an ass."

I fidgeted with the hem of my too-long lesbian-like sweater. "You totally are an ass."

"Look. I'm sorry. I've had a long day and I'm tired."

"I wasn't going back to my dorm," I replied, not sure what to make of his apology. I felt myself softening again.

"Where to?" he said and started the engine.

"The animal shelter on Barnes Street?" I asked.

He nodded and pulled away from the curb. I stared out the window as we passed through the campus. The heavy rain was bringing down some of the gold and burnished leaves from the trees that lined the streets. They littered the ground like sprinkles on an ice cream sundae.

A bit of fog was rolling in and the day was turning dark. I shivered a little as my wet shirt pressed against me. A warm blast of air brushed over me, and I glanced down to see Romeo adjusting the vents so I would have most of the heat.

I didn't say anything because it wouldn't make up for his butthead ways earlier.

"So why are you going to the shelter?" he asked.

"I volunteer there several days a week."

"You go every night after tutoring?" he questioned.

"No, but since we quit early, I have time tonight."

There was a beat of silence as we turned out onto the main road away from campus. "You like animals, huh?"

I leaned my temple against the glass of the window. It was cold. "I love them."

"You said you had a scholarship. Is this what it's for?"

Wasn't he full of questions? "Yes, I'm studying to be a vet."

A few moments later, the car slid up to the curb in front of the shelter. I could see the lights were still on, and I smiled. "Thanks for the ride."

My hand paused over the handle when he shut off the engine. "What are you doing?" I asked warily.

"I'll walk you in."

"That's really not necessary," I rushed out. I didn't want him here. This was my place. My sanctuary.

He popped open his door, and I hurried to say, "But you'll get wet."

His arm disappeared into the backseat and came back with his hat. "I'm already wet." His smile was rueful.

I had no choice but to get out and hurry toward the door. Romeo was already there, and he held it open as I rushed past him inside.

Michelle was at the front desk and she looked up in surprise. "Rimmel! I didn't expect you tonight." Then her gaze went to Romeo as he came in behind me. Her eyes widened and she glanced at me with a question in her eyes.

"I had a little extra time tonight and thought I'd stop in to see if there was anything I could help with." I prayed she told me to clean up poop or something that would scare Romeo away.

"Everything's been done. We're closing up in an hour."

"Oh," I said, feeling dejected. "Well, I'll just go say hi to Murphy."

Michelle smiled. "I'll be back in the office, filing paperwork." Then she glanced at Romeo again.

He stepped around me and held out his hand. "I'm Roman. I go to school with Rimmel."

Michelle shook his hand and smiled. "So nice to finally meet a friend of Rimmel's!"

I wanted to groan out loud. Instead, I walked back toward the room where the cats were kept. Everything was tidy like Michelle said and there really wasn't anything that needed done. I spoke hello to a few of the cats who looked up at me as I wandered toward the corner where Murphy was.

When I sank down on the floor in front of his cage, he looked up and saw it was me. It made me feel warm inside when he got up and walked to the door. When the door swung open, he stepped out into my lap.

I laughed. "Hey there, Murphy." I stroked his velvety fur and he began to purr. "I missed you today," I told him as he pushed his nose against my hand.

I felt rather than saw someone hovering behind me, and Murphy looked up over my shoulder. I leaned back and glanced up. Romeo was hovering in the doorway, watching me with unreadable eyes.

I sighed. "Wanna meet Murphy?"

He came into the room and Murphy darted back into his shelter. Romeo's footsteps faltered, and I waved him forward. "It's okay. You're just new."

Many of the other cats got up and went to the doors, looking at him with interest, but not Murphy. Murphy was too used to being ignored and sometimes sneered at. It made me feel sad for him, but part of me also identified.

I leaned back into the opening and held out my hand for him. He rubbed his nose against it, but I didn't move to grab him. That would only scare him more.

"Sit," I told Romeo.

He looked around like he wasn't sure what to do, and I giggled. He smiled and then sank down behind me on the tile.

"You like it here, huh?"

"It's my favorite place," I replied honestly. I didn't feel as guarded, like a door to my insides opened up when I was here and I felt it was okay to let him see just a little.

Murphy crept a little closer to the door, but I didn't let on that I knew. Instead, I started scratching behind his ear.

"That cat sounds like a lawn mower," Romeo quipped.

I laughed again. "Yeah, he kind of does."

My hair was wet and felt heavy against my back, making my shirt wetter than it already was. I pulled back my hand and lifted the heavy mass up and away from my shoulders and face using a hair tie around my wrist to secure it into a messy bun at the top of my head.

The air brushed against my neck and I shivered.

"Your shirt is soaked," Romeo said.

I shrugged and leaned back to pet Murphy some more.

"Rimmel," he said softly. Whatever I heard in his voice caused something in me to stir. I turned toward him, my body answering the call in his tone.

He didn't say anything. He just looked at me. His eyes roamed my face like he'd never seen it before. I felt the blush creep up from the bottom of my neck and work its way up until my cheeks felt warm.

"What?" I said, my voice coming out more as a whisper.

"Nothing. I just wanted to look at you without your hair in the way." He continued to stare, unapologetic. When I couldn't take any more, I ducked my head, causing a strand of hair to fall loose against my cheek.

Romeo leaned forward and lifted my chin with his fingers. My eyes connected with his and this… this current went through the room. His fingers slid from beneath my chin and tucked the hair behind my ear. "You're beautiful," he said, a hint of surprise in his tone.

A rush of warmth filled my chest, but then reality came crashing back and I snorted. "Are you trying to get me to do your work again?"

He winced and his hand fell back to his lap. "I mean it."

I was saved from having to reply when Murphy crawled back into my lap. I smiled and stroked down his back and turned to face Romeo. "This is Murphy." The affection was clear in my voice.

"Is he yours?" Romeo asked, holding out his hand to the cat. Murphy smelled him tentatively.

"He would be if I didn't live in a dorm."

Romeo moved slowly, sliding his hand back to rub the cat behind his ears. The loud purring started up again. "So are all these cats homeless?"

"They're up for adoption."

"How long's Murphy been here?"

I lowered my gaze and my stomach rolled. "He came right after I started volunteering over a year ago."

He paused in petting and looked up. "That long?"

I nodded and cleared my throat. "People tend to overlook him."

"His eye," he murmured.

Emotion clogged my throat so I didn't speak. We sat there in silence for long moments. And then Murphy climbed off my lap and climbed into Romeo's. He seemed taken aback by the cat's easy affection.

"He likes you," I said, my voice thick.

"He's pretty cool."

I got up, unable to sit here like this with him anymore. It was affecting me too much. I reminded myself not to get taken in by his smile and the fact that Murphy liked him.

I grabbed a bag of cat treats out of the cupboard and passed them out among the cats. Then I held one out to Murphy, who was content in Romeo's lap.

He perked up and stood, arching his back in a stretch as he sniffed at the treat. "It's your favorite," I told him. He took it in one bite and then licked his lips like he wanted more.

"Oh no you don't," I told him. "One's enough."

I felt Romeo's stare and I looked up. Sometimes I forgot just how blue his eyes were and then I would realize all over again and it would make my stomach flip.

The sound of muffled barking came through the walls, and Romeo blinked. "You have dogs here too?"

I nodded.

"Can we see them?"

"Sure," I said and lifted Murphy out of his lap. I tried not to notice how my arm brushed against his chest as I lifted the cat.

"I'll see you tomorrow, Murph," I said and set him back in his shelter. Immediately, he went to the back and curled in a ball.

I led him to the room across the hall where the dogs were kept, but before I could pull open the door, his voice behind stopped me. "Here."

I looked and he was shrugging out of his varsity jacket and holding it out for me. He might as well have been growing another head because his action was totally foreign.

"You're wet and freezing," he said when I only stared.

"I'm okay," I argued.

He looked down at my chest and his eyes grew a little heavy. I followed his gaze and wanted to die.

Okay. So maybe I was a little cold.

Or a lot.

My nipples were drawn into little pebbles that you could totally see through my wet shirt plastered against me.

"Uhhh," I stuttered. I needed to take the jacket. I was putting on a show for him. But I couldn't. My shirt was so wet it would just get the inside of the dry coat wet too.

Romeo cleared his throat and gestured to the coat again. "It's just a jacket, Rimmel."

I spun around, putting my back to him, and yanked the oversized shirt over my head. I was wearing a tank top beneath it, and while it was damp, it wasn't wet like my shirt. I tossed the top aside and reached around me for the jacket. He slid it into my hand with a warm chuckle.

I pulled it around me and bit back a groan because it was like being wrapped in an electric blanket. The material swallowed me whole. I didn't have to worry about showing too much in this because there was so much fabric I was totally concealed.

It hung well past my hands and almost to my knees.

He grinned when I turned around. "You're gonna get lost in that thing."

It was so warm and it smelled just like him. Whatever comeback I was going to make died on my lips.

I showed him the dogs and we spent some time playing around with them. It didn't surprise me that Romeo liked them. They were all high energy and sort of wild just like him.

After a while, Michelle poked her head in and said she was going to lock up.

"C'mon," Romeo said, "I'll drive you back to campus."

"You don't have to do that," I rushed to say. "Michelle usually gives me a ride."

"But I'm here now."

And what about when you aren't? The thought was like a knife in my chest. I told myself to hang on to that feeling because there would come a time, like probably in ten minutes, when he would be gone and life would be the way it always was.

He seemed to take my silence as some kind of agreement, and we went back out into the main room where I gathered up my things, including my shirt.

Michelle's eyes went right to the jacket I was wearing and then her gaze bounced between me and Romeo. I caught her eye and shook my head slightly, wanting her to get the idea out of her head immediately.

"I'll see you tomorrow," she said, opening the door for us.

When I was out on the sidewalk, Michelle called out for Romeo. When he turned back, she said, "You're welcome back anytime, Roman."

I gave her a death glare and hoped it gave her nightmares. Judging from the smile on her face, it wouldn't.

The ride back to campus was short and quiet. I couldn't help but sink into the soft, warm seat and breathe in the scent of his jacket. When we pulled up in front of my dorm, my eyes were heavy and threatening sleep.

"How'd you know which one I was in?" I asked sleepily.

"Lucky guess."

"Oh. Well, thanks for the ride."

I started to climb out.

"Rimmel?"

"Yes?"

"I really am sorry about before. Thanks for letting me hang with you tonight."

Hang? Is that what we'd done?

I got out and hefted my bag on my shoulder. Then I remembered his jacket. I waved my arms as he backed up, and he hit the brakes. I rushed around the front of the car, his headlights blinding me, and dropped my bag at my feet so I could shrug out of the jacket.

"Here," I said, handing it to him through the window.

"Thanks," he said, not looking at my face, but instead at the little tank I was wearing. I picked up my bag and held it in front of me like a shield and backed away from the car.

He sat in the lot and watched me until I disappeared inside.

I could hear the velvety purr of his engine all the way up the stairs as I walked to my room.

CHAPTER TWELVE

ROMEO

Rain cut through my headlights, making slashing marks in the air as I drove home. The image of Rimmel sitting Indian style on the tile floor with that cat in her lap and her hair piled on her head refused to go away.

Yeah, I'd had the urge to check her out before. I mean, shit, I checked out every woman I saw. But I never really thought I'd see that.

I felt like it was the first time I'd looked at someone and really *saw* them.

It left me shaken.

I was just tired, that's all. My body was done and my brain was trying to pick up the slack. Tomorrow this would be a memory, and I certainly wouldn't be haunted by the image of Rimmel and a cat.

I'd only waited for her because of the text.

The challenge.

Yeah, it was initiation for the Omegas. But it almost felt like some kind of unspoken personal challenge between Zach and me. A dare. I lifted my mouth a little at the thought because this wasn't grade school. Hell, this wasn't even high school. This was college. Technically, we were adults. We didn't dare each other.

But still, I wouldn't back down.

Zach thought he played a good hand. He thought I'd been dealt a raw deal. I had to admit, yeah, I was pretty handicapped. I mean, shit, she was like socially inept. She became nervous just when someone looked at her too long.

And she was always falling over. Her clothes looked like sacks, she freaking snorted when she laughed, and her hair…

She is beautiful.

The thought came out of nowhere and shocked me into next week. The car jerked to a stop in the driveway, and I sat there while the engine idled and stared out at the rain sliding down the windshield.

Even as I wanted to deny it, my mind refused. It wasn't the first time I'd thought it either. Hadn't I just told her the very same thing?

But it never really hit home. Maybe I hadn't heard my own words.

They were loud and clear right now.

I shook my head. I couldn't really understand. She wasn't beautiful.

But she is.

She lifted her hair up off her face and the room literally stopped. It was like there was a sudden vacuum sucking me in until the only thing I could see was her.

Rimmel's face was shaped like a heart. She had high cheekbones, wide eyes, and a chin that gradually tapered in. Her lips were full and pouty, and if she ever took those glasses off, the impact of her eyes would be astounding. As it was, they were stunning behind the glasses. She had a small nose, almost perky, and her skin was so creamy it almost looked like the cream my mother liked to pour in her coffee.

And the curve of her neck… I'd never noticed such a thing before. But when she turned back to the cat, I could see it. She was so small-looking. Delicate and fine-boned. Her neck was sloped gently and curved out to give way to her shoulders. I wanted—no, I itched—to drag my fingers along that spot. To flirt with the hair at the nape of her neck and to take my teeth and nip at the perfectly smooth skin.

When she got up to show me to the dogs, I couldn't tear my eyes off her. Her shirt was soaked and it plastered to her frame. The cold made her nipples erect and I could barely take seeing them without being allowed to touch.

So I offered her my jacket. To cover her up, to let me get my head on straight.

But it backfired.

She went and took off her shirt.

Holy shit did my cock spring to life when she pulled away that fabric. Even though she kept her back turned, I still got quite a glimpse. Her arms were willowy, her waist narrow and trim, giving way to softly flared hips.

Honestly, she wasn't at all my usual type. I liked a girl with curves, a girl I could grab. Rimmel wasn't all that curvy, but there was something about her that I couldn't stop looking at. Heat flared in my stomach and spread like I'd just drank a giant shot of whiskey and the burn of alcohol was spreading through my limbs.

My varsity jacket hid most of her body, but it didn't douse my reaction. It swallowed her up and the only thing I could think of was being on top of her, my body covering hers, completely swallowing her up.

I guess it was a good thing I suddenly found her attractive. I did have to sleep with her. It certainly would make it easier.

I hadn't expected to like her though, not genuinely. I had a lot of friends, but not many of them I would consider genuine. Most of them liked me because of my status. Because of the game. Because being around me gave them something.

I played along. Hell, I enjoyed it. But deep down I knew where the line was drawn. Braeden was the closest friend I had. And I would count Trent among that list. Along with a handful of other guys on the team. But that was it.

There had never been a girl before.

A girl I actually was intrigued by. A girl I wanted to learn more about.

I learned something tonight. I learned something I didn't think anyone ever got to see. Her vulnerability. Her softness. The way she looked at the animals, the way she acted with them, it made me slightly jealous. Sure, everybody liked me, but no one ever looked at me the way she did that cat.

As I watched her with him, I realized she identified with it. He was sort of the outcast of the shelter. No one wanted him because he looked different, because maybe they thought he wasn't as good as the other cats.

But when he showed affection, he purred louder than any cat I'd ever heard. He'd turn his green eye on you and really look. When he saw I was going to be kind to him, he accepted me immediately.

Was that how Rimmel felt? Did she feel overlooked? Like an outcast?

Thunder rolled overhead, and I realized I was still sitting in my idling car. I shut it off and dashed through the rain into my house, flipping on the lights as I went.

I knew I could get her into bed. Especially after seeing her tonight. All I had to do was draw her in, notice her, make her feel special.

It would be almost effortless. I should have been happy, smug and grinning like the Cheshire cat.

But I wasn't.

CHAPTER THIRTEEN

RIMMEL

The library seemed a lot busier than usual and it made me slightly uncomfortable. One of the great things about a library was the peaceful, quiet atmosphere.

Yeah, it was still quiet in here (for the most part), but the air in the building was anything but peaceful.

I took up a spot in the back, the last table left, and sank into the chair. I was dressed in a pair of loose jeans, purple Converse, and a loose white T-shirt topped with a long purple cardigan that I bought two sizes too big. The sleeves were long and I pulled them over my hands as I sat there curling my fingers into the extra material.

I'd worn my hair up today.

I usually only put it up when I was in my room or at the shelter cleaning. My hair was dark and unruly. I knew if I cut some of the length off it would probably be more manageable, but then I wouldn't have it to shield myself with.

But the way Romeo looked at me…

The other night in the shelter, I hadn't really thought twice about pulling up my hair. It was wet, heavy, and on my nerves. I guess thinking back now, it was a little startling that I didn't think about being in the same room with him and how pulling my hair up might leave me feeling exposed.

Maybe I would have thought that if he hadn't looked at me that way. But he did. The change in his eyes was definite. The blue was as amazing as always, the kind of blue that you didn't often see. It darkened as his gaze fastened on my face and didn't let go.

Usually, I would have ducked my head, but I couldn't. I felt like he was seeing me, like the *real* me. And I felt like maybe he liked it.

He called me beautiful.

The only person that ever called me beautiful was my father. Except for several years ago… but I wouldn't think about that.

So when I got dressed today, I pulled it up into a messy-looking topknot. As I'd gone through the day, a couple strands had fallen out against my neck and one occasionally brushed my cheek, but I didn't fuss with it.

Ivy had been surprised. I could tell by the way her eyes widened when I walked past to grab my sweater. She even told me it looked nice, almost trendy.

Earlier this morning, I passed by Romeo's friend, the one from the other day. He did a double take, then lifted his hand in a wave. "Looking good today, tutor girl!" he shouted.

People turned to stare.

I almost rushed in the bathroom and pulled my hair down. But I didn't. Maybe it was time I stopped hiding all the time. I was almost nineteen. I wasn't a kid.

I knew how to handle people and certain situations. I shouldn't let the past define me anymore.

But some habits were hard to break.

A couple girls walked by where I was sitting and started whispering and rushed away. Odd. I looked around and something became clear.

These people weren't here to study.

They were here because he was coming. Romeo.

Way more than half of the people in here were girls. They were all dressed to impress and some were fussing with their hair and lip-gloss.

I remembered a recent Buzz that came through the Alpha App. Something about Romeo being at the library and how the library was getting busier. Well. That notification just increased the traffic.

I also saw the Buzz about the mystery girl in his Hellcat. It wasn't a mystery, though. It was me. I wondered what all these girls would say if they knew that.

Were they here because they were curious and hoped to see some girl on his arm? Or were they hoping to come here to draw his attention and *be* that girl?

Right next to me someone cleared their throat.

I jumped about a mile out of my seat and threw my arms out in surprise. The arm where the person was standing smacked into their middle, and I heard an *oomph*.

"I'm sorry," I rushed out. "You startled me."

"What the hell?" the girl snapped, and I turned all the way around to stare up at her. She had icy blue eyes, long honey-colored hair, and a full face of flawless makeup. She was rubbing her palm over her middle where I smacked her.

"You shouldn't sneak up on people," I said.

An incredulous look crossed her features. "I wasn't sneaking."

"Well, I didn't hear you." I pointed out.

She dropped her hand from her belly and regarded me with a scrutinizing gaze. I saw the way her lips sneered at my makeup-free face, my glasses, and my unfashionable outfit. And then her gaze shifted, almost like she had sized me up and decided I wasn't anything for her to worry about.

It kinda pissed me off.

"Are you Romeo's tutor?" she asked.

I should have known this was about him.

"Yes."

"Well, where is he?" She perched a hand upon her hip.

Did she think I was his keeper? "I assume he's on his way."

"Well, when he gets here, you should go." She glanced behind me, and I knew her friends were probably nearby listening.

"And why is that?"

"Because he's going to be busy with me."

"He's coming here to study." I pointed out. This girl was irritating.

Her eyes narrowed and her mouth thinned. "You don't have a chance in hell with him."

"I never said I wanted one," I shot back. Was this girl actually implying I was here for something other than tutoring? I was here because I had to be, not because I chose this and certainly not because I wanted Romeo.

"Listen here, nerd," she said, towering over me, using the fact that I was sitting to try and intimidate me.

It was sort of working, but I didn't want to show it. "He'd never go for a girl like you."

"Sorry, I'm late again," Romeo said as he walked toward the table. I turned and looked at him, but he didn't look at me. He was looking at the girl.

Had he heard what we were saying? God, I hoped not.

"Romeo…" The girl's voice was dripping with honey. "Are you here to study? I am too. Maybe we could do it together."

Her friends had come closer to the table now. Everyone was looking at him, hanging on his every word, even the ones he had yet to see.

He glanced at the few girls just off to his side and gave them a charming smile. They all practically melted into a puddle. Then he turned back. "Sorry. Can't. Coach's orders."

I felt my shoulders relax a little. For a moment, I thought he might ditch me to go with these girls. The idea of that really shouldn't have bothered me, but it did.

"I won't tell if you won't," she giggled.

I rolled my eyes.

She saw my reaction and glared at me. I could see something mean forming on the tip of her tongue. Romeo slid right between us, putting his back toward the girl and blocking her from my view. "It's really crowded in here tonight," he said, looking at me.

I nodded.

"Wanna go somewhere else to study?"

I couldn't see the girl behind him, but I sure heard her sharp intake of breath. A little bit of bitchy came out inside me and I smiled. "Yeah, that'd be great."

He waited for me to gather my stuff and then moved back to let me stand. When I was ready to go, he turned toward the girl behind him and smiled. "Later."

She mumbled something I didn't hear as Romeo draped his arm across my shoulders and steered me to the door. About every eye in the entire library stopped to stare at us. My face felt like it was on fire because it burned so badly from embarrassment.

Romeo didn't seem to care or even notice we were getting more stares than a man dressed in drag. He didn't even seem uncomfortable to be seen with me.

supposed to sleep with her and complete rush if the other girls were trying to scare her away?

"Do you really want to go study?" she asked, bringing me back into the moment. My phone beeped again, reminding me I hadn't looked at it yet.

"Yeah," I answered. "I have a ton of homework."

"Where do you want to go?" she asked.

I was already lighting up the screen on my phone. The first thing to pop up was the newest notification from the BuzzFeed. *Stick to your circle.* I shook my head and deleted it. As I did, a text popped up.

STEAL SOMETHING FROM THE DEAN'S OFFICE.

BRING TO THE PARTY FRIDAY NIGHT.

I stared at the challenge for long moments, clenching my jaws. Zach wanted me to steal from the dean. Not only that, but I was supposed to keep it until Friday? If I got caught, I could get kicked out of school. My chances at the NFL would be gone before they even got started.

"Romeo?" Rimmel said from the other side of the car.

I glanced up.

"Is something wrong?" Her voice was genuinely concerned.

"Nah." I lied. "Just checking my messages."

"We can cancel today's session if you want."

I couldn't. I needed the time to get closer to her. I'd just have to take care of this other thing later tonight.

"It's all good." I dropped the phone in the cup holder and pulled out onto the street.

"Where are we going?" she asked.

I gave her one of my charming smiles. "My place."

Her eyes about fell out of her head, and I chuckled.

"Maybe we should just go back to the library."

"You'd rather go back there with those vultures than go to my place?" I asked, some of my smile slipping away. Did she really dislike being around me that much?

She cocked her head to the side and looked at me. "Do you have any roommates?"

"Nope."

She visibly swallowed. "We'll be alone?"

I slowed the car and leaned over into her personal space. "What's the matter, Rimmel?" I whispered. "Are you afraid to be alone with me?"

She pursed her lips. "Of course not."

"Good." I snapped back into my seat and pressed on the gas.

She made a hissing sound and I laughed. I had her. She was trapped.

Silence lapsed for a few minutes as she turned to stare out the window. "Can I ask you something?" she said, her voice tentative and low.

"Yep."

She kept her face turned away, and I knew whatever she wanted to ask was something she wasn't sure she should. "Why aren't you back there with those girls?"

"What makes you think I want to be?" I returned. The vulnerability but also underlying confusion actually made something inside me cave a little.

She snorted. "Everyone calls you Romeo for a reason." I opened my mouth, but she held up her hand to say, "And it's not because it's a variation of your actual name."

I grinned. "You noticed that, huh?"

Rimmel rolled her eyes and turned back to the window.

"Maybe I wanted to be here with you," I answered.

She stiffened in the bucket seat. Her small fingers curled around the edge of the leather. Maybe it was the wrong thing to say. Maybe it sounded too much like a pickup line. I saw the disbelief in the set of her shoulders, in the tension of her jaw. I wanted her to believe me.

Not because I wanted to sleep with her.

Because it was true.

"Those girls back there, hell, the guys too… they only want something from me," I said. She didn't say anything, but I knew I'd caught her attention. I knew she was listening intently, so I continued. "Sometimes I wonder if it's really me they like, or if it's the football star, the guy with the nice car, or the guy who can get them into parties."

I fell silent. I didn't mean to say all that. I only wanted to make her believe me. I hadn't meant to spill the thoughts buried deep in my mind.

* * *

My hands tightened around the steering wheel, flexing a little against the leather. I was acutely aware of Rimmel beside me, so when she moved, I knew it right away.

She rolled her head against the seat so she was looking at me instead of out the window. "It's the blue eyes."

It took a minute for me to realize what she meant. I threw back my head and laughed. "Are you saying you like my eyes, Rimmel?"

She turned away again, but she whispered, "Maybe."

Something inside me eased. The panic I'd felt moments ago about my accidental confession no longer seemed like an issue. Her reaction—or lack thereof—was exactly what I needed. It made me feel like maybe those worries, the ones I held so deep, weren't as bad as I thought they were.

And she liked my eyes.

Really, I wasn't surprised. My eyes were pretty damn amazing.

I turned into the long curved driveway that led around the side of the house, and Rimmel straightened in her seat. Nervous energy seemed to vibrate right off her, and I suppressed a smile.

She was so expressive. I never noticed until I started to really pay attention to her. Most people I was sure didn't realize because you had to really look at her to notice. But I was beginning to like it. I was beginning to want to do nothing but watch her. Every time her mood changed (which was like every five minutes) it was a new experience. I felt like I was seeing this house for the first time through someone else's eyes.

And she was intimidated.

Most people I brought here ooohed and ahhhed over the sweeping pristine driveway, columns lining the main house, the picturesque landscaping, and the amazing backyard. It was an impressive home and it left an impression on people.

But not Rimmel.

She didn't care about all the things everyone else did. If anything, she went against it.

"My mom is a perfectionist," I explained, wanting to distract her. "She likes everything to look perfect all the time."

"It is beautiful," she said politely.

I parked the car and pointed through the windshield to the guest house. "That's my place. I live out there by myself."

"It must be nice to not have to share a bathroom." She stuck out her tongue. A flame of desire ignited low in my gut.

I cleared my throat and got out of the car. Rimmel followed along behind me as we walked around the pool. I noticed the wide arc she made around the edge and the wary look in her eye. "Don't like to swim?"

"No," she said tightly, and then a wall closed over her features.

"Want a soda?" I asked, walking through the living room and into the kitchen.

"Sure," she replied, stopping at the island and dropping her bag on the floor.

I grabbed two cans of Coke out of the fridge and turned. "Heads up," I called and tossed it to her.

She threw up her hands and ducked. The soda hit the back of the barstool and bounced on the floor.

"You were supposed to catch that," I pointed out as she unfolded her arms from her head.

"You were supposed to hand it to me." She glared.

I shook my head and came around the island to pick up the can. I held it out in front of her face and flirted with the top. "Think it will explode if I open it?" I wagged my eyebrows.

She backed up a step. "Don't you dare."

I lifted the tab on the top just slightly. She shrieked and moved to rush by me, holding her arms up to protect her face from the spray. I laughed and caught her around the waist, dragging her back as I set the can on the counter.

"I'm not cleaning up the mess that will make."

"Jerk!" she said and lifted her arm to smack me.

I wrapped my other arm around her, pressing her hands down against her sides. She struggled for a second. Then she seemed to realize how close we were and her body went still.

I could smell the shampoo from her hair, feel the rapid beating of her heart against her chest, and hear the unsteady breaths she was dragging into her lungs.

One of my hands flattened against her back and slid down so it rested in the hollow of her waist, just above her ass. My fingers flexed and her head tilted back so she could look up into my face.

Fuck, she was small. She didn't even come to my shoulder. I imagined in that moment she looked a lot like she did the other night with my jacket on. Engulfed. Owned. Claimed.

But this time it wasn't by my jacket.

It was by my arms.

Her eyes showed surprise, but beneath that emotion I saw something more. I saw desire and need. I saw attraction.

The urge to kiss her slammed into me so hard my arms jerked her closer. Her breath whooshed out of her and her eyes rounded.

Slowly, I lowered my head, taking my time and anticipating the moment. My gaze fixed onto her full lips and I imagined sucking them into my mouth and rubbing my tongue over their softness.

Just breaths away from our first touch, she sucked in sharply and ducked her head. The hair piled high on her head whacked me in the mouth, and I drew back slightly. Rimmel's forehead dropped to my chest, and her hand came up to twist in the cotton of my T-shirt.

Why did she pull away? I could feel her desire. I could practically taste it.

The moment was gone so I peeled my arms away from her and stepped back. "I'll get you another soda," I said, noting the raspy quality of my voice. On my way, I grabbed up my own soda, popped the top, and took a healthy swig. The cold, spiky caffeine prickled the back of my throat and erased some of the spell she'd just cast over me.

"So what kind of homework do you need help with?" she asked, sitting at the bar in the kitchen and tucking her legs beneath her. Her cheeks were flushed and the glasses were slipping down her nose.

If she were anybody else, I'd have her in bed right now.

What if she was a virgin?

The thought was so abrupt and so shattering that I spun around and grabbed the edges of the sink. I squeezed the rounded granite and stared out the small window that looked into some trees behind the house.

She probably was a virgin. I mean, look at her. It wasn't like I'd never taken a girl's virginity before. Frankly, it never seemed like that big of a deal.

Until now.

* * *

Was I going to be able to take her virginity because of a dare? An initiation?

I had to.

My reputation. My status. My pride was all on the line.

"Romeo?" A small hand lightly touched the small of my back. All the muscles in that area tightened and my eyes slid closed. When I didn't pull away, her touch grew a little bolder and her fingertips pressed into my shirt. "Are you sick?"

She was standing so close her sweater brushed against my side. Concern radiated off her as she leaned around to try and catch a glimpse of my face. I turned my head and looked at her.

Our eyes collided and my entire world seemed to realign.

Ahh, fuck.

CHAPTER FIFTEEN

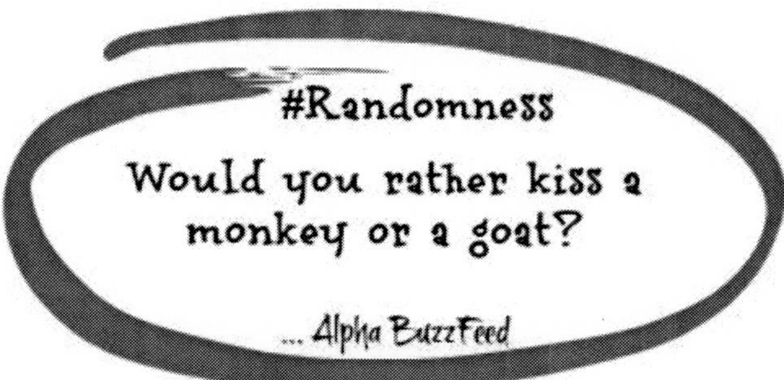

RIMMEL

I thought he was going to kiss me.

For a second, I saw it in his eyes. I wondered if that same look had been reflected back at him.

But when he leaned in, I ruined it. My stupid brain got in the way and stopped him.

I wish I hadn't. I wanted to know what it would be like to kiss Romeo. I'd imagined it more than once. I also wondered what it would be like in his arms.

I knew now.

It was the same feeling I got when I watched my favorite movie for the hundredth time. The same feeling I got when I was tired and cranky and wanted nothing more than to go home and put on my favorite ratty hoodie. It was that feeling I got when I finally was able to put it on.

Relief.

Comfort.

Familiar.

Even though he was almost entirely muscle, being wrapped up in him wasn't rigid; there was enough softness to him that made me want to curl closer, to run my hands around to his back and tug him just a little bit nearer.

But he let go and I stepped away. I don't know how long it took for my heart rate to return to normal, but when it had, I noticed him hunching over the sink like he was suddenly ill.

Didn't it just figure?

I practically melted in this guy's arms and he got sick.

Way to make him want you, Rimmel.

I shook my head. There were so many things wrong with that single thought it scared me. I pushed it aside and moved into the kitchen behind Romeo. My hand hovered over his back for long seconds before I got up enough nerve to actually touch him.

When he didn't pull away, I increased the pressure of my hand. I spoke to him. I don't recall what I said.

He looked at me.

Yes, he'd looked at me many times before. But never like this.

I felt as though a hand punched into my chest and squeezed. The look laid bare in his sparkling blue eyes was raw and intense. It awakened feelings in me I thought I'd buried a long, long time ago.

Romeo turned from the sink. One of his hands curved around my hip and tugged me just a little bit closer. My limbs grew heavy, like I was sinking in a pit of sand. He leaned down and I stretched up.

This time I wasn't going to pull away.

"Roman." An unfamiliar voice broke into the heavy curtain of desire between us. "Oh!" the woman exclaimed in surprise when she saw he wasn't alone.

We jerked apart like lightning struck between us.

"Mom," Romeo said, his voice slightly strained. I turned my eyes on his mother as she stood there staring at us.

Clearly she was surprised. I couldn't understand why. Surely I wasn't the first girl to ever be in his apartment. And we weren't even… well, we were studying.

Well, sort of.

"I saw your car and thought I'd come see if you wanted to join your father and me for dinner," she said, fingering a golden necklace around her throat.

She was a beautiful woman with blond hair, a perfectly made face, a fresh manicure with red fingertips, and dressed in a red sheath to match. Her eyes weren't blue like Romeo's, and I wondered if he'd gotten those from his father. She was taller than me by several inches and looked like she worked out on a regular basis because she wasn't just thin; she was toned.

I remembered what Romeo said about her being a perfectionist about the way the house looked. Clearly that perfectionism extended to her own appearance.

"I'm a little busy right now, Mom," Romeo replied. "But thanks."

"Who are you?" his mother said frankly, eyeing me without apology. I wanted to cringe, but I didn't. If this woman thought appearance was everything, then she must be dying inside as she looked at me.

I stepped forward and extended my hand. It was covered by the purple material of my sweater. I grimaced and shoved it away, offering my hand once more. "I'm Rimmel."

For a brief moment, I thought she might refuse my hand, but then she reached out and lightly grasped my fingers. "I'm Victoria, Roman's mother."

"Nice to meet you, ma'am."

Her eyes narrowed slightly when she pulled back. She didn't like me. It was painfully obvious. My stomach clenched a little. I knew I shouldn't care what her opinion of me was, but I did. This was one of the reasons I chose animals over people. I cared too much. It made me feel sick inside when people looked at me the way she was right now. I couldn't understand why others were so judgmental of each other. I was entirely too sensitive and it was easier to just blend into the background and go unnoticed.

"You got to college with my son?" she asked.

Romeo stepped forward so I could feel the solid wall of him just behind me. I told myself not to enjoy the feeling, to realize he wasn't standing there for me, but because his mother was speaking.

"Thanks for the offer, Mom. Save me a plate? I'll come in and eat later."

Just like that, she dismissed me. Her eyes flicked behind me to settle on Romeo. "We'll talk when you come in."

He agreed and then after another tense moment, she turned and left. I let out the breath I hadn't realized I was holding and turned. "Wow, she's…"

"Intimidating?" he finished, the corner of his mouth turning up. "She's not that bad when you get to know her."

Pain pierced my heart and a small cloud of sorrow swept over me. I turned toward my bag to get out a pencil and notebook.

"Hey," Romeo said softly. He caught my hand and pulled me around. I glanced down at where we touched and stared at the difference in size of our hands. "Did I say something?"

I shook my head. "Maybe we should get to work."

His fingers tightened on mine before he let go. For a second, I hoped he would yank me into him and give me that kiss I'd lost out on twice now.

But he didn't.

We spent the next hour and a half studying. It was hard to focus here in his house. The only light came from two pendants hanging over the island where we were seated. The lights everywhere else in the house were off. The darker it got outside, the more definitive the bubble of light was that we sat in. Like we were in our own little world and beyond it was nothing but darkness.

At one point, I pointed to something on his paper and our hands brushed together. Our eyes met and another one of those heavy moments passed between us. By the time I was packing up my things, my nerves were slightly frayed and my skin was humming.

I didn't know that being alone with him would affect me this way. We finished later than usual because we got a later start. Well, that and I don't think either one of us looked at the clock once.

"I'll drive you back to campus," he said, pushing his notebook aside and standing up to stretch. When he reached his arms over his head, the hem of his T-shirt rode up and I could see a taut expanse of skin across his waist.

Those muscles on either side of his hips were visible again, creating a deep V shape that disappeared down into his jeans.

I bit my lower lip as heat blossomed in my center.

He must have noticed my reaction because his eyes darkened and he slowly lowered his arms. His cell began ringing from somewhere in his pocket and broke the moment.

He swore lightly and pulled it out to look at the screen. "It's Braeden," he said before answering.

"Hey, man," he said.

I picked up my bag and slung it over my shoulder and pointed toward the door. "I'll wait outside."

He nodded and went back to his call. I moved slowly through the dark living room until I made it to the door. Outside was cold. It was never this cold in Florida in October.

My breath puffed out in front of my face and I wrapped my arms around myself for added warmth. I really needed to start remembering a coat. It just wasn't something I ever thought about because in Florida I never had to.

I glanced out at the pool. There were lights glowing from within the water, making it look like an inviting lagoon.

I stayed back away from it and moved around toward the driveway. There were trees lining his property and dotting various points in the landscape. All the leaves were golden and burnished orange. A crisp breeze blew through the night and a few quivering leaves fell and floated silently to the ground.

This house was beautiful. It looked austere and well kept, but not so cold that it was uninviting. I grew up in a small three-bedroom home where the only tree in our yard was a palm tree and the grass was brown most of the year because it was always so incredibly hot.

Maryland was a beautiful state. The trees, the air—

A slamming noise from behind had me spinning around. I glanced at the house, thinking Romeo had finished his call, but it wasn't him.

It was his mother.

She was heading toward me from the back door of the main house. Light spilled out over the concrete from the door she'd left partially open.

"I'm just waiting for Rome-Roman to take me back to campus. He's on the phone," I told her as she stopped in front of me. I didn't want her to think I was out here doing something I wasn't supposed to.

"Why are you here?" she asked coolly.

Her question caught me off guard a little. "Umm, we were studying."

Her face turned sour, like she sucked on an entire lemon. "I'm not stupid, you know."

I gave her a blank look. *What?*

"I know my son is very popular. I know he dates."

A pit formed in my stomach. She couldn't possibly think I was dating Romeo. I didn't have to say anything because she just kept on talking.

"You aren't the first girl he's brought home." She crossed her arms over her chest. "He usually sneaks them in and out and thinks his father and I don't see." She rolled her eyes. "He's almost twenty, he's an adult, and he keeps his… relationships quiet so I never say a word."

"I don't understand why you're telling me this." My stomach was feeling twisted and I didn't want to hear about all the girls Romeo brought home.

"You're the first one I've actually seen. The first one he didn't try to hide."

Obviously, she thought I was lying about studying. I wanted to laugh. I wanted to hold out my arms and say *look at me!* But I didn't. I had pride and I also knew Romeo didn't think I was that terrible looking. If he did, I wouldn't have seen that look in his eyes before.

"I won't have you"—she paused to look me up and down—"or any other low-class girl come into my home and try to take advantage of my son. He has a bright future ahead of him, an important one, and I won't allow anyone to distract him from that."

I swallowed. She thought I was a gold-digger? She thought I wanted to somehow benefit from Romeo?

I laughed. I laughed so hard I snorted.

She stared at me like I had five heads.

"Don't worry," I said, drawing up my meager stature and height. "Your son is safe from *low class* like me."

She stiffened. I glanced back at Romeo's house.

What the hell was I doing here? I mean, really. I shouldn't have come. I shouldn't be here. I shouldn't be feeling things for a guy who could never reciprocate. This was wrong. It was just all so wrong.

It wasn't going to happen again.

I couldn't let it.

Tears burned the backs of my eyes and I blinked them away.

His mother was still standing there studying me. It seemed like some of the fight had left her face. But I didn't care. It didn't matter.

"Tell Romeo," I said, not bothering to correct myself and use his full name. "That I found my own way home."

I turned and walked away, keeping my head held high and my shoulders back. I walked that way until I disappeared around the curve in the driveway along the side of the house. Once I stepped into the darkness, I allowed my shoulders to slump.

***

A lone tear fought its way past my furious blinking and trailed over my cheek. I wiped it away and ran.

I ran to the end of the driveway and out onto the street without ever looking back.

CHAPTER SIXTEEN

#DormDrama
Someone got caught cheating last night.
His relationship wasn't the only thing
that went up in smoke.
#Bonfire #GotMarshmallows
... Alpha BuzzFeed

ROMEO

When I went to find Rimmel, she wasn't anywhere in sight.

But my mother was standing in the driveway near the Hellcat, staring off down the empty driveway.

"Where's Rimmel?" I asked, palming my keys.

She turned to me. There was a shadow of regret in her eyes.

"Mom?"

She blinked and she was her normal composed self instantly. "She left. Said to say she found her own way back."

Worry slammed into me. It was the same feeling I got when a running back found an opening and mowed me down on the field. "Where did she go?" I asked harshly.

Mom's eyes widened. "Down the driveway."

I rushed toward my car, fumbling with the handle to get inside.

"Just let her go," Mom called behind me.

I stilled as anger overcame the worry. In seconds, I was towering over her with a hard look in my eyes. "What the hell did you say to her?"

She lifted her chin. "Don't you talk to me like that."

"So help me," I growled, and she drew back. "You let her run off into the dark, in a neighborhood she doesn't know, by herself?" I spat. "You better pray nothing happens to her."

"You care about her."

She was as shocked by her words as I was.

"Yeah," I said, turning back to the Hellcat. "Maybe I do."

"She's not good enough," Mom called.

My fists clenched and I turned in the open doorway of my car. "You don't even know her. She's the only person I've met in years that hasn't wanted one single thing from me."

"She wants something," Mom vowed like she knew.

I gave her a sad look because I couldn't believe she would act this way. "She doesn't have anyone, Mom. Not one friend. I would think a person like you—a woman with so much—could have at least afforded a small amount of kindness."

A stricken look paled her face, but I ignored it and turned away. She was still standing there when my headlights bounced over her as I turned and sped down the drive.

I found her on the next street over, heading in the direction away from campus. It might be funny if it didn't scare me so fucking bad. Yeah, I lived in a nice neighborhood, but that didn't mean these streets were exempt from crime.

Anyone could have driven by and seen her. Rimmel was no match for anyone. She was too small, too gentle, and too innocent to protect herself.

I was going to have to do it for her.

She didn't look when my headlights shone directly behind her, but her steps quickened when she realized I wasn't just going to drive past.

It was freezing outside and all she was wearing was that stupid too big sweater and T-shirt. It hung well past her butt and her thin legs almost looked like twigs sticking out from beneath it. The bag on her shoulder probably weighed more than she did, and I clutched the steering wheel at the sudden bout of anger that lit inside.

She had to know it was me behind her. The Hellcat's engine was the smoothest purr I'd ever heard. But still, she didn't turn around.

She was angry.

I guess I couldn't blame her. My mom was a friggin' piece of work.

I swerved out around her and hit the gas to shoot forward. Up ahead, I pulled to the side of the road and slammed it in park. I swung open the door and jumped out, but I then leaned back in to rummage in the backseat for something.

When my hand closed over it, I straightened and turned toward Rimmel. She was standing down the street a little ways, just staring at me through the darkness. She made no move to come any closer, and the way she shuffled her feet told me she wasn't sure what to do.

But I sure as hell was.

I left the car running, the door open, and the headlights on. I stalked toward her down the street, not once taking my eyes off her. I stopped just shy of bumping into her. I was so close she had to tilt her head all the way back to look up at me.

I said not one word when I reached out and relieved her of the bag and dropped it on the road beside me. Even in the darkness, I could see how pale her cheeks were, how her lower lip trembled just slightly from the cold.

I lifted the item in my arms and worked my hands in it. Then I slid it down over her head. "Up," I murmured, and she lifted to push her arms through the oversized sleeves of my Alpha hoodie.

The soft, thick fabric fell over her, and I felt her sigh against the warmth.

"Don't ever do that again," I ordered, but the words came out hoarse and low.

She tilted up to look at me again, her eyes wide beneath those damned glasses.

I wouldn't wait another second. Not one.

I cupped her jaw, my fingers splaying out against the sides of her head, and then I crushed my mouth to hers.

CHAPTER SEVENTEEN

Love is in the air tonight.
The #BuzzBoss can feel it.
Can you?

... Alpha BuzzFeed

RIMMEL

Oh my God.

He kissed me.

CHAPTER EIGHTEEN

#KissandTell

Who've you been kissing lately?

Reply to @BuzzBoss

... Alpha BuzzFeed

ROMEO

If you'd kissed one girl, you'd kissed them all.

Not true.

The second my lips touched hers, everything else melted away. The street, my car, the initiation. Everything.

Her mouth was soft and inviting. I was demanding, almost desperate, but she didn't seem to mind. She opened for me instantly, and my tongue swept inside, staking its claim. I gripped the sides of her face like she was my lifeline as I slanted my mouth over hers again and again.

Rimmel's hands came up to wrap around my forearms as if to hold me in place while the kiss went on and on. The fullness of her mouth begged to be nipped at, which I did so hungrily at her bottom lip. Her fingers dug into my skin and she reached up on tiptoes so she could get a little bit closer.

Never in a million years would I have guessed the amount of passion her small body could hold. But now I knew. And I was selfish. I wanted it all. I wanted it all for myself.

Our lips met again, crushing against the other, as I released her face and locked my arms around her back. Her body melted against mine, but it wasn't enough. I wanted more.

I palmed the sides of her waist and lifted. She came willingly, wrapping her legs around my waist and flinging her arms around my neck.

The heat of her core pressed against my middle had my cock straining against my jeans as need hammered my bloodstream until I thought I might burst.

I ripped my mouth away and looked at her. Her eyes were heavy and dazed, her lips swollen and pink. My God, she was beautiful. More beautiful than anyone I'd ever seen.

I tightened my arms around her, holding her tight. Possession was like a set of impenetrable handcuffs as it enclosed around me.

She let out a small sigh and wiggled her bottom so she was closer. The action had my gut clenching and the urge to carry her around to the hood of my car and bury myself deep inside her right here on the street took hold of me.

I started walking before I even realized what I was doing.

A car drove by, slowing a little as it went around us. Reality came crashing back and I realized we were on the street. Rimmel wasn't some lay I could just do on my car out here in the open. She deserved better than that.

"Fuck," I muttered and then reversed my steps. She started to slide down my body, back to her feet, but I bent to pick her back up. I growled a little deep in my throat and clutched her to me. Her legs came back around me just as snug as before, and I carried her and the bag to the Hellcat.

When she was seated in the passenger side, I reached around her and pulled the seatbelt across. The back of her head was resting against the seat and her hands were lost in my hoodie. Once the belt clicked into place, I pulled back and looked at her, sweeping my eyes over her face.

Before going around to get in the driver's seat, I dropped a quick kiss to her lips.

Neither one of us said a word on the short drive back to campus. When her dorm came into sight, my stomach tightened a little. I wasn't ready to let her go.

When I parked, she started to tug her arm out of the hoodie. I reached over and stopped her. "No you don't."

She looked at me with a question in her eyes.

"Keep it. Wear it to the game Saturday night."

"The game?" she asked.

I threaded my fingers through hers and lifted her hand to my lips. "You're gonna come watch me play, aren't you?"

"Uhhh," she stuttered.

I gave her one of my charming smiles. She sighed. "Yeah, maybe."

I knew she'd be there. Just the thought of knowing she was there watching made me want to play better than ever.

She glanced down at the hoodie. It was the football team's colors, deep royal blue and golden yellow. It read Property of Alpha Football across the front.

"You're sure you want me to keep this?" Her voice was wary.

"I'm sure," I said definitively. "I'm beginning to think you don't own a coat."

She giggled. "I do. I just always forget it. We never needed one in Florida."

I tucked a strand of hair behind her ear. "You're from Florida?"

She nodded.

"Your mom probably isn't a piece of work like mine." I meant it as a joke, something to make her smile.

Sorrow wrapped around her like a thick blanket. "My mom died."

"Oh, baby," I murmured, leaning close to press my forehead against hers. "I'm sorry."

"It was a long time ago," she whispered. "I was eleven."

"*Shit*," I swore under my breath. She grew up without a mother. I couldn't even imagine what that must have been like.

I felt her stare on me so I lifted my gaze to meet hers. Our faces were so close it looked like she had one large eye instead of two.

"I *do not* want your pity." Her voice was firm.

I couldn't help but smile. She had a little Hellcat buried beneath her hood. "No pity here." I drew back and kissed her forehead.

Rimmel sat back and pushed her glasses up on her nose. "Romeo, what happened?" she whispered.

I knew she meant between us. Hell, I was sort of wondering that myself.

All I knew was I couldn't deny the way she affected me.

"Something," I murmured.

"Something," she echoed.

She pulled away and started to get out of the car. I caught the sleeve of the hoodie and tugged. "Tell me you aren't going to pull away," I said. A part of me was worried the minute she left this car, the bubble of whatever was between us, she would get scared and run away.

Her teeth sank into her lower lip and she regarded me. I could see the doubt already creeping in around her eyes.

"Tell me, Rimmel," I demanded. I wouldn't let her out of this car until I heard it from her lips.

"I promise."

I barely heard the words, but she said them. Something inside me eased a little. "I'll wait 'til you're inside the building," I told her.

She looked back on her way inside the dorm. My hoodie totally dwarfed her small frame and I liked it. Just seeing it on her made me feel triumphant.

I wondered how long it would take her to figure out it had my name and number on the back.

I grinned to myself. I hoped she didn't notice until she wore it somewhere that everyone could see. Then they would know she was mine.

* * *

My phone beeped and I looked down at it as she disappeared inside.

I'M HERE. WHERE ARE YOU?

Shit, I forgot I told Braeden to meet me.

BE THERE IN A FEW

I didn't drive back home. I just went across campus.

I had a burglary to accomplish.

CHAPTER NINETEEN

#SwoonAlert
If Romeo showed up at your window, would you let him in?
#ReportsOfRomanceOutsideTheDorm

... Alpha BuzzFeed

RIMMEL

What the hell just happened?

I felt fuzzyheaded and drunk, only I hadn't drunk one drop.

Kissing him was what I imagined an atomic bomb would be like. His lips completely obliterated everything around them.

One minute I was standing on the street, feeling angry and hurt, and the next… the next I was wearing his hoodie and promising not to run away.

I didn't even know it could be like that. So intense. So electrifying. My head still swam and my knees felt weak. What did it mean?

Other than he was like the world's best kisser.

Romeo acted like it was going to happen again. He asked me to wear his hoodie to the game. He wanted me there.

He made me promise not to run.

But what about him?

I don't think he understood what he was getting himself into. He'd been caught up in the moment, in that incredible kiss. He was likely driving home right now and shaking his head. He was probably already regretting what happened.

I opened the door to my room and crept inside, closing the door silently behind me. When I turned, I let out a breath. Ivy wasn't home. Thank goodness. She'd take one look at me and know something happened. Then she would demand to know what it was until I caved.

I wasn't ready to tell anyone. I wanted to keep this night to myself even for just a little while.

Morning would come. Should I keep that promise? Should I believe there was something between Romeo and me? What if I did and he hurt me? What if he laughed? I didn't want to go through that. It hurt too much.

After I set my bag aside, I pulled down the covers on the bed and turned out the light. I changed into a pair of cotton boxers and a white tank for sleep, hesitating a moment before pulling off Romeo's hoodie. I draped it over the end of my bed before climbing in and lying down.

I wished I knew what he was thinking right now. I didn't know what to do. If only my mom were still here, I could call and ask her for advice.

I missed her.

I missed her every day.

I worried about Romeo for a while before I started reliving that kiss, the way he held me in his arms and carried me to the car. I thought I was too keyed up to sleep, but I drifted off with tingling lips.

I don't know how much later I was roused by a sound. It was probably Ivy sneaking in past curfew and trying not to be loud about it. I burrowed down into my blankets a little bit farther and slipped back into sleep.

Tink, tink, tink.

My eyes popped open. That wasn't any sound Ivy ever made sneaking in before.

Tink, tink, tink.

I rolled over in bed and listened some more. It sounded like something hitting against glass. When it didn't stop, I pushed up and flicked on a small lamp beside my bed. I looked across the room to Ivy's bed and noted she still wasn't home.

I glanced at the clock. It was after two a.m. She must not be coming home.

The noise continued, this time louder. It was coming from over by the window.

I got up and crept over and peered down into the grass.

I wasn't wearing my glasses, they were next to the bed, so my vision was slightly blurry, but I would know Romeo anywhere.

What the hell was he doing?

I unlatched the locks on the window and pushed the glass up. "Rimmel," he whisper-yelled from beneath.

"What are you doing?" I whisper-yelled back.

"I'm coming up!" he said and started backing up like he was going to jump.

I know I wasn't wearing my glasses, but my eyesight wasn't that bad. How did he think he was going to make it up here? A rustling sound below drew my attention away from Romeo. Braeden was down there too. He was standing beneath the window like he was ready to give Romeo and boost.

They were insane. They must be drunk.

Before I could tell them to stop, Romeo launched himself forward and used Braeden as some kind of launching pad. His hand just cleared the window ledge and he swung back and forth like he was going to fall.

"Romeo!" I gasped and rushed forward to grab his hand.

His other hand swung up and gripped the ledge, giving him a much more solid hold. He glanced up at me with blond hair falling over his forehead and mischief in his gaze. "Hi."

I giggled. "Hi."

"Where's your glasses?"

"I don't wear them to bed."

He smiled. "Move back so I can come in."

I released his hand and backed up. Seconds later, he swung himself into the room with ease and straightened.

"Day-um." He whistled, keeping his voice low as he looked up and down my body.

The tiny shorts and tank left very little to the imagination.

"You look hot," he growled and came at me.

I backed up a step and he caught me around the waist. Both of us fell back and landed on my bed. I laughed and looked up. But he wasn't laughing or smiling.

His gaze was intense and it made my heart skip a beat.

"What?" I whispered. Maybe he'd come to tell me how much he regretted earlier.

"Has anyone ever told you just how beautiful you really are?" He breathed.

The bottom fell out of my stomach and I shook my head.

"That's a damn shame," he muttered and lowered his head to capture my lips.

I surrendered to him immediately. The feeling of him on top of me was so delicious that I shivered. His hand slid down to my hip and pulled me more firmly under him as he explored my mouth lazily.

It wasn't the same kind of desperate kiss as before, but it rocked my world just the same. He kissed me so thoroughly that my legs began to shake and the center of my panties were moist. I could feel the rigid length of him pressing against the front of his jeans, and it made me shake more.

When he pulled back, he stared down with soft eyes and a small smile on his lips.

"Are you drunk?" I blurted out. Then I winced. *Way to play it cool, Rimmel.*

He chuckled low. "Nope."

"So you're really just kissing me because you want to?" I asked. Once again with the mouth vomit. When would I ever learn?

"Ah," he said, sitting up and putting his back against the wall. His legs were so long that his feet still hung off the side of the mattress. "Already having morning-after doubts and it's not even morning yet."

"Technically it is." I countered.

He laughed and reached for me. I didn't pull away. I couldn't. I was powerless to the need he created in me. Romeo settled me in his lap and tucked an arm around me. "I like kissing you."

He reached down and fingered his hoodie on the bed. "You sleeping with this?" His voice grew raspy.

I shrugged. "Maybe."

He growled, wrapped his arms around me, and buried his face in my shoulder. "You really test my limits," he said. Then I heard him mumble, "Already."

"Your limits?" I asked, pulling back to look at him.

"If you were any other girl, I would already have you naked and beneath me."

His words should have shocked me. Maybe made me angry.

They didn't.

They turned me on. I shivered with newfound desire.

He groaned and sat me aside and stood from the bed. "You're killing me, Smalls."

"Smalls?" I giggled.

He grinned. "That's what we call the small players on the team."

"I'm not on your team." I pointed out.

"No. But you are mine." The ownership in that statement made my blood run hot. This was moving fast. Like way fast. He must have seen the fear on my face because his eyes softened and he dropped down beside me and took my hand.

"I can be intense sometimes," he allowed. "I don't mean to freak you out."

"It's okay," I murmured, looking at our joined hands.

"When I set my sights on something, I tend to just go for it, full speed ahead." He brushed the pad of his thumb across the back of my hand. "We'll take it slow, okay?"

"You and me?" I said, still not really believing this was happening.

"Yeah." He smiled.

I should have said no. I didn't want to. I hadn't wanted something this much since well, *ever*.

"Okay."

He gave me an enthusiastic kiss and then bounded up from the bed. "I did come here to kiss you again." He began. "But that's not the only reason I'm here."

I was still trying to catch up to the fact that there might be an us. "Okay?" I asked tentatively.

"I need a favor."

CHAPTER TWENTY

#LateNightMusings

If you sext, do you get a phoner?

... Alpha BuzzFeed

ROMEO

Braeden was waiting for me exactly where we said to meet. I pulled the Hellcat slowly down the dirt road that led to the bonfire party spot. No one ever came out here during the week. He was leaning against his huge truck when I parked right beside it.

"Sorry I'm late, man," I said.

"Everything cool?" he asked, eyeing me from his comfortable position against the truck.

"Yeah, it's cool." Normally, if I was late because of a hook-up, I would brag and we would laugh. But I didn't want to tell him who I'd been with. I felt like I wanted to keep it to myself just a little bit longer.

"So what's up?" Braeden asked, not pressing me for the details. "Why did you want to meet out here?"

"I didn't want anyone to see us," I replied.

He straightened from the truck, his interest piqued.

"I gotta do something. Something I could get in trouble for if I got caught."

"For the rush?" Braeden assumed.

I nodded yes at the same time I said, "I'm not supposed to say."

"Got it," he replied immediately. "You need help?"

"I need a lookout."

He nodded.

"Dude, if we get caught, there won't be much I can say to help either one of us."

He grinned. "Even better."

That's one of the reasons I liked Braeden so much. He was crazy as hell.

"Beer's on me this weekend," I promised.

He pumped his fist in the air. "Sweet!"

"We need to go to the faculty and admin building. I need to get in the dean's office." I started to say more but stopped because Braeden started laughing. The wicked gleam in his eye made me laugh too.

"Dude, you need to rush a frat. You'd eat the shit up they make you do."

"I like my freedom," he drawled. "I'm a wild stallion, can't be tied down to nothing. Not even a kickass frat."

"What about Missy?" I taunted.

A slow smile spread across his face and he ran his hand through his thick, eternally messy dark hair. "Dude, she's fucking hot." Then he held out his hands like he was squeezing something. "And she's so good in bed."

I slapped him on the back. "You're totally whipped."

He knocked my hand away. "Shit, like hell I am."

I could have stood here and ribbed him all night, but we had shit to do, and the longer I dragged it out the more anxious I got. "Okay, so let's take your truck across campus and park in a lot near the building, but not too close. We can jog over. I just need you to stand lookout in case someone comes. Just text me or something to let me know I gotta get out of there."

It only took a few minutes to drive to an empty lot and park. It took even less time to jog to the building. I left my varsity jacket in the truck and Braeden did the same. Both of us were dressed in jeans and dark-colored shirts so we blended into the night fairly well when we stuck to the shadows of the building.

The good thing was the streetlights on this side of campus were fewer and farther between because classes weren't held over here and there weren't any dorms. Students wouldn't have any reason to come over this way at night.

Unless of course you needed to steal something.

When we got to the building, we tried the back door, the one that faced the parking lot. It was locked. Adrenaline pumped through my veins as we scaled around the perimeter, looking for a way in. When every single door appeared to be locked, I felt myself start to sweat. I had to get inside.

"Pssst," Braeden called from several yards away. He motioned for me and when I got to his side I saw that he'd managed to get a window open. It wasn't a huge one, but I could shimmy in.

"The fuck did you do?" I whispered, pointing to the way the metal frame around the old window was bent and the lock was somehow popped out on the inside.

He grinned. "I got skills."

I held up my fist for a pound. Then I mouthed, "Wait here."

I hoisted myself up into the window and shoved my feet in first. I had to wiggle a bit to get my shoulders to pass through the opening, but after a few tries, I dropped down onto the floor with a soft thud.

I was in someone's office, but I knew it wasn't the dean's. It wasn't nearly big enough or nice enough for the head of the college. I moved stealthily through the room and peered out into the hallway. It was dark and empty.

I slid along the walls. It was eerily silent and still inside. There was no light at all, so I used my cell phone to provide enough to see. Everything smelled like floor polish with maybe a hint of lemon. Except it didn't make it smell fresh. It smelled like the cleaning crew just added the lemon to take away the harsh smell of the cleaners.

It didn't work.

Maybe when we left we'd leave that window open in a poor attempt at airing out the place before everyone showed up to work in a few hours. Poor people. No wonder half the faculty at this school was cranky as hell. They were probably high off stanky cleaning fumes.

One of the hallways widened at the end to create a square, open room, kind of like an entryway. The wall to my left was lined with chairs and what appeared to be a sad-looking fake plant. On the other side was a wooden desk set up with various office supplies.

This must be the dean's personal secretary. I glanced ahead at the large double wooden doors with a plaque on the front. I shined my phone at it and the polished gold reflected back at me. DEAN.

Bingo.

I tried the handle and it didn't turn. What the fuck could he possibly have in his office that warranted locking his door?

I leaned my forehead against the wood and let the light on my phone click off. After a few moments of debating, I went and searched the secretary's desk, thinking maybe she had a key.

She didn't.

But she did have a drawer full of paperclips. I snagged one and bent it around so it was straight like a wire. Then I went back to the office door and used my phone to shine on the door handle.

Seconds later, the sound of a lock popping free echoed through the hall. I looked behind me to make sure no one was there and then slipped into the room, closing and the door behind me.

The dean's office was big, which wasn't a surprise. The most dominant thing in the room was the massive desk sitting in the center. Behind it was a wall of windows covered with closed blinds.

I wasn't about to take a tour of the place. I just wanted to get the hell out of there. I surged forward and shone the light on his desk, looking for something I could take. My gaze settled on his nameplate, which was basically a long block of wood with his name engraved on it.

I grabbed it as my cell vibrated in my hand.

I glanced down.

GUARD!

Shit.

The sound of footsteps echoing down the hall, drawing closer, caused my heart to jump in my throat. I raced around the other side of the desk and slipped beneath it.

Seconds later, the handle on the door jiggled and opened. The only sound I could hear was the thundering of my pulse. I didn't even breathe, just pressed myself beneath the desk and hoped the guy didn't come all the way in. He didn't, but the bright beam of his high-powered flashlight roamed about the room, inspecting the corners, suspicious.

After what seemed like eternity, the light clicked off, the door shut, and the sound of footsteps faded away.

I let out a breath but sat there for a while just to make sure the guard wasn't coming back.

When I was sure he was gone, I crept to the door and let myself out. I stuffed the nameplate in the waistband of my jeans and rushed back into the office where I'd come through the window.

Braeden wasn't there when I dropped onto the ground. I rushed around the side of the building and almost got caught in the beam of security's headlights. I dropped to the ground and rolled into the shadows.

Security drove away.

The sound of muffled laughter burst from behind.

I jumped up and turned. Braeden stepped out from behind some landscaping, his white teeth flashing in the dark. "Dude, you should have seen your face."

"Fuck you," I said with a grin.

"Did you get it?"

"Yeah, let's go."

Once we were in the safety of Braeden's truck, he turned to me. "Now what?"

Now I had to hold on to this until the frat party on Friday night, but I didn't want it at my house. I didn't trust Zach. I wouldn't put it past him to call in some lame tip to the dean about the missing item from his office. The next thing I'd know, people would be pounding on my door and searching for this stupid piece of wood.

Yeah, no. I wasn't going down like that.

I needed somewhere to keep it.

Somewhere no one would think to look.

I rolled my head toward Braeden. "Let's go to Cypress Hall."

He gave me a strange look. "The chick's dorm?"

I smiled.

CHAPTER TWENTY-ONE

#Spotted
One sweet Hellcat was seen outside the girl's dorm.
#SomeonesGettingLucky
... Alpha BuzzFeed

RIMMEL

"You *stole* that from the dean's office!" I heard myself shriek, and I stared at the nameplate he held out for me to see. I jumped up from the bed and paced the small space in front of Romeo.

He was absolutely nuts.

"Why the hell would you do that?" I asked.

Then I stubbed my toe on the edge of my desk.

"Ow!" I hissed and doubled over while bouncing around on one foot.

"You're like a one-woman show," Romeo remarked from behind me. His voice was clearly amused.

"I need my glasses," I muttered, hopping around and reaching for them somewhere near my bed. I knocked something over and it fell to the floor.

"Whoa there, graceful," Romeo said and scooped me up in his arms.

I let out a little squeak in surprise. "Put me down."

"No," he said mildly. "You are a danger to yourself."

I made a *hmph* sound and he snickered. The bed sagged beneath his weight as he sat down. I moved to scramble off his lap, but he locked his arms around me and wouldn't let go.

"I'm rushing a frat. The Alpha Omegas," he said.

I glanced up; our faces were so close I could feel his breath mingling with mine. "Are you supposed to tell me that?" I asked.

"No."

"So you're saying you took this as part of rush?"

"Yes."

"Why would they make you do something that could get you in serious trouble?" I asked. That just seemed stupid.

"Because it's a frat," he said, like it was obvious.

Then I realized I was dealing with a bunch of men. "Right."

"Anyway, I just need somewhere to keep it 'til Friday."

"What's Friday?" I asked, suspicious.

"A frat party."

"Oh." I thought about when I went to pick up Ivy from the bonfire and the people crowded around him. Something in my stomach churned, and I twisted out of his lap to stand. Somehow during everything that happened tonight, I forgot who Romeo was.

He was popular. He partied. He played football. He had girls vying for his attention. There was no way I could compete with that. I was just a phase. A way to pass time while he was being forced into studying.

I needed to remember that. I couldn't let him in.

Well, not any further than he'd already gotten.

"Hey," Romeo said softly and came to stand behind me. I didn't bother to turn around. "You okay?"

"I'm fine," I said. I certainly wasn't about to admit that for a little while, I was letting my heart take over for my head.

"Hell-o up there!" Braeden's voice floated through the still-open window.

Romeo went over and looked down at him. "I'm coming!" He turned away from the window and picked up my cell that was lying on the table by my bed. With my glasses.

I crossed to pick them up and he handed them to me. Everything came into focus when I slid them into place.

"What are you doing?" I said, noting my phone in Romeo's hand.

"Putting my number in here." I watched him deftly type away. "In case you need me."

"I'm not going to need you."

He grinned and looked up. "Okay, then. In case you *want* me." Then he produced his phone and held it out. "Put your number in."

Well, I guess it couldn't hurt. What if he needed to cancel tutoring?

I was a lousy liar. I totally wanted to give him my number. Just like I totally wanted him to kiss me again.

I was in *so* much trouble.

I punched it in and handed the phone back. "Give me the nameplate," I said and held out my hand.

His smile lit up the entire room, and I found myself smiling back. After he handed it to me, he stepped up close so barely any space separated us.

He kissed me slowly. His lips were gentle as they took over mine. He kissed me until my knees went soft and everything in my head had gone blank.

"I'll see ya later," he whispered against my lips.

He leapt out of my window like he was some kind of cat. The muffled sound of laughter floated up as he and Braeden took off.

I shut the window and hid the nameplate beneath my mattress. Then I climbed back in bed. His scent was on my blankets.

I knew I shouldn't. I knew he was nothing but trouble. But I still fell asleep with a smile on my lips.

Ivy stumbled in the door just before seven a.m. Her shirt was buttoned up crooked and her shoes were on the wrong feet. Her hair looked like she rolled around half the night in bed…

Which she probably did.

Just not her bed.

Someone else's.

"I'm so tired." She groaned and collapsed on her bed.

I was standing in front of my dresser, looking for something to wear. For the first time in a long, long time, I wasn't grabbing the first thing my hand closed around.

I'm not sure what that meant.

Okay, yes, I did. I just wasn't ready to admit it to myself.

"Did you get any sleep last night?" I asked her.

"Ugh. Not enough." She groaned and rolled around on her blanket. "I can't even skip because I have a test this morning."

"Want me to make you some coffee?" I offered.

"I love you," she moaned. I knew she was only kidding and grateful for the coffee, but even still, her words made me feel a pang.

For years I'd told myself it was okay to be a loner. That I didn't need friends because they just hurt you anyway.

But deep down, sometimes I thought it would be nice to have one.

I pushed away the thoughts and went over to the little coffee maker in the corner of the room. It was a Keurig, so all I had to do was add in a little pod and hit a button.

Seconds later, the scent of coffee filled the room. It smelled good, and I decided to have one too. I grabbed a bottle of creamer out of the mini fridge and poured a generous amount in both mugs, then carried one over to Ivy.

"You're my hero," she said, taking the cup and swallowing some down.

I went back over to my dresser and stood sipping out of my cup, pondering my meager wardrobe.

"Are you trying to decide what to wear?" Her voice was sort of awed.

I sighed.

She appeared beside me and reached deep into the bottom drawer and pulled out a pair of dark jeans with the tags still on them. I looked at them curiously. I didn't even remember I had those.

"How'd you know those were there?" I asked.

She rolled her bloodshot eyes. "I went through your clothes."

My mouth fell open. She shrugged. "Please," she said, like I should be surprised. "You know I had to see if you had anything worth borrowing."

"I'm sure you found lots," I said and grinned.

She cringed. "You need a serious wardrobe overhaul."

Apparently she isn't the only one who thinks so, I told myself as I grabbed the jeans. My grandmother sent me these like a year ago. She was always trying to send me cute, trendy outfits, and I never wore any of them.

I yanked the tag off the pants and slid them up my bare legs and under the large T-shirt I had on. "Ugh, they're too tight," I said once they were buttoned.

Ivy laughed. "They're skinny jeans. They're supposed to fit like that."

I went to the full-length mirror and lifted the shirt to study my reflection. They didn't look too bad. At least with these, I wouldn't trip and fall over the too large hem.

"I wish I was that skinny," Ivy said from her bed.

"I look like a boy," I muttered. I didn't have many curves. I'd been small all my life.

"There's a shirt that goes with the jeans in there too," she said.

It was really sad that she knew more about what was in my drawers than I did.

I rifled through the drawer again and sure enough, there in the back was a plain long-sleeve cotton top. It was sinfully soft to the touch and a shade of blue that reminded me of Romeo's eyes.

I pulled off the shirt I'd covered up with after my shower and added a tank top over my bra. The blue shirt wasn't tight, thank goodness, but it wasn't overly large either. It sort of skimmed over my body and ended at my hips. The sleeves were too long (as usual) and that made me feel a little more comfortable because I was able to tuck my hands inside like I did with everything I wore.

"Nice," Ivy said with a yawn.

I decided standing here worrying about my clothes was a waste of time and I turned away from the mirror and grabbed my lip balm to smooth over my lips. I remembered how cold it was last night and fished around under my bed for a pair of cozy boots that really looked more like slippers to me than shoes. But a lot of people wore them around here, and I had to admit they did keep my toes from freezing. I pulled them on, enjoying the way my jeans fit down inside them with ease. Usually, I had to jam my pants down in there and it was uncomfortable and lumpy.

Ivy was watching me with a curious look, and I suppressed the urge to blush like a mad woman. She got up and grabbed a large brush off her dresser and came toward me. Without saying anything, she started brushing through the thick mass that was still partially damp from my shower. It took too long to blow-dry it all completely, so I rarely did.

"You know your hair would be gorgeous if you spent a little time on it," she said as she worked.

"I don't have time to mess with my hair," I said awkwardly.

"Every girl has time to mess with her hair," Ivy rebutted.

"Maybe I just don't care what people think."

"It isn't about what other people think," she said. "It's about the way *you* feel. Being put together on the outside makes you feel better on the inside."

I couldn't really argue with her because I didn't know if she was right. I hadn't bothered with my appearance in so long I didn't know what it would feel like to actually try.

Ivy wandered over to her side of the room and sprayed something on her hands and then worked it through my hair. She divided it into two sections and started braiding the length of it. It made me think of when I was a little girl and my mother used to braid my hair.

A thick lump formed in my throat and I sipped at my coffee, trying to make it dissolve.

When Ivy was done, she stepped back and looked at her handiwork. "Much better."

I got up and went to the mirror. It was a little unsettling to see myself this way. She styled my hair in pigtail braids, but it didn't look juvenile. She somehow managed to make them look thick and bouncy. The unbraided ends curled out around the hair bands and fell against my chest. The top was side-parted and had a little bit of height at the crown, and a few short pieces at my hairline curled against my forehead. The style seemed to draw attention to the shape of my face, and my glasses didn't take over my eyes. Added with the clothes that actually fit and a pair of boots that didn't appear lumpy, I actually looked like all the other college girls that walked around campus.

Without the makeup, of course. I wasn't even going to bother with that stuff. Not today anyway.

"Thanks," I told Ivy, still looking at my transformed hair.

She didn't reply, and that's when I noticed the utter silence. Ivy was standing there beside my bed with the Alpha hoodie in her hands. I must have been sitting on it and when I got up, it caught her eye.

She was holding it out and staring at something. Her reaction was a little odd. I mean, it was just a hoodie. She couldn't possibly know where I got it.

Still clutching the sweatshirt in her hands, Ivy looked up. "How did you get Romeo's football hoodie?" Her voice was hushed, like I'd committed some heinous crime.

"How did you know it was Romeo's?" I asked, slightly uncomfortable.

She held it out to me so I could see the back, his name and number in plain sight.

Oh. Would have been nice if I'd noticed that. A little bit of shock rippled through me as well. I mean, he obviously knew it had his name and number on the back, yet he still told me to keep it. He told me to wear it. He acted as if he wanted people to see it.

"Rimmel!" Ivy demanded.

I glanced up. "What?"

"You have *Romeo's* football hoodie on your bed. *Explain*!"

"Oh. Um, I got cold at tutoring." It wasn't exactly a lie. I had. Besides, I had no idea what to say.

"The douche you're tutoring is *Romeo Anderson*?" she exclaimed. "Why didn't you tell me!" she burst out.

I started to answer, but she was pacing and then jerked to a halt and cut me off to say, "That explains the BuzzFeed and why Romeo is suddenly hanging out at the library."

Then she gasped.

I jerked because it was so dramatic.

"*Ohmigod!*" she rushed out in one breath. "*You're* the mystery girl in the Hellcat."

Damn BuzzFeed.

"Well!" she demanded again. All traces of her utter exhaustion were long gone. "Say something!"

"Oh, I didn't realize I was part of the conversation," I muttered.

"Rimmel." Her eyes narrowed. Then they widened again. "Is that why you were worrying about your clothes? You like him!"

I started shaking my head furiously.

"Yes!" she demanded. Then she glanced down at his hoodie still clutched in her paws. I had the sudden urge to snatch it from her. "Does he like you, too?"

I snorted as my stomach flipped over. I thought about the kisses, about how he crawled in through the window just hours before. If Ivy knew he'd been here in this room, she'd probably collapse. "I highly doubt it," I said and gently pulled the hoodie from her hands. "And the clothes are just because I got tired of tripping and falling over all my baggy stuff."

She gave me a pitiful look. “It sucks to like someone who doesn’t like you back.”

“Yeah,” I said, her words piercing my heart. I wish they didn’t hurt, but they did. And so did the look in her eyes. She felt sorry for me. Like she knew there was no way in hell he could ever like me. It’s like she thought he’d given me his hoodie out of pity.

Ivy was watching me closely. I could feel her penetrating gaze. I turned away and grabbed my bag. It was still a little early for class, but I didn’t care. This room was stifling.

“Hey,” she called out as I reached for the door.

My hands tightened around Romeo’s hoodie. I hadn’t planned to bring it with me, but the thought of leaving it here with her made me sick.

“Yeah?”

“You going to the game Saturday night?”

“Do I ever?” I asked. Truth was I did plan on going because Romeo asked me to. I just planned to sit where no one would notice me.

“You should come. Me and Missy are going.” Her eyes sparkled. “She’s dating Braeden. He’s on the team too.”

I nodded.

"You know him?" She seemed surprised all over again.

"I've met him."

She nodded easily. "Well, yeah, definitely come. You can sit with us. It'll be fun."

Suspicion overcame me. I didn't like feeling that way, but I couldn't ignore it. "Why would you want me to come with you?"

The question caught her off guard and she looked up. "I thought we were friends."

Friends.

"Yeah," I said, stuffing down the unexpected emotion that burned up the back of my throat. "Sure. I'll sit with you at the game."

She gave me a wide smile and waved. "Awesome. Now I better hit the showers. It's going to take a long time to fix all this." She gestured to herself and stuck out her tongue.

It was colder outside than I expected. I thought for sure once the sun was up it would chase away the worst of the autumn chill. It seemed that more leaves had fallen to the ground overnight and people shuffled through them on the sidewalks, rustling sounds filling the air. My cheeks stung a little as the breeze blew and bit into them.

I glanced down longingly at the hoodie in my arms and thought of putting it on. But I didn't. I adjusted it so Romeo's name didn't show and pulled it a little closer to my chest.

Judging from the reaction I got from Ivy when she saw it on my bed, I could only imagine what everyone else would say if I walked through campus with his name plastered on my back.

I certainly didn't want to see the same look of pity Ivy gave me one hundred times over.

CHAPTER TWENTY-TWO

Got Info?
Keep the #BuzzBoss in the know
Contact me via the #AlphaApp

...Alpha BuzzFeed

ROMEO

It was almost three a.m. when I put my key in the door to my place. I was freaking dog tired. Between the grueling practice, classes, raiding the dean's office, and everything that happened with Rimmel, I wanted to pass out for a week.

I stepped inside and didn't bother with the lights. I tossed my bag on the floor and launched my keys somewhere in the vicinity of the couch. I was going to skip my workout in the morning. The last thing I wanted was to be too worn out to perform in Saturday's game.

I bypassed the kitchen and headed straight to my room. All of a sudden, a feeling of unease crept up the back of my neck and caused me to pause.

Just as I was about to turn, something slammed into me and I was tackled to the ground. It didn't hurt because my training kicked in immediately and I knew how to take the fall.

Immediately, my arms went around the waist of my attacker and I hugged him, flipping us both over so I was on top. I'd caught him off guard, and the guy beneath me looked up in surprise. I threw my fist down, putting all my weight behind it, and caught him in the jaw.

He groaned and tried to buck me off. I raised my hand again, adrenaline and rage making me crazy. When I swung down, something stopped me from connecting. A hand caught my wrist and twisted it behind my back.

"Easy!" someone yelled. "Think of Saturday!"

What the fuck…?

The hands grabbing me loosened, but I was being gripped now from all sides. I started to struggle, but I was severely outnumbered. I was shoved down onto the ground, my hands were cuffed, and a bag was tied over my head.

"What the fuck is this!" I demanded, struggling as they brought me to my feet. I kicked out and connected with something. Sick satisfaction filled me for making someone hurt.

I wanted to make these fuckers bleed.

"What crawled up your ass and died?" someone said.

Everyone laughed.

They were fucking Omegas.

Some of the fight left me, but not all. What kind of assholes jump someone in their own home?

Zach probably put them up to this.

"Search him," someone else ordered. They kept their voice low and hushed. I couldn't see, but I really thought it was Zach.

Hands patted me down and checked my pockets. They were looking for the nameplate. I smirked because they weren't going to find it.

"It's not here," someone else said.

"Check the bag," the guy I thought was Zach ordered.

I heard all my shit being dumped all over the place, and my hands clenched behind my back. After several minutes of my place being tossed, they determined what they wanted wasn't here.

"Looking for something specific?" I said through the bag over my head.

"Bring him and let's go," Zach ordered.

"Don't fucking hurt him," someone else said roughly. "He's gotta play Saturday."

"Don't get your panties in a wad, Trent," someone behind me muttered.

"Shut it," Zach demanded.

This was some jacked-up shit.

I could only assume I was being taken to the same place I was the night we were introduced to rush. I didn't bother fighting them. I wanted to know what was going on. When we finally arrived to wherever they brought me, the bag was yanked off my head and I blinked to take in my surroundings.

All the other pledges were here too. A little of me relaxed because at least I wasn't being brought somewhere to get jumped. We were in the same basement-looking space as before, except this time there weren't tons of lit candles. Lamps and lights hanging above a few pool tables in the back were on instead.

"Fellow Alphas," Zach said, spreading his arms wide as he looked at the frat members off to the side. Then he scanned the pledges. "Wannabes. I have brought you all here tonight for a little check-in. And for some of you, a check-*out*." He glanced at a couple guys and smirked. "We're a little more than halfway through this year's rush, and as predicted, some of you are made for this and others… well, you suck!" he yelled the last word and all the members laughed.

This guy was such a douche. How the hell did be become president? I glanced around at the members, my eyes stopping on Trent. He looked at me and I saw the irritation in his eyes. Clearly he was wondering the same thing.

"You have all been given challenges and most of you have complied. Branneman!" he yelled and looked toward the end of the line where a dark-haired male stood.

"Yes?" he replied.

"You didn't complete the last challenge we gave you. You're out."

His body jerked and his jaw hardened. "Ye—" He began, but Zach cut him off.

"No excuses!" He motioned to a couple of the members and they stuffed a bag over Branneman's head and escorted him out.

Zach locked eyes with me. I held his stare and refused to look away. "Cox, too!" Zach snapped.

Two guys down from me, another bag was stuffed on a surprised head and he was escorted out as well.

"Max was escorted out of the pledge group last week," Zach added and then looked at the rest of us. "And so you all remain."

Was he going to get to the point already? I was exhausted, and by the time I got home, it was going to be daylight.

"I know some of you have already taken your assigned woman to bed. I hope you got pictures, losers, because if you don't, the same fate those men just endured awaits you."

My shoulders stiffened at the reminder of this "assignment." I wanted to get Rimmel into bed more than I ever had anyone, but I didn't want to do it like this. I was never the kind of guy who was bothered by one-night stands, casual sex, or drunken hookups. As long as it was consensual, I was down. But having to sleep with a woman to get myself into an exclusive club, a woman that was chosen for me, a woman I essentially had to use, left a bad taste in my mouth.

I don't know why it didn't bother me before, but it suddenly did now.

Wait.

Yes, I did know.

Rimmel.

"Show of hands," Zach called. "Who's finished this challenge?"

Several hands went up. Everyone looked around. A lot of gazes landed on me. I didn't flinch. Hell, I wasn't even embarrassed I wasn't the first.

"Well, well, well..." Zach said, pacing over to stand in front of me.

"Looks like *Romeo* might be losing his touch."

I gave him a look that said I was bored.

"What's the matter, *Romeo*?" Zach taunted. "Is the nerd too much of a challenge?"

I felt my lip curl when he mentioned Rimmel.

"The clock's a ticking." Zach got up in my face. "Less than two weeks to seal the deal."

I didn't say a word. I just stared him down.

"I gotta tell ya," he boasted, stepping away from me and addressing everyone else. "I don't think you can do it. She's probably cold as ice."

One. More.

All he needed to say was one more fucking word about her and I would pound him.

A couple of the pledges laughed. Probably not because it was funny, but because they wanted to kiss Zach's ass.

"Tomorrow night we're having a frat party at Omega. Be there. See what life will be like when you're one of us." Zach looked at me again. "Did you get what you were supposed to?"

"Of course," I replied.

"Where is it?"

"Somewhere you won't find it," I said smoothly.

"You were supposed to bring it," Zach challenged.

"To the party tomorrow, not here. Not now."

"You have it when I say you have it!" Zach snapped.

Dude needed a beer.

He needed to chill the fuck out.

"C'mon, Zach. We all saw the text. You said the party." One of the members who was not Trent spoke up.

Zach shot him an angry look but said nothing.

"The night before the inductions into Omega, you will be brought back one final time. Have your proof that you slept with your assigned female. If you have it. You're in." He glanced at me. "If you don't? You're out."

Bags were shoved on all of our heads once more. Hands grabbed me and spurred me forward.

"Rick," Zach said behind us.

The hands guiding me stopped. The bag was ripped off my head again, and I found myself looking into Zach's eyes. "Bring the girl tomorrow night," he said.

The last thing I wanted to do was bring Rimmel into a room full of these assholes. "What the fuck for?"

He smiled. It looked more like a sneer. "I'd like to meet the nerd. I hear you've become quite smitten."

The more he talked about her, the more he implied he knew her, the more pissed off I got. I lunged forward and shoved my face right up in his. Satisfaction speared me when his eyes widened just a fraction. He wasn't as tough as he thought he was.

"Well, since you seem to know everything," I said, dead calm, "then you must also know that I take care of what's mine. You might be president of this frat, but I own the campus. Do. Not. Push. Me."

An arm wrapped around me from behind and towed me back. "You said what you needed to say, man," Trent said. "Let's go."

"Bring her," Zach called after us. "I mean it."

The bag was stuffed back on my head, and I stiffened. "Chill," Trent murmured and led me from the building.

As soon as the cold air hit me, I reached up and ripped the bag off my head and swung around. Trent and three other Omegas were standing there looking at me.

"That guy is a total douche," I spat.

No one disagreed.

"You're supposed to keep that on," Trent said.

I ignored him. "So is he that much of an asshole to everyone or just me?"

The guys all looked around. Trent sighed. "I'll take him home," he told the others.

They all nodded and left.

"This shit ain't worth the hassle," I told Trent as I looked around. The Omega house loomed in front of us. We were in the backyard near what looked like an old shed. Off to the side was one of those old-looking doors that lifted out of the ground. It reminded me of the *Wizard of Oz* and the shelter they ran to during the tornado.

That must be where we'd come from. That must be the hangout of the Omegas.

"C'mon," Trent said, and I fell into step beside him as we walked toward a black SUV parked nearby.

When we were in the car, Trent turned over the engine and said, "I've never seen him hate someone so much."

"Yeah, well, the feeling's mutual."

Trent shook his head. "He's pushing it with you. We've all warned him. He keeps it up and it's borderline hazing."

"No one will tell," I said. And it wasn't like I was the type to run and tattle either. I could handle Zach. I could handle any hazing he might decide to dish out. What I couldn't handle was him messing with Rimmel because he knew it would get to me.

"You'd be surprised," Trent said and drew my stare.

"What do you mean?"

"I mean the Omegas haven't been too happy with their leadership in a while."

I grunted. "What a surprise."

"Look, we all see that he's going out of his way to make it hard on you. You have more friends here than Zach. He just doesn't realize it."

"I won't have him messing with her," I said. There was no give in my words.

I felt his sidelong stare as we drove silently for a few minutes. Then he sighed. "Yeah. I thought that might be the case."

We pulled up to my house not too much later. The sky would soon start lightening with the rising sun.

Trent put it in park and looked at me. "Look, just get through rush. Once you're inducted, we'll take care of Zach."

"What do you mean?"

"I mean the reason he didn't want you last year is because he knew once you made it in, we'd all outvote him as president."

I glanced at him. "You want me as president?"

"Dude, you're like the most popular guy on campus. The party follows you. Not to mention you're the quarterback for the Wolves, and if you take presidency now, the Omegas will have a steady leader for the next couple years."

Basically, he was saying if I became president of the Omegas, the already popular, exclusive frat would just become more so.

Maybe he could sense my hesitancy. Or maybe he just knew I was really pissed off, because he said, "You know the Omegas have connections with the NFL. A couple of our alumni, retired Omega, are NFL vets."

I knew that. It's the main reason I wanted in. The NFL was my end goal, and this was a way in.

"Fine," I said and opened the door. "I'll see you at the party tomorrow."

"I'll be there."

I leaned back in before shutting the door. "Thanks for having my back. I won't forget it."

"I know," he replied.

He drove off down the driveway, and I went inside. I walked through the mess they made in my house, kicked off my shoes, and fell into bed.

I had classes in a couple hours and I had to be there. Coach wasn't too lenient on players who missed them during the season.

But the last thought that passed through my head before I fell asleep was of Rimmel.

CHAPTER TWENTY-THREE

Public Service Announcement:
After what the #BuzzBoss saw today, it's safe to say flesh colored pants are NEVER in style.
#Wrong #EyeDoucheAnyone?
...Alpha BuzzFeed

RIMMEL

By lunch, it wasn't any warmer than it had been this morning. I was grateful for the boots on my feet because if I was just wearing sneakers, I knew my toes would be frozen.

The sky was dim and gray, the sun only peeking through every so often. The air was blustery; the wind would whip up out of nowhere and brush its cold promise of winter against my cheeks. Brightly colored leaves scattered the ground and somersaulted across campus as everyone moved from class to class.

I skipped breakfast and was starving by the time my lunch break rolled around. Classes had seemed endless today, so I filled some of my time working on assignments while the teachers droned on and on.

The eating hall (or so I called it) sat almost in the center of campus. The building was two massive levels with the campus store filling the lower floor and the eating hall on the top. I guess it was really more of a food court than an eating hall, like the kind you might find at a nice mall.

I walked up the stairs and glanced around, trying to decide what I felt like eating. Around the perimeter of the room were various types of restaurants and eateries. There was a pizza place, a taco place, a deli that made sandwiches and offered a variety of chips. There was a place called The Market that offered salads and fruits, granola bars, and fancy bottled waters. There was also the typical burger joint and a place that had chicken. Over on the far side was a smoothie bar that had a never-ending line. There was even a coffee bar, which was also always packed.

I settled on grabbing a Cobb salad from The Market, a cup of fresh seasonal fruit, and a granola bar (for later). Once I had all that, I got in line at the coffee bar and waited ten minutes to get a pumpkin-flavored latte. They weren't very popular in Florida, but here in the North, they were practically gold.

The cold I was having a hard time adjusting to, but the pumpkin latte? Yeah, no problem there.

When finally I was handed my coffee, I wrapped my one free hand around it and sighed at the warmth that seeped into my fingers. It was busy in here, like always, and I thought longingly of going back to my room to eat, but I was too hungry to trudge all the way over there first.

I began scanning the room for a somewhat quiet seat, when I saw someone waving in my direction—Ivy. When she saw I noticed, she motioned for me to join her and her friend Missy (who was at the bonfire last weekend).

I couldn't help but notice the curious stares I got as I walked across the room. It had been happening all day. I knew it was because of the way I looked. There wasn't anything spectacular about it, but it was better than I usually appeared. In my early class, one girl I'd never talked to before even told me she liked my hair.

As I walked, I glanced down at my messenger bag and the hoodie I tucked over the top, making sure it wasn't slipping free and Romeo's name wasn't suddenly visible.

"Rimmel, hey," Ivy said, giving me a smile when I approached.

"Hey, Ivy," I said and then turned to her dark-haired friend. "Hey, Missy."

I barely knew Missy at all, only from the few times I'd picked Ivy up and she was with her.

"Hi," she said and gave me a little wave and a curious stare.

"Sit!" Ivy said, gesturing toward an empty seat at their table.

I set down my food and coffee and lifted my bag off my shoulders and draped it over the back of the chair. I saw Ivy glance at the hoodie, and I tucked it into my lap when I sat down. I didn't want it to get knocked onto the floor if someone passed by. After all, it wasn't my shirt and I didn't want it to get damaged.

Yes, and pigs could fly.

Truth was I didn't want Ivy putting her hands on it. Or waving it around for everyone to see.

"How did your test go?" I asked, remembering she said she had one this morning.

"Crap, I hope I passed," she said and picked up a giant coffee to sip at it.

Whatever "magic" she worked this morning to make herself look more awake worked. She was dressed in a pair of skintight dark jeans, a white sweater, and an infinity scarf with a red chevron pattern. Before I sat down, I noticed she was wearing her favorite cowboy boots. Her hair was pulled up into a high ponytail that bounced when she talked and her makeup was carefully applied to hide the dark circles under her eyes and give her a dewy, wide-awake look.

Missy was equally as beautiful. Her dark hair was long and sleek, and I couldn't help but wonder how she got it so perfect. Her wide gray eyes were done with taste, and she was dressed in jeans, a white top, and a leopard print velvet blazer. I wasn't one for animal print, but that blazer was totally gorgeous.

"I love your top," I told her.

She beamed. "Thank you."

"So, Rimmel," Ivy said as I broke into my salad and started eating, "have you seen him today?"

"Who?" I asked.

"Romeo," she said, like it was obvious.

"I don't tutor him on Thursdays," I said. "Just Monday, Wednesday, and Friday."

"Oh, well, that's still three days a week," she said. "I wish I was smart so I could tutor him."

I laughed and so did Missy.

Ivy grinned and took a bite of her sandwich. "You still coming to the game with us?"

"Sure," I said.

"I like your hair," Missy told me.

I felt myself blushing. "Thanks, Ivy did it."

"You totally need to do my hair like that," Missy told her and launched a Cheeto across the table.

Ivy picked it up and ate it.

A tray with like half a pizza on it and a giant soda plopped down on the table beside Missy, and I glanced up.

"Ladies," Braeden said, taking the last empty seat at the table. If he was surprised to see me sitting there, he didn't show it.

"Hi," Missy said, giving him a smile. He leaned over and kissed her.

"So, like, are you two dating or what?" Ivy said.

Missy gasped. "Ivy!"

Braeden laughed. "We're having fun."

Missy nodded, but I had to wonder what she thought of the "having fun" label. Judging from the way she looked at him, she really liked Braeden.

Braeden took a sip of his monster soda and glanced at me. "Tutor girl," he said.

"Football boy," I shot back.

He grinned. "I didn't know you guys knew each other," he said, gesturing between the three of us.

"We didn't know you knew Rimmel," Ivy said.

Braeden shoved a huge bite of pizza in his mouth and said something no one understood.

"Ivy and I are roommates," I told him as he chomped.

He gave me a thumbs-up and kept eating.

All three of us sat there and watched in awe as he housed his food. When I was sufficiently grossed out, I turned back to my salad.

"You ladies going to the Omega party tomorrow night?" he asked a few minutes later.

"Of course!" Ivy and Missy replied at the same time.

When the conversation didn't continue, I realized they were waiting for me to reply. "Uhh, I don't think so."

No one tried to talk me into it, so I figured they also agreed that me and a frat party didn't mix. I finished my salad and munched on fruit. Braeden was really entertaining and pretty much kept all of us laughing. I was glad because I wasn't good at conversation.

We were sitting near a window that seemed pretty drafty and every time the wind blew outside, some of the cold air would seep in and wrap itself around me. I finished eating and reached for my coffee, grateful it was still warm enough to heat my fingers.

Braeden's phone rang and he grabbed it up and answered. My stomach fluttered a little, wondering if it was Romeo. "Where you at, man?" Braeden said into the phone.

He listened for a few minutes and made a few sounds that I had no clue what they meant. After several minutes, his eyes slid to me. “Funny you should ask,” he said. “She’s actually sitting right here.”

Ivy and Missy both looked at me. I shrugged. Beneath my ribcage, I felt like there was a ball bouncing around inside me, causing everything beneath my skin to vibrate. There was only one person Braeden and I both knew that could be asking about me.

“Uhh.” He looked at me again and then said, “Nope.”

He listened for what seemed like forever, and I knew Ivy and Missy were just as curious as I was about what Romeo was saying on the other end of the line. Braeden leaned up out of his chair and looked down at me. He smiled. “Yep.”

Braeden’s eyes narrowed slightly as he listened some more. “Yeah, I got it. Okay. Later.”

“Rome wants you to turn your phone on,” he said, setting down his cell.

I’d completely forgotten I’d turned it off before classes this morning. I fished it out of my bag and powered it on, setting it on the table beside my cup.

A few minutes later, it beeped with a Buzz notification and a text. I picked it up and looked at the text.

GOING HOME AFTER MORNING CLASS 2 SLEEP. TXT U LATER.

I felt everyone watching me and I knew they saw the small smile on my lips and the redness in my cheeks. I cleared my throat. "I need to get to class."

I rose out of my seat, and at the same time, so did Braeden. He came around the table and took the hoodie out of my hands.

"What are you doing?" I asked.

He shook it out and stuffed it down over my head. I gasped, but it was muffled by all the fabric going over my head. When my face finally popped out, I gaped at him. "What the hell are you doing?!"

"Romeo said he told you to wear it," Braeden said with a straight face.

"To the game," I protested.

Ivy gasped. "You didn't tell me that!"

I gave Braeden an evil look, promising him payback. He grinned.

I started to take it off, but he shook his head. "He just told me to make sure you put it on."

"What the hell for?" I demanded, putting my hands on my hips. The sleeves were too long and they covered my hands and the shirt fell way past my butt.

"It's cold out."

Was he serious right now?

"I don't want to wear this," I growled.

He smiled. "I know." He hesitated, then went on to say, "Mad respect for that."

I wasn't entirely sure what that meant, but he didn't elaborate.

"Just wear it." He sighed.

"You don't understand," I said low so only he could hear.

His eyes flashed with understanding and something else I didn't really know. "I understand more than you think," he replied equally as low. Then in a louder voice he said, "If Rome wants you to wear it, then you should."

Ivy leaned around Braeden to say. "If you don't leave that on, I will beat you."

I rolled my eyes.

People were staring. A couple girls walked by, and I heard Romeo's name on their lips. Everyone saw. This place was no better than a high school. It would probably be on the Buzz later.

"Fine," I muttered. I wasn't about to draw even more attention to myself by making a scene and refusing to wear it.

Braeden grinned.

I hoisted my bag up and over my shoulder and went to gather my empty lunch containers. Ivy shook her head. "I'll get it."

"That's okay."

She touched my arm, and I looked up. "That's what friends do."

I nodded. "Thanks."

"See you later," Missy said. I gave the table a wave and then left the building. People actually stared as I went.

I was grateful for the cold air when I got outside, though it wasn't nearly as cold now that I was wearing this sweatshirt.

Too bad I was going to have to take it off.

My phone beeped and I pulled it out and looked down.

LEAVE IT ON.

I wanted to laugh. How the hell did he know I was going to take it off as soon as I left Braeden's sight? I quickly typed my reply and hit SEND:

IT HAS YOUR NAME ON IT.

YEAH, I KNOW.

I pictured his crooked smile when I read what he said.

BUT PEOPLE WILL THINK WE'RE TOGETHER.

THAT'S THE POINT.

His last reply nearly made me drop my phone. I sent the screen dark and stuck it in the front pocket of the hoodie.

Why would Romeo want everyone to think we were together?

CHAPTER TWENTY-FOUR

#Buzz is #24's hoodie was walking around campus today, but he wasn't the one in it.

... Alpha BuzzFeed

ROMEO

Coach got me out of my one afternoon class. I went to his office to "talk" about the upcoming game, when really all I wanted was for him to look at me and demand I go home to sleep.

It worked. He declared I looked like dog shit and then sent me home. He would make sure I wasn't penalized for missing one class, and I knew he'd still let me play.

It didn't get me out of practice, though. If anything, he ran me harder than usual. But at least I'd gotten a few hours of sleep beforehand.

Once practice was over and we were all showered, most of the guys went out for pizza, but I hung back. Braeden did the same, promising he'd catch up to them in a few.

I was throwing stuff in my duffle and Braeden leaned nearby, watching me. "You know her roommate is that girl you hooked up with a couple weeks ago at the bonfire," he said.

"I kinda figured, but I wasn't sure." I grimaced. Of all the girls on campus, why did I have to hook up with Rimmel's roommate? "We just messed around. I didn't bang her."

"Hey, man, I don't care if you had a threesome on the dean's desk," Braeden said. "But you know she's sniffing around Rimmel now. That could be a problem."

I told Braeden about rush and how I was supposed to sleep with Rimmel. I wasn't supposed to, but fuck Zach's rules. That guy was an asswipe. I also told him about the fact Zach wanted her at the party tomorrow night and how I knew he chose her to make rush hard on me. I was worried what kind of shit he was going to pull at the party to drive a wedge between her and me.

I didn't tell him about the talk I had with Trent. About me possibly being made Omega president after I was inducted and everyone went against Zach. It seemed like I should deal with one issue at a time.

I felt the weight of Braeden's stare as I closed up my locker and shrugged into my jacket. "Obviously you got something to say," I told him, looking up.

"She didn't want to wear that hoodie today," he stated, staring at me. Was there a bit of challenge in his eye?

What the fuck was this about?

"And I told you I wanted people to know she was with me. We both know Zach won't be able to mess with her as much if people think she's mine. They'll watch out for her."

"Or it will put a bigger target on her back," Braeden deadpanned.

Was he talking about Ivy or something else? My eyes narrowed and something very close to anger simmered just beneath the surface. "I'm not sure I like your tone," I bit out, stepping a little closer.

Braeden stepped off the locker he was lounging against and drew to his full height, facing me. He was a big guy, but I was taller.

"You're my best friend, Rome. I'm loyal to you. But I like that girl. There's something about her… She's innocent and *real.* She's the only girl I've met on campus who wouldn't chew off her own arm just to claim some kind of connection to you. I don't want to see her get hurt because you're in a pissing war with the Omegas head asshole."

"What the fuck do you mean you *like* her?" I growled.

His eyes widened just a fraction. "You're into her."

"What?" I said, most of my fight draining away.

"I thought you were just using her to get into Omega. I figured you were having a good time with the challenge of getting a nerd."

"She is *not* a nerd." I growled again, all my anger resurfacing in one second flat.

Braeden smiled. He slapped me on the shoulder, but I knocked away his hand. "Chill," he said. "I see now I was wrong. You're into her."

"*Fuck*!" I spat and my shoulders slumped. I was into her and it was creating some kind of war inside me. A war between the guy I was and the guy everyone wanted me to be. It never used to be a competition. I was happy to be that guy. The player, the football star, the charmer.

I was those things.

But I was more. Maybe I didn't realize that until Rimmel started tutoring me weeks ago.

"Don't worry, man," Braeden said. "You chose good."

I glanced up at him. "How can you say that? Do you have any idea how stuck I am right now?"

"Look, maybe she isn't the type everyone expected you to get with, but I for one am glad. You need someone to bring you down off your throne a little."

I gave him a hard look. He grinned. "It's the truth. Besides, we can bring her in. We'll watch out for her."

Braeden didn't get it. This wasn't just the guy meets girl from different social circles and falls in love.

Hell, I *was not* in love with her. But I did like her. I liked her a lot. But she was supposed to be the girl I used to get me into Omega. Omega was my shortcut into connections, my way into the NFL.

Braeden didn't understand that. He didn't realize that right now it felt like I had to choose.

I had to choose between the only thing I ever wanted, the NFL, or a girl who somehow bypassed my "keep 'em at arm's length" code.

When I didn't agree with him, when I said nothing at all, he frowned. "Hey, man. You know I don't *like* her *like* her. Not like that. I just meant she was pretty cool for a girl. In a friend way."

He thought I was jealous and still mad about what he said. I didn't bother to correct him. I forced the heaviest of my concerns deep down and grinned. "That's good to hear," I said. "I wouldn't want to have to pound your face."

"Like you could," Braeden shot out.

We both grinned and left the locker room.

"You coming for pizza?" he asked out in the parking lot.

I shook my head. "Nah, I have something to do."

Braeden gave me a knowing smile. "Tell tutor girl I said hi."

I gave him the finger and tossed all my shit in the back of the Hellcat. I didn't want to hang with all the guys tonight. Suddenly, being so popular seemed like a pain in the ass.

I left campus and headed a few blocks over to the animal shelter. I knew that's where she would be.

Maybe once I saw her, the war inside me would quiet.

CHAPTER TWENTY-FIVE

Even #Nerds need love. Word on campus is there's a certain #Nerd looking to score big. Stay tuned for the show.

... Alpha BuzzFeed

RIMMEL

Even after all the work was done and the entire shelter was clean, I wasn't ready to go. The quiet, un-chaotic atmosphere was exactly what I needed tonight. Michelle was in the back, taking care of some paperwork, and the other girls had gone for the day.

I decided to hang out with Murphy for a while. It seemed like eternity since I'd seen him last. I still came here almost every day, so technically, it hadn't been long at all, but I guess all the things happening lately made my days seem fuller.

I wasn't sure what to feel anymore.

The last few weeks had changed things for me in ways I didn't really understand. I used to be focused on school. On animals and just keeping my head down. I was still completely dedicated to becoming a vet, and school was still very important to me… but it seemed like lately it might not be enough.

Emotions stirred in me, emotions I thought I stuffed down so deep they'd disappeared. A couple weeks with Romeo, a few bone-melting kisses, and a lunch with two girls, and I realized they had been there all along. Waiting. Lurking. Watching.

I liked Romeo. More than I wanted to. How much longer could I fight it? The minute he touched me, I seemed to turn to mush. It's like everything my head knew to be true was pushed aside by my overeager heart.

Romeo was dangerous to me. Not in any physical sense, not even a threat to my future. I *would* see my dream of becoming a veterinarian come to life. Nothing would stop me from that.

But on an emotional level, Romeo was possibly an atomic bomb. He scared me. He scared me more than any guy I'd ever met, even the one from years ago. Maybe because this time I knew whatever piece of me I let him have I would never, ever get back.

How could I surrender any part of me to him?

Dangling right here before me was an entire life. Friends. A guy. Something more than just me, myself, and I.

I wanted it.

How would I know I could trust him? How could I trust any of them?

I sighed and looked away from the open textbook in front of me, not even bothering to try and read it anymore. Murphy was curled up in my lap, and I stroked his velvety fur and leaned my head back against the wall. "I wish I knew what to do, Murphy," I whispered.

I closed my eyes and concentrated on the vibrations against my legs from Murphy's machine-like purr and tried to clear my mind. A few moments later, Murphy stopped purring and I felt him lift his head.

I opened my eyes and looked across the room.

Romeo was standing in the doorway, watching me. Our eyes collided. We stared at each other for a long time. I don't really know what he was looking for, but I was searching for something, anything that would tell me how he really felt.

He was wearing a pair of washed-out jeans that hung dangerously low on his narrow hips. His deep-royal and yellow-gold varsity jacket was open to reveal a black T-shirt with some sort of faded logo on the front. His hair was damp like he'd just come from a shower and it was tousled and messy on top like he'd been running his fingers through it.

His shoulders were the same wide width as always, but beneath his captivating blue eyes was a hint of darkness, giving him a slightly weary look.

"Hey," I finally said, breaking the silence.

"Hey," he replied, coming farther into the room. Neither of us said anything else as he dropped down in front of me, mirroring my Indian-style pose. His knees bumped against mine he sat so close, and my stomach flipped over at the casual touch.

Murphy abandoned my lap and climbed into Romeo's. He glanced down, lifted half his mouth, and scratched him behind the ears. "Figured you'd be here," he said.

"Just getting some studying done. Hanging out with Murph," I replied.

"Can I hang out too?" he asked.

"Sure."

I don't know why things suddenly seemed awkward between us. I didn't know what to say or how to act. Just because we kissed a couple times didn't mean we were dating or together. He kissed lots of girls. I knew I wasn't anyone special. What I didn't understand was the hoodie. Why he wanted me to wear it so badly. I heard the whispers this afternoon. No one had ever been spotted wearing it around like that.

"You're not wearing my shirt," he said, as if he knew where my mind had gone.

"I didn't want to get hair all over it." I gestured to Murphy.

"I just got done with practice," he said, and it seemed it was more to fill the silence than anything else.

"You look tired," I said honestly.

He gave me a sheepish look. "I'm fucking exhausted." Then his eyes sparkled. "But don't tell anyone that. I got a rep to protect."

I smiled, but it didn't last long. He did have a rep to protect. It was exactly why I couldn't understand that he was here with me.

My phone went off beside me. Seconds later, Romeo's went off as well.

I picked mine up and looked down at the latest Buzz. I felt the blood drain from my head. It was about me. The BuzzBoss called me a nerd. No, worse… a *hashtag nerd.* Pretty soon I would be trending all over the Alpha social waves.

Everyone thought I was going after Romeo.

I snorted because it was freaking ridiculous. The loud sound caused Murphy to look up from beneath Romeo's hand.

He was staring down at his screen too. I knew he was seeing the same notification I was.

His eyes lifted to mine. I jumped up, taking my book with me, and strode to where my bag was and started packing everything up. When I turned, he was at my elbow, Murphy in his arms.

"It's just the stupid BuzzFeed," he murmured. "No one pays attention to it anyway."

I laughed. "Do you even believe that?"

His gaze was unreadable when I reached for Murphy and pulled him against my chest. "You should go."

"You're mad."

"Yeah, maybe I am."

"I didn't write that Buzz," he said.

"It's not the stupid Buzz!" I cried. Then I felt contrite. I sighed and took Murphy over to his shelter and placed him gently inside. After I made sure everything was closed up, I grabbed my stuff off the table, his hoodie one of those items.

"I'll drive you back to campus," he said.

"I don't think that's a good idea."

His eyes narrowed.

Michelle came out and saw us standing outside the cat room. "Romeo," she said with a wide smile. "Did you come to give Rimmel a ride?"

"Yes," he said smoothly, looking at me with a dare in his eyes.

"Good, I won't feel bad that I have to stay late."

"Is everything okay?" I asked.

"Everything's fine," she said. "We have an animal coming in from another county and he won't be here until late."

"I should stay." I began. "You might need help."

She was already shaking her head. "I can handle this. Besides, you have class tomorrow."

"I'll get her home," Romeo said, placing his palm on the small of my back. My skin tingled beneath my shirt, and I felt like he was branding me.

"See you Saturday!" Michelle gave me a wave and disappeared.

"C'mon," Romeo said softly, guiding me toward the door.

I went with him because I didn't feel like walking. Outside, the air felt bitter and I gritted my teeth against it.

"You don't like the cold much, do you?" he said, gazing down at me.

"I'm from Florida. Cold like this is just unnatural."

He chuckled. "You could put that on, you know," he said, gesturing at his hoodie.

"I'm good," I replied and went over to climb into his Hellcat. The interior was still warm from when he drove over, and I sighed as I leaned back.

"You hungry?" Romeo asked when he got in. "I'm starving."

"Sure," I said.

He drove to the nearest drive-thru and ordered a bunch or burgers, some fries, and two milkshakes. "Is your roommate at your dorm?" he asked.

"I doubt it. She never is," I replied.

"Good. We can eat there."

He wanted to come upstairs?

"I'm not sure," I said, recalling all my doubts.

"We need to talk, Rimmel," he said softly. "You're pissed and I want to know why."

I snorted and pushed my glasses up on my nose. "You know why."

"Maybe. But I want to hear it from you."

No one was in the hall when we walked to my room. Thank goodness, because I could only imagine the kind of stir that would create. I hurried to let us in and held my breath, praying Ivy wasn't here. She wasn't, and I relaxed when the door closed behind us.

Romeo kicked off his shoes, flung his jacket over the end of my bed, and practically dived onto the mattress. It looked small with him in the center.

"Make yourself comfortable," I said sarcastically.

He grinned and took a huge bite out of one of the burgers. As he chewed, he patted the mattress beside him. I hesitated but gave in and sat down because he had the food.

After rubbing some yummy-smelling hand sanitizer on my hands, I unwrapped a burger and took a small bite. Romeo was already on his second burger.

"Those jeans you're wearing are hot," he said around a bite.

I glanced up and noted his heated gaze and I felt it down to my core. Something stirred inside me and it felt a hell of a lot like desire.

I took a pull of the chocolate shake, hoping it would cool the flames. It didn't seem to help, because he watched my lips wrap around the straw and his eyes darkened until they were sapphire pools.

I shivered.

He sat up and put his back to the wall and moved the bag of food onto his other side. He held out his arm like he wanted me to come closer. I moved just an inch, but it was enough. He caught hold of me and scooted me into his side beneath the crook of his arm.

My legs stretched out beside his on the bed. My feet didn't even make it to the end of the mattress and his hung over. He looked so much more powerful than me as I compared our bodies. It made me wary and a little mad all over again.

"Tell me what's eatin' ya," Romeo said, reaching for another burger.

I debated and then I thought, *Why not?* This was the way I was feeling. It wasn't going to go away. I needed to speak up for myself because if I didn't, no one else would.

Plus, maybe it would scare him away.

If it did, I wouldn't have to feel like this anymore.

"I wore your shirt around campus this afternoon," I said. "I left it on like you asked."

"You probably looked cute as hell," he murmured.

"Well, I sure did get a lot of looks and whispers."

"Is that what you're upset about?" he asked, still eating.

"When I was finished with classes for the day, I stopped back by the food court." I began. "To grab something for later, and someone stopped me."

He paused in eating and his body tensed next to mine.

"It was some girl," I said, and he relaxed immediately. It made me curious and partially alarmed that he thought it might be someone else. "She had long black hair and was a lot taller than me."

"Could be anyone," he said.

I poked him in the ribs. "You saying I'm short?"

"Calling it like I see it, Smalls," he quipped.

I told myself not to be charmed.

"She'd seen the shirt. Your name," I said, the charm evaporating like water on a hot day. "She told me you were going to get bored, that you always get bored, and when you did, I would be just another notch on your belt."

"Rimmel." Romeo said my name with a sigh. He abandoned the burger to its wrapper and put his free arm around me to pull me closer. My body melted into him until I realized I couldn't let him hold me. Not right now. I'd let everything and anything he said become the truth.

I pulled away and he let me go. I slipped off the bed and stood.

I felt his gaze but didn't turn to look at him. I couldn't. His blue eyes would weaken me.

"Girls are going to be jealous. The ones I hooked up with and the ones who want to," he said.

I glanced at him then. "You've hooked up with a lot of girls," I said.

"Yes, I have." He looked straight at me.

I wasn't expecting that. I wasn't expecting such a straightforward, honest reply. He said it without trying to sugarcoat it. He said it without trying to soften the blow with his smile.

The wall I was holding up between us cracked.

I took a breath and kept going. "That's the thing, Romeo. You could have any girl you want. Why are you here right now? Why did you insist on my wearing your name today?"

His eyes narrowed like something I said pissed him off. "Are you saying you aren't good enough?"

I laughed and spread my arms out wide. "Seriously?" I said. "Look at me! I'm not tall and long-legged. I don't like to party. I don't have model perfect hair or designer clothes. I don't wear makeup. I snort when I laugh and I wear glasses."

"So you think I'm superficial?" he said, the muscle in his jaw ticking as he looked away.

"No. Yes," I said, confused. "I don't know!" I yelled.

"So let me get this straight," he said. "You're pissed because girls are being petty, the BuzzBoss is calling you a nerd, and because in spite of it all, I'm still here?"

"Yes!" I shot out.

Why are you still here?

He scrubbed a hand over his face like he was tired. I was tired too. Suddenly, I was so very tired. He materialized behind me. I felt his heat against my back. His solid arms wound around my waist and pulled me into his chest and he lowered his chin to my shoulder.

"What do you want from me?" I whispered.

He turned his head and pressed a kiss into the crook of my neck. My eyes slid closed. "Right now?" he breathed, his words fanning out across my skin. "Right now I want to kiss you."

Excitement raced down my spine and my toes curled against the floor.

"Can I kiss you right now, Rimmel?"

I nodded. Maybe I shouldn't let him touch me or kiss me, but I wanted him desperately.

He pulled back and guided me around. He didn't move like he was hurried; instead, he stepped up as close as he could. Our toes bounced together and he slowly wrapped his arms around me, pulling me in so my back arched, and pushed my waist into him farther. One of his hands slid up my back and cupped the back of my neck, tilting my head back so I was totally open for him.

I got caught in the blue web of his eyes. I got tangled up in just the feel of him against me, and a cloud of desire settled over the room.

"You asked me why I'm here," he murmured, leaning in so he was so close his lips brushed mine as he spoke. "This is why I'm here, Rimmel. Can't you feel it too?"

My eyes drifted closed and I nodded. The small movement bumped our lips fully together and neither of us pulled away.

Once connected, we were fused together. My arms came up to wrap around his neck, and I leaned up on my tiptoes to get better access to his mouth.

Romeo groaned deep in his throat and deepened the kiss. Sparks of electricity burned me and heat pooled in my center. His tongue slipped between my lips and smoothed over my teeth to tangle with my all too willing tongue.

My brain grew fuzzy and my limbs heavy as he continued to work my mouth like he knew exactly how to make my body succumb to him. When I felt my lungs were going to burst, he broke contact but didn't pull away. As I pulled in deep breaths of air, his lips slid across my jaw and toward my ear, where he tugged my lobe with his teeth and sent chills of pleasure racing across my skin. My arms fell from his neck and grabbed his biceps as he explored down my neck, licking and biting as he went.

I moaned as he slid back up, and I turned my head to kiss him again. Romeo lifted me so my feet weren't touching the ground and laid me across the bed, coming over me with his considerable size. I gazed up at him with passion-laced eyes, and he smiled down at me with slightly swollen lips.

I reached for him and he met me halfway, stroking my tongue with his as his hand found the hem of my shirt and slid up across my stomach.

I stilled because the sensation was new, and he drew back slightly to look down. "I won't do anything you don't want."

It took a moment for his words to penetrate my foggy brain, and I nodded.

"I just want to touch you, baby," he rasped, his voice hoarse. "Is that okay?"

I arched up against his hand, giving him my answer and better access to my skin at the same time. My body was on fire beneath him and his touch was like the cool water that calmed the flames. His lips fused to mine once more and we kissed endlessly as his fingertips dragged across my stomach and teased the waistband of my jeans.

His hand was so big that when he laid his palm flat over my stomach, it nearly covered my entire abdomen.

He murmured something unintelligible against my mouth as he explored upward until the tips of his fingers caressed the underside of my jaw.

The rest of his body was alongside mine, we touched from my feet all the way up. He leaned over me so I could feel his weight, but enough of him was on the mattress so I wasn't being squished.

The second his fingers brushed the fabric of my bra, the flames he'd been keeping under control raged. The desire in my blood tripled and I made a small sound in the back of my throat. I wanted more. I wanted so much more.

Romeo pulled back to look down but kept his one hand where it was. With his other hand, he reached up and gently pulled my glasses off, carefully setting them off to the side. Then he leaned down and pressed ultra-soft kisses to each of my fluttering eyelids.

A soft sigh expelled from my lips and his fingers spasmed against me like he was trying to hold himself back. "Okay?" he asked, inching up a little ways.

My breasts felt swollen with need and I whispered, "Yes," as I threaded my fingers through his hair and pulled him back down to me. His hand slid all the way up and cupped my small breast. He palmed it entirely, giving it a gentle squeeze and making my hard nipple ache. The pressure of his kiss increased, and I tightened my fingers in his thick blond hair. I loved the way it felt between my fingers. I reveled in the softness.

The sensations running through my body were almost overwhelming. My fingers and knees shook with need and my stomach jumped around even as another part of me urged for more. Romeo's hands were gentle but gave so much pleasure. He massaged my breast and ran his finger beneath my bra strap against the smooth skin of my shoulder. Cool air brushed over my exposed abdomen, and the kiss we shared went on.

I wiggled beneath him, wanting even more, and my hands left his hair to cup his jaw. He pulled back and stared down at me. The room was dim, but even in the faded light, I saw how much I affected him.

He was attracted to me; that much was painfully clear. If I couldn't see it in his eyes, I could certainly feel him against my hip. He rocked against me restlessly as he stared down at my face.

I couldn't look away. I was captivated by him.

As he watched me, his fingers delved into the edges of my bra cup and tugged the fabric down. It gave way, and his palm covered my bare breast and squeezed. My eyes slid closed and my head fell to the side. He nuzzled my neck as his fingers found my nipple and rolled it between his fingers.

My hands no longer held him. They had fallen to my sides, but when he once again moved against me, I gripped his hips and my lips reached for his once more.

His kiss was my entire universe, so much so that I didn't hear the door open. I didn't hear Ivy's surprised gasp. I would have gone on kissing him if he hadn't lifted his head.

He looked up, his body stiffening only slightly, and I looked to see what caught his attention.

"Crap!" Ivy said, her body frozen in the doorway and surprise written all over her face.

I ducked my face into the space between Romeo's shoulder and jaw, hiding because she caught us but also because I was still quivering with need and didn't want her to see.

"Hey," Romeo said. "What's up?"

"Uh, um…" Ivy stuttered. I smiled into his neck because Ivy was *never* speechless. "I can just come back."

"It's cool," Romeo said, his voice still a little deep with passion. "You can stay."

Disappointment flared in me, but then I realized it was for the best. I was getting far too carried away. Romeo adjusted my bra under my top and pulled his hand free. Already my skin ached for him, missed his touch. I was still hiding against him, and he chuckled and wrapped an arm around my waist to drag me along with him as he sat up against the wall.

I peeked at Ivy and saw she was debating on what to do. I noticed a couple girls walking down the hall, trying to see what she was looking at.

"Close the door, Ivy." I reminded her.

"Right." She did and then walked into the room. Her gaze kept bouncing back and forth between Romeo and me like she almost couldn't believe her eyes.

A funny feeling wormed its way into my stomach, and some of the things I'd been worrying about before we started making out reared their ugly heads.

Then I remembered the night at the bonfire Romeo had walked Ivy to the car. "Do you two know each other?" I said, sitting up a little. Romeo kept his arm wound around my waist.

Ivy opened her mouth, but Romeo spoke before she could. "We go to the same parties. We made out a couple weeks ago, didn't we?"

Ivy flushed. She glanced at me. I was surprised too. Surprised he would just call it out like that. It was almost like he was just putting it out there so it wasn't between us.

That wall inside me cracked again.

"Um, yeah," Ivy said. "At the bonfire."

Romeo nodded. "Missy's dating Braeden."

"They're just having fun," Ivy and I replied at the exact same moment.

We both looked at each other and laughed.

Romeo grinned. "Ah, yeah. That sounds like Braeden."

"I thought that was your motto too?" Ivy said, lifting her sculpted brow at him.

"That's what they say." He didn't confirm or deny, and it frustrated me.

The only thing I'd learned tonight was that my body burned for him.

He slid off the bed and straightened his clothes. He seemed to fill up the small space. Ivy clicked on a lamp on her side of the room and dropped onto her bed to watch us. Romeo's eyes slid down to my chest and he smiled slowly. Then he lifted his hoodie off the floor and tossed it to me. "It's cold. You should put this on."

I glanced down at my chest and grimaced. Both my nipples were so hard you could see them through my clothes. I grabbed up the shirt and shot my eyes toward Ivy, but she couldn't see. Her view was blocked by Romeo.

"Walk me out?" he said, shrugging into his jacket.

"Sure," I said. After I put on the shirt, I grabbed the bag of food we'd only half eaten and picked up his shake and handed it to him.

"Here." I blushed. "You didn't really get to eat."

"Funny thing," he said, stepping close. "I'm not that hungry anymore."

Across the room, I thought Ivy might die.

"I'll be right back," I told her, stuffing my glasses back on. She shook her head and mouthed, *Oh my God.*

I grinned. I couldn't help it.

We stepped out in the hall and everything went quiet. Various sets of eyes all turned and fastened on Romeo.

"Ladies," he said and gave them all his megawatt smile.

Then he draped an arm around my shoulders and led me to the stairs.

As the stairwell door closed behind us, the entire hallway burst into chatter.

CHAPTER TWENTY-SIX

ROMEO

"So you and Ivy?" Rimmel asked when we stepped out of the building and onto the sidewalk.

I mentioned it on purpose up there. I wanted her to ask about it. I was concerned Ivy might be using her to get to me.

Arrogant? Yes.

Impossible? No.

I felt a stark need to protect Rimmel. Besides, trying to hide my one-time make-out session with her roommate or any girl on this campus was stupid. Word got around way too fast. The last thing I needed was for some bitch to corner Rimmel on campus and spill a bunch of details that they embellished just to make her angry. Shit, it already happened today.

When I first found her tonight, I could feel the space between us. I hadn't liked it. It made something in me feel hollow.

"There is no me and Ivy. There never will be."

"But you two hooked up?"

"We made out. I did more with you tonight than I did with her."

She ducked her head into my chest, and I smiled. She brought out these tender feelings in me I'd never experienced with anyone before. I used the hand that was already draped over her shoulder and tugged on her braid. "Some girls are probably gonna say shit, Rim," I said. "Some bitches be devious."

She giggled and looked up at me as we stopped beside the Hellcat. "Some bitches?"

I grinned. "Just keepin' it real."

She shook her head. I dropped my arm from around her and caught her chin with my hand and looked in her eyes. "When that happens, come to me. I'll tell you the truth, even if I think it's something you don't wanna hear."

She searched my eyes, looking for something. I don't know what. I saw the doubt in her gaze, the wariness. It made my gut tighten. But then again, the words I just spoke made me feel that way too.

I was painting myself into a corner. I was an asshole. Here I was telling her I'd be honest when I wasn't entirely. Yeah, I'd be honest about all the women I'd been with. But how could I tell her about the frat? About what I needed to do to secure my pledge?

She would never speak to me again.

"Okay," she replied softly, drawing me out of my own head.

"You still mad at me?" I asked, releasing her chin.

She cocked her head to the side. "Mad? No. Confused? Yeah."

"I can work with that," I said.

She smiled.

"I gotta go to the Omega party tomorrow night. Come with me."

Her smile fell away. "That's not my thing."

"Am I your thing?" I gave her a smile.

"I'm not sure yet."

I put a hand over my heart like I was wounded. In reality, it made me respect her. Most girls fell all over themselves to give me the answer I wanted to hear. If I had asked anybody else to go with me, they would have said yes before I was done asking.

And she wasn't even playing hard to get. She was just being herself.

"C'mon, you might have fun."

She made a face. "I doubt it."

"I'll be there."

"And fifty of your conquests," she muttered.

I grinned. "Somebody's jealous."

She gave me a look. "Maybe fifty of mine will be there too."

I knew she was kidding, but just the words made me churn with a feeling I did not like. It was so swift I was shocked into silence.

"Romeo?" she asked when I just stood there. "I was just kidding. You could have at least pretended to be horrified."

I grabbed her hand and brought it up to my lips to press a kiss to her palm. "I don't like the idea of anyone touching you."

Her eyes dropped to her hand.

"Come with me tomorrow," I said, letting my lips brush against her when I spoke.

"If I don't like it, will you bring me home?"

"Yes." But I was going to make sure she had a good time.

"Okay," she agreed tentatively.

When I tugged her hand, she tumbled into my chest. I leaned down and took my time kissing her.

When I pulled back, she was breathless. "People are probably watching us through the windows."

"So?"

She shook her head and gave me a bewildered look.

"Remember what I said. If anyone bothers you, come to me. If you can't find me, go to Braeden."

"I can take care of myself."

"I know. But I want to."

"I'll see you tomorrow," she said, not agreeing or disagreeing.

"Hey, can we skip tutoring? I want to go home after practice and get ready. We can study later this weekend."

"Sure."

I watched her step up onto the sidewalk away from the Hellcat. Her thin legs stuck out from beneath the oversized shirt and the writing was huge across her back. My chest swelled a little when I saw my name practically branding her.

"Hey," I said, and she turned back.

I rushed forward and caught her around the waist, lifting her off her feet so she was level with my face. She laughed and the sound filled me up inside. "Kiss me."

Rimmel reached out and slid her hand slowly over my shoulder and to the back of my neck. Her small fingers dipped into the hair at the base of my head and tugged me closer. She glided her soft, luscious lips over mine and tentatively dipped her tongue where they parted. I opened for her willingly and soon both of us were breathing hard, gasping for air.

I swore under my breath when I realized we were outside. It was just supposed to be one kiss. Clearly, I couldn't kiss her without losing it.

I sat her down on the pavement and held on until I knew she was steady on her feet. "I'll wait 'til you're inside," I said.

She went and I drove home.

On the way, I realized something.

Seeing her didn't quiet the war inside me. It only made it worse.

CHAPTER TWENTY-SEVEN

RIMMEL

Ivy was waiting for me in our room like I knew she would be. When I walked in, she practically attacked me.

"*Ohmigod,*" she gushed, running her words together. "You *have* been holding out on me!"

I gave her a look. "What do you mean?"

"He did *not* give you that hoodie because you were cold."

I sighed. “Look, I don’t know what’s going on between us, if anything.”

“Didn’t look like ‘if anything’ to me.” She pulled out her phone and held the screen out for me to see. “Even the latest Buzz is about you two.”

Hashtag heart? That was totally charming.

But I needed to remember we weren’t together, not officially.

“It probably didn’t look that way when you were making out with him at the bonfire,” I said coolly.

She snapped her mouth shut. I rummaged around to get some PJs. Once I found them, I grabbed my little tote full of my bathroom stuff and went to the shared bathroom to brush my teeth and get ready for bed.

I wore Romeo’s shirt to the bathroom, then I put it back on once I had my sleep shorts and tank on. Everyone stared at me. I ignored them all. The thing was I was better off doing this than hiding in my room. I’d been hiding for the last almost six years of my life. I was tired of it.

A couple girls smiled at me on the way out and I smiled back. I couldn’t help but wonder if they were only being nice because of Romeo.

Ivy was in her pajamas when I got back to the room. I set my stuff aside and grabbed my book and got into bed.

"About Romeo…" she said.

I looked up. "Is that why you're suddenly being nice? Because you think being near me will give you another shot with him?"

She was taken aback by my frankness. I sort of was too. But Romeo seemed to be concerned about girls and how they were going to treat me. And part of me wondered who else he was worried about so much that he felt the need to plaster his name on me like I was a piece of property.

"I've always been nice to you." Her voice was mildly hurt, and I had a pang of doubt.

"Yeah." I agreed. "You have. But you've never wanted to sit with me at lunch or asked me to go to a football game."

She glanced down into her lap. "Honestly?"

"That would be nice," I said.

"When I first saw his shirt on your bed and you said you were tutoring him, the thought ran through my mind."

I nodded.

"But that was before I saw him with you. He's totally into you."

"Don't sound so surprised," I muttered.

She gave me a look. "We both know you aren't his usual type."

She was right. It was the same thing I kept telling myself.

"I don't really understand either." I admitted.

Her face softened. "Your wardrobe could use some serious help. And a brush would definitely help your hair," she said, and I laughed. "But you're a really good person, Rimmel. You just need to let people in."

I frowned.

"You've kind of been closed off. You don't make it easy for people to get to know you or be your friend."

I couldn't argue with that because I was closed off. I had been for many years. The reason I didn't have any friends was because I never let anyone close enough.

"Romeo's kind of been the ice breaker. He makes you a little more approachable."

That surprised me. "He does?"

"Well, duh." She rolled her eyes. "He is so totally gorgeous."

I giggled. "He really is hot."

We both laughed.

"I won't lie. You being with Romeo and us being friends will totally help my social life," she said after we quieted. "But even if you weren't with him—or whatever you are—I would still hang out with you."

"Really?" I asked, looking her in the eye.

"Really."

I believed her. She didn't try to feed me some lame story about how she was happy for me and how we'd always been the best of friends. I felt like she said the truth.

Besides, it would be nice to have a friend.

"Thanks, Ivy," I said.

She smiled. "So are you coming to the Omega party now?"

"He asked me to."

She squealed. "Good! Now I'll have someone to hang with when Missy gets all hot and heavy with Braeden."

"She really likes him, huh?"

Ivy nodded. "Oh yeah, more than she'll admit, but I know."

"Yeah. I noticed too."

"I just hope she doesn't get hurt. Guys like him don't always stick around."

Her words speared me. I knew we were talking about Braeden, but Romeo was his best friend. They were certainly a lot alike.

My face must have given away my thoughts because she immediately said, "I'm sorry. I shouldn't have said that."

I smiled. "No. It's totally fine. It's true. I hope Missy doesn't get hurt."

And I also hoped I didn't either.

The next day seemed to drag by until classes were over and I went to the shelter. When I was there, time always seemed to fly. Ivy texted me early in the evening… and kept texting until I told her I'd come home and help her pick out an outfit.

She couldn't possibly want my help. We both knew I was a total fashion victim.

I was getting nervous for tonight. I'd never been to a frat party before. I wasn't really sure what to expect. I told myself it was probably a lot like the bonfire when Ivy called me to come pick her up. That didn't seem too bad. It seemed like there was a lot of places I could find to hide out.

After I spent some time with Murphy and a few of the other cats, I went back to the dorm. Ivy had clothes all over her bed and piled on her floor. She easily had triple the amount I had.

"What took you so long?" she said when I walked in. "I have nothing to wear!"

"Looks like you have half a department store," I observed.

"I am *not* wearing shorts," she said, looking over her stuff. "I froze my ass off last time."

"So wear jeans," I said and sat on the bed. My stomach fluttered with anxiety and I glanced at the clock. I wasn't sure what time Romeo was coming to get me, but I knew it wouldn't be for a while yet.

I hadn't talked to him all day. I kind of liked the break. Not that I didn't want to talk to him—I did. I thought about him constantly. But it was nice to have a breather and actually be able to think for a little while without being taken in by his compelling sapphire eyes.

Ivy pulled out a pair of strategically ripped-up jeans in a faded blue shade and shimmied them on. She had a lot more curves than I did and filled out her jeans in all the right places.

"I like those," I said. "You look good."

"Yeah?" she asked and looked in the mirror.

I nodded. Then she went rummaging through her tops and tried on about five—that all looked good—before she decided on one that was tight, low-cut, and black. Next she added about twenty bracelets to her wrist, a pair of gold hoop earrings, and a pair of black boots.

She made looking good seem effortless.

"What are you wearing?" she asked as she plopped down in front of a makeup mirror and picked up her foundation.

"This?" I asked.

She spun in her seat. "No. Absolutely not."

"What's wrong with it?" I asked.

"You're wearing sweatpants," she said like it was obvious.

"It's cold out…" I said.

She muttered something under her breath and picked up her phone and hit a bunch of buttons. Then she turned back to the mirror and started making up her face. "Put on those black leggings you have."

"What black leggings?" I asked.

She rolled her eyes. "The ones you sleep in."

"You want me to wear pajamas?" I gaped. That was worse than sweatpants.

"Leggings aren't sleepwear." She paused, then added, "Well, to anyone but you."

I gave her a look.

"Did you buy them in the pajama section at the store?"

"No," I said and sighed.

"Put them on," she ordered. "Then put on a white T-shirt. The least baggy one you have."

I didn't argue because I really didn't care what I wore. I did worry about how cold I was going to be in just a T-shirt, though.

She finished up her makeup a few minutes later, looking gorgeous as always. "Sit," she said, pointing to the chair she just vacated.

"I'm not wearing makeup," I said. I had no idea how to apply it or where any of it went.

"I'm going to do your hair," she said.

I was okay with that. I plopped down and she pulled it out of the bun and started brushing it out. It was so long it fell halfway down my back. It was dark, the color of chestnuts, and once she had it all brushed out, it shined in the light.

Ivy produced a large wand-looking thing that was plugged into the wall and started wrapping my hair around it. "Seriously," she said as she worked, "if I had hair like this, I would totally rock it every day."

"You'd totally be annoyed by it every day." I corrected.

"It's all about the products," she said and launched into some lesson about shampoo and conditioner. I only half listened.

Halfway through curling my hair, there was a knock on the door, and my stomach dropped. Was that Romeo already?

"Come in!" Ivy called, and Missy slipped into the room. She had a small tote over her shoulder.

"Hey," Ivy called. "Look at this bitch's hair," she said, stepping back and pointing at me with that thing in her hand.

Missy shook her head and sighed. "It's a damn shame."

"Does it look bad?" I worried, trying to crane my neck to see in the mirror.

Ivy pushed me back in the seat. "Hell no. It's awesome. That's why it's a shame. You don't even appreciate it."

Missy made a sound in the back of her throat like she agreed.

"Did you bring it?" Ivy asked her.

"It's in my bag."

She nodded and kept working. They chattered on about Braeden and other people they knew who I did not, and I totally tuned out. I was glad Ivy had someone to talk to other than me for a change. I really liked her, but she talked a lot.

After what felt like forever, she put the curling thing down and made me flip my head upside down. She ran her fingers through the locks, messing up everything she'd just done. Made no sense to me.

When I flipped it back up, she and Missy made appreciative sounds and she added some kind of clear, slippery stuff to her fingers and worked it in. Then she sprayed it with a bunch of hairspray she promised wouldn't make my hair feel stiff.

I didn't tell her this was the first time I'd ever had someone style my hair (other than the day she braided it). I barely ever went to get it trimmed. That's why it was so long. When I did, I just left the place with it still wet and let it air-dry.

"I'm totally jealous," Ivy said, standing back to admire her work.

"Thanks for doing that," I said, praying I didn't look like a Chia pet or something.

I stood up to go look in the mirror.

"Wait!" Missy said and jumped up from my bed. She was wearing a pair of black skinny jeans, sky-high heels, and red top with a thin black belt that fastened just below her breasts. She reached in the bag she brought and withdrew the velvet leopard blazer she had on the other day. "Here, wear this," she said.

I looked at the jacket and then back at her. "You want me to wear that?"

"You said you liked it," she replied.

"I do."

She nodded. "You can totally borrow it. It will make that outfit."

"Thanks," I said, getting a little choked up. All this girl time was making me emotional. I slipped it on. It was just as soft on the inside as it was on the outside.

"Looks so good." Missy beamed.

"Here," Ivy said and handed over my brown fur-lined boots.

"Do those match?" I asked.

"Yes," both girls said simultaneously.

I slid them on, grateful for the warmth. Then I went to the mirror to see.

I did a double take at my own reflection.

It seemed impossible it was me.

But it was.

I just stood there and stared, unable to say anything.

Ivy and Missy high-fived and then went back to talking about whatever.

My hair never looked so pretty. It hung in loose curls over my shoulders and down my back. It was parted off to the side and looked shiny and sleek, just like I always wanted it to (but it never did). For once, my black-rimmed glasses didn't appear to take over my entire face, but seemed to have a bit of balance. I turned a little to admire the way the glossy curls fell down my back and caught the light.

The black leggings totally worked as an actual outfit. They were comfortable and didn't make me feel like I was trying to be someone I wasn't. They hugged my body because that's what leggings did, but the tan boots came halfway up my calves and the white T-shirt was loose enough that it covered most of my butt. The blazer was a little looser on me than it had been on Missy, but it still looked nice. It seemed to make me look like I had more of a shape than I actually did. It ended up above my hips and the warm brown and black seemed to play off my hair and boots.

My face was makeup free, but I went to my bag and pulled out some vanilla lip balm and smoothed it on to give my lips a slight shine.

It's amazing how a hairstyle and a beautiful outfit could make me feel. I wished my mother could see me. I wondered if she would have been proud.

Just thinking of her reminded me of something I'd kept in the top drawer of my dresser, hidden away for years. I went to it now and pulled it out carefully, sliding it over my head, taking care to slip it beneath all my hair. I turned to Ivy and asked, "Does this match?"

She turned and smiled. "It's perfect."

Missy nodded.

It was a pendant on a long gold chain, made to look like a cameo brooch. It was large and oval, with a black background and an ornate golden frame. In the center was the silhouette of a woman carved out in white. The detail on the lady was amazing.

The piece had been my mother's. I still remembered her wearing it.

Tonight would be the first time I'd ever let myself wear it anywhere other than my room.

A few minutes later, there was a knock on the door. My pulse jumped and my stomach dropped. I knew it was Romeo. I could feel it.

Ivy gave me a look and bounced to the door to answer. "Hey," she said, still holding the door only partially open. I heard his deeper voice on the other side and my teeth sank into my lower lip.

"She's over there," Ivy said and opened the door all the way.

My palms felt sweaty and I resisted the urge to wipe them down my thighs. My eyes glued to his face the second he appeared and my nerves increased tenfold as I wondered what he would think about the way I looked.

His eyes saw me, then kept going, totally passing right by. My ego stung a little because I hadn't earned just a little bit of a longer look.

But then he seemed to jerk and his eyes flew back to where I stood.

I smiled.

His eyes widened and recognition slammed into him. He hadn't realized it was me. But now he did. He stepped a little closer as Ivy giggled, and his stare ate up my face and hair. Then his gaze traveled down my body all the way to my toes, reversed, and traveled back up again.

"Holy shit," he breathed. Then he seemed to catch himself and hurried to say, "You look beautiful."

I laughed. "Thanks."

"Well, my work here is done," Ivy said. "When you get to the party, Rimmel, come find us."

"You aren't riding with us?" I said nervously.

Romeo frowned but then turned to the girls and said, "You can if you want."

I worried Missy's eyes might fall out of her head. And when Romeo's gaze seemed to settle on her, it only got worse. "Braeden picking you up?"

"No," she answered. "I'm riding with Ivy."

"All right," he said, motioning to all of us. "Let's go."

"I don't mind driving," Ivy hurried to say. "You two can be alone."

He seemed to debate and glanced at me. His eyes roamed my body again, and he frowned. "No," he finally said. "Ride with me. Then Rimmel won't have to try and find you in the crowd."

Ivy looked at me as if to ask if it was okay. I nodded.

"We'll meet you downstairs," she said, and she and Missy left the room.

Romeo looked at me and rubbed a hand over the back of his neck. "I knew you were beautiful, but damn,

Rimmel," he muttered. "I'm kind of having second thoughts about taking you around all those drunk frat guys."

"Do I really look that different?" I asked.

He cocked his head to the side. "Actually, you look more like you than I've ever seen."

I wrinkled my nose. That didn't make sense.

"I mean, your outside matches your inside."

"Thank you," I said, touched by the statement.

"So everything with you and Ivy?" he asked.

"It's really good."

He nodded. I moved to walk past him, and he caught me around the waist. His lips crushed against mine instantly, kissing me fiercely.

I melted against him and kissed him back with everything I had. His hands came up to bury themselves in my hair and he groaned low in his throat. I reached between his jacket and shirt to wrap my arms around his waist.

After a few minutes of intense kissing, he released me and set me away.

"If we don't leave right now, we never will."

At the door, he stopped and turned. "I need the thing I gave you to hold."

I dug it from beneath my mattress and held it out. He grinned and reached for it, but I hesitated, then glanced inside the front of my blazer. There was a pocket, so I slid the nameplate inside. "I'll hold it 'til we get there."

"You sure?" he asked.

I nodded.

He held out his hand and I placed mine in his.

"You ready for your first frat party?" he asked.

Ready or not, here I come.

CHAPTER TWENTY-EIGHT

ROMEO

The Omega house was one of the largest frat properties on campus. It was set sort of back off the road and a very green yard stretched out beside and behind it. Large, mature trees filled the space around the house, giving it a more private feel, even though it was located on the edge of campus.

Omega House was a large stone building. Just looking at it, you knew it was filled with history. There was a plaque on the wall by the wide double front door indicating it was one of the oldest buildings on campus.

It looked like a giant box with rectangular windows running along the entire front on both the first and second floors. The stone wasn't the perfectly cut man-made kind; instead, it was in various shades of tan and brown and was rounded, making it look like it was literally dug out of the ground and used to build a formidable home.

The front door was a weathered shade of royal blue, and on each wide door was a sign with the Omega symbol in the center. Long, wide concrete steps led up, giving way to a large concrete patio. The landscaping was exceptionally nice considering a bunch of guys lived here. It was obvious the campus paid for the upkeep of the exterior.

Large evergreen bushes flanked the ends of the building and assorted plants in varying shades of green grew along the front. Out in the back was the building I remembered from before, the one with the secret club down below.

I couldn't see it now as we pulled into the parking lot and I found a spot, but I knew it was there. Music was pumping through the night when I opened the door and climbed out of my Hellcat. The driver's seat was pushed forward, and Ivy and Missy unfolded themselves from the back. I watched Ivy closely, taking in her reaction to getting a ride with us.

After she straightened her top, she glanced at me and smiled. "Thanks for the ride, Romeo."

There was no gleaming agenda in her eyes, and it made me feel better. "Anytime."

The two girls moved off to stand at the end of the car and were already yapping away, but it wasn't lost on me that Rimmel was still hiding in the passenger seat.

I walked around and opened her door. With wide, dark eyes, she looked up at me through her glasses.

My heart nearly stopped when I first saw her tonight. In fact, my eyes had skipped right over her, dismissing the fact it *was* her. I'd never seen her look more beautiful. Maybe her friendship with Ivy wouldn't be such a bad thing after all. She was glowing, and I knew it wasn't just because someone curled her hair.

I wanted to see more of this side of her. Not only because she looked damn hot, but because she looked so happy.

* * *

I could feel the nerves rolling off her, and I leaned down inside the open door and smiled. I was sort of nervous too. I wasn't sure what to expect tonight when I walked in with her. I was damn proud to have her on my arm, but I also didn't want anyone else looking at her.

"Want to hold my hand?" I asked and grinned.

She snorted and whacked my outstretched fingers. "Let me out."

When she was beside me, I reached for her hand, lacing our fingers together, and slammed the door to the car. She glanced down at where I held her. "You don't have to do that."

"I know." My fingers tightened around hers.

The four of us walked through the lot and up onto the sidewalk that led down to the house. I could hear people laughing and cheering. A crowd materialized off to the side, but I didn't give them much attention because there were people all over this place. They spilled out the front door and onto the porch of the house.

Rimmel stumbled a little as she walked, and I released her hand to wrap an arm around her waist. She patted my stomach. "Romeo," she whispered.

I glanced over and everything in me stilled.

The dean was walking toward us with two campus security officers. "Mr. Anderson," the dean said with a tight look on his face.

"Is there a problem?" I said, releasing Rimmel and stepping slightly in front of her.

Ivy and Missy stopped walking and stood off to the side, watching with wide eyes. I wanted to tell them to leave, but I held my tongue. If things went bad, I would need someone here with Rimmel.

"I'm very sorry to approach you like this," the dean said, and our eyes connected. I saw that he didn't want to be here, yet he was. "I realize this is quite the insult to such an active and promising student here at Alpha U, but a matter was called in to the campus police and it is this university's duty to follow up."

Ah. I see. So whoever sent them here went around the dean and straight to the campus police because they knew the dean wouldn't entertain causing trouble for his star athlete.

Fucking Zach.

"It's not a problem," I said easily, totally relaxed. "You have a standard to uphold."

"We received an anonymous call about a theft in the dean's office," an officer said, stepping forward. "Of course we went to his office to confirm that something was indeed missing. It seems his nameplate is gone."

Rimmel's hand reached under my jacket and curled against my back. I knew she was thinking of the object they were after and its presence in her jacket.

"As I said…" The dean spoke to the officers. "I'm not sure what happened to it. The cleaning service could have knocked it off the desk and broken it."

"We have to follow up on all leads in the matter of theft," the officer replied.

"Of course." The dean motioned at me.

"What does this have to do with me?" I asked like I was bored.

"We have reason to believe you're the one who took it."

I laughed. "Like I don't have anything better to do than steal shit from the dean?"

The officer who had said nothing so far looked embarrassed. His friend, however, would not be deterred. I would bet money that Zach paid him to do this here and now.

A small crowd had gathered not too far from where we stood and watched with apt attention. Zach was not only trying to keep me out of the Omegas, but he was also trying to destroy my reputation.

Sneaky bastard.

"Please empty your pockets," the officer said.

"Are you serious?" I asked sharply.

Everyone looked at the dean, who looked like he had a bad case of diarrhea. "I'm afraid he is."

I shrugged. "Sure. No problem." I turned slightly toward Rimmel and curved my hand around her elbow to lead her a few steps to stand beside Ivy. "Stay here."

Her eyes were anxious when she looked up at me. I winked.

I made a show of reaching in my varsity jacket pockets, showing that they were empty. Then I slid it off my shoulders and tossed it to the officer. "Feel free to check the inside," I told him.

As he did that, I handed my cell to Rimmel and pulled out the pockets of my jeans. Then I took off my shoes and held them upside down and lifted the ankles of my jeans to show I had nothing in my socks.

"Roman," the dean said, worry in his tone, "you don't have to go that far."

"Yes, I do," I said. "I want to be sure everyone here knows I am no thief." I said it loud enough that whispers broke out across the watching crowd.

Then I reached for the hem of my shirt and pulled it over my head in one fluid movement. A couple girls over on the porch whistled and hooted. I waved at them.

I held out my arms and spun, letting the shirt hang from my fingers. "I think it's pretty obvious I'm not concealing some block of wood."

Then I stopped and grinned. I reached for the buckle on my jeans. "Shall I take these off too?" I directed the question to the officer with my jacket.

He flushed. "That won't be necessary."

Everyone was silent when I put my shoes and shirt back on. When I reached for my jacket, the officer said, "I'm going to need to search your vehicle."

I laughed and tossed him the keys. "Have at it. It's the green Challenger over there."

"We know which one it is," the quiet officer muttered.

I glanced at Rimmel and her friends. "You ladies go ahead. I'm going to watch Barney and Fife here to make sure they don't scratch my paint."

Ivy and Missy glared at the officers before turning to walk away. Rimmel hesitated, her eyes never leaving me.

"It's all right," I said. "I'll be right behind you."

"Who's that?" the officer said, stepping closer to look at Rimmel.

My annoyance level skyrocketed. I spun, blocking her from sight. "No one you need to concern yourself with."

"Well, if she's with you—"

"She's not," I said, hard.

The dean stepped in. "We did not come here to harass our students."

I stared the officer down until he lamented and turned toward my car.

Of course they found nothing. All they accomplished was looking like a bunch of idiots. When the one leading the witch-hunt mentioned searching my room, I laughed.

"I live on private property, not on campus. If you want to search my place, you're going to need to call my father, Anthony Anderson. You might know him?" I asked. "He's a lawyer."

"That won't be necessary," the dean said immediately. "Gentlemen, I think it's obvious the tip you received was a waste of everyone's time."

The officers left and before the dean followed, he looked at me apologetically. "I'm sorry about this, Roman."

"Thanks," I replied.

Three steps toward the party, I heard the officer say, "Is that a frat party? Maybe we should—"

"No," the dean said loudly. "You've already made us look like big enough idiots for one night. Let's go."

On my way inside, the crowd gathered around as I passed by. I spent long moments shaking hands, laughing, and shooting the shit with people I didn't really want to talk to.

I wanted to get to Rimmel. And then I wanted to pound Zach.

Inside, the crowd was considerable, but it wasn't hard to find her. My eyes seemed to know exactly where to look. She was standing over by the keg in between Ivy and Missy with a beer in her hand.

She looked totally out of her element. When she saw me walking toward her, the relief in her eyes was clear.

"What happened?" she said over the loud, thumping music.

"Nothing." I grabbed the beer out of her hand and took a healthy drink. "It's all good."

I handed the cup back to her and she took a small sip and made a face. "How do you drink that stuff? It's nasty."

I grinned and drank the rest. "C'mon," I said, draping an arm across her shoulder. "I'll get you something less nasty."

People eyed her when we went across the room to a giant tub filled with ice and bottles of drinks. I pulled out some fruity girl drink and popped the top before handing it over. She tasted it and gave me a smile. "That's better."

"Rome," Braeden called, materializing out of the crowd and coming up beside us. "What's this about the po-po hassling ya outside?"

"Fucking cops," I said and grabbed a beer.

"They searched him," Rimmel said, taking another sip of her drink.

Braeden seemed to just notice her, and when he realized who it was, his eyes widened. "Da-yum, Rimmel. Girl, you clean up good."

One of the guys standing behind Braeden turned and glanced at her over his shoulder. "I'd do her," he yelled, and all his buddies laughed.

I grabbed him by the back of his neck and dragged him backward, tossing him up against the counter. "The fuck you just say?" I growled.

My reaction drew some stares because I usually played it so cool.

"I d-didn't mean anything, Romeo. I'm d-drunk," the guy stuttered.

"Romeo," Rimmel said from beside me, but her voice only made it worse. We'd only been here five minutes and already the guys were checking her out.

Braeden wrapped an arm around my waist and towed me back. "Dude, chill."

I stared down the asshole as I drank my beer and tried to calm my sudden anger. He didn't move, just stood there and watched me warily.

"Get the hell out of my sight," I spat. He took off and disappeared into the crowd.

Even after he was gone, anger seemed to crowd beneath the surface of my skin. Zach was starting to get to me. Hell, this entire night was.

Trent stepped up to the keg, and I joined him. "You need to rein Zach in," I told him.

"What'd he do now?"

"Tried to get me arrested."

Trent choked on his beer. "He what?"

"He needs to be brought down a couple pegs."

"Man, I'm sorry. No one knew he would go that far," Trent said.

As if he knew we were talking about him, his voice echoed through the room. “Omegas rule!” he roared. Everyone cheered and held up their drinks.

I found him in the crowd and watched him take a seat on a couch in the next room as his buddies settled around him.

I turned to Rimmel, who was talking to Ivy, Missy, and Braeden. “I need the plaque,” I said in her ear.

She reached into her jacket and pulled it out. I took it and started across the room.

“Romeo!” Braeden called, but I kept going.

The crowd parted for me as I went, and soon I was standing across from Zach, who looked up and smirked. “Romeo. You made it.”

I tossed the nameplate at him. It hit his chest and bounced up, knocking the beer out of his hand. It overturned and sloshed all over him, soaking his shirt and part of the girl plastered to his side. She shrieked and jumped up, brushing quickly at her clothes.

“What the hell is your problem, man?” Zach growled.

“Nothing. Just following orders. Giving you what you asked for.” I sneered. “And just a warning, if I go down for something you ordered, I'm going to take you with me, and it will be one bumpy bitch of a fall."

Zach shoved to his feet and stared me down. "Omegas have honor."

I smirked. "Didn't you know? There's no honor among *thieves*."

Zach's eyes narrowed. "I have no idea what you're talking about."

"You're playing stupid now?" I said casually. "I honestly thought you were better than that." I shook my head and turned.

"Drinking rally!" I yelled and held up my beer. The entire house erupted into cheers and yells. Cups and bottles filled the air.

People started chanting my number. *Twenty-four, twenty-four, twenty-four!*

I turned back to Zach and smirked. His eyes turned dark, and I got some satisfaction in seemingly getting the popular vote in his own living room.

Rimmel was looking a little green around the edges when I went back to her side. I glanced at the drink in her hand, but it was still full.

"You need some air?" I asked.

She nodded enthusiastically. I took her hand and we weaved through the house to the back door, stepping out onto an old stone patio with grass growing up between the pavers. The air was cold and the wind was picking up.

"Ah, for once I'm grateful for the cold," she said, taking a deep breath.

"You okay?"

She nodded and turned her face away. A couple people ran by me, laughing, and I took her elbow and moved to the edge of the patio. "Hey," I said and tipped her chin up to make her look at me.

"We've been here like ten minutes and you've almost been arrested and in a fight *twice*. I'm scared to know what the rest of the night is going to be like."

I felt my expression soften. The fear in her eyes was real. "You were worried about me?"

"Duh," she said and rolled her eyes. "You *are* my ride."

My mouth opened, and she burst out laughing. "You should see the look on your face."

I smiled and pulled her close, anchoring an arm around her back. "That wasn't funny."

"Yes-huh." She grinned and her head tipped back. The long strands of her hair draped over my arm.

"You were worried 'cause you like me," I said low.

Even in the muted light, I could see the blush on her cheeks.

"Say it," I whispered.

Her eyes focused on something behind me. "People are staring," she murmured.

"And…?"

"And it's—"

I cut off her words with a kiss. It was meant to be an innocent, quick touch of lips, but the second I came into contact with her soft mouth and tasted the strawberry on her tongue, everything else fell away.

Need slammed into me so hard it almost knocked me over. The sounds of the party fell away and all I could think about was what she felt like in my arms.

I heard my phone go off in my pocket. Rimmel's did the same. Then in the very back of my mind, I heard the dinging of an endless amount of smartphones.

I ignored it all.

I only broke away from her when someone bumped into me from behind, forcing me to pull back to keep our balance. "Sorry," someone slurred and kept going.

Rimmel was dazed, and I chuckled.

The back door slammed against the house with a sharp crack and someone yelled. "Where the hell is the nerd that suddenly got hot?"

I stiffened. Rimmel's eyes cleared and filled with confusion.

Her phone went off again, and she pulled it out of her blazer and glanced down at the screen. She snorted loudly and shook her head.

"What?" I asked.

She turned the phone so I could see the latest Buzz. It was about her. I swore under my breath.

"I heard she was out here, putting the moves on number twenty-four!" the guy yelled again.

Some guys laughed and someone else chimed in to add, "You know that ass has to be fine to get his attention."

People laughed, and I went rigid and turned around. My eyes landed on several guys wandering out near the grass. Of course it was Zach's followers and one of them was a fellow Omega.

He glanced over and saw me; his face screwed into a smile. He swaggered over, probably thinking he looked cool when he really looked like he had a full diaper.

"I gotta hand it to ya," he said. "You got some game."

"You need to step away," I said, my voice dead calm.

Some of my friends and people I knew stepped forward as if to show I wasn't alone. I gave them all a grateful, subtle nod.

"Why don't you step aside and give us all a look at her?" he said, ignoring my warning.

I kept my body firmly planted in front of Rimmel and crossed my arms over my chest.

Braeden materialized beside me, taking up the same braced position. "What seems to be the problem?" he asked.

"No problem. Just came to see the nerd who got hot," the guy replied. I think his name was Jack.

"There aren't any nerds out here," Braeden countered.

Ivy came out the back door, followed by Missy. They were both clutching their phones. When they saw me, they rushed around me and to Rimmel. "The BuzzBoss is totally talking about you!" Ivy said like she was impressed.

"All I did was comb my hair," Rimmel remarked.

I wanted to laugh.

Zach materialized behind his crew, and they parted to let him come to the front. "I'd be interested in meeting your date tonight as well, Romeo. After all, I did invite her."

"He invited you?" Ivy asked Rimmel behind me.

This guy was seriously asking for it. He was doing everything humanly possible to screw things up for me. So I called his bluff.

I stepped aside and reached for Rimmel's hand, drawing her forward. "Rimmel, this is Zach. He's the president of the Omegas."

Zach's eyes latched onto her and a little bit of surprise sparked through them. Then his lips curved into a smile I instantly wanted to wipe off his face. He came forward, his stare never once leaving Rimmel.

"I have just one question," he said.

"What?" she replied.

My hackles rose just because he was speaking to her.

"You give it up to him yet?" Behind him, his crew laughed.

Rimmel didn't say anything; she just stood here with pink cheeks.

"Because you know when you do, he's gone." Zach finished.

I didn't even have a chance to talk myself out of it. Hell, I barely even thought. I just heard his words and saw the calculating and nasty look in his eyes, and I was done.

Even though I was beyond angry, I moved Rimmel out of the way with care, placing her beside Braeden, and then I spun, plowing my fist into the side of Zach's jaw.

He went down immediately, like a scarecrow in the wind.

I stood over him as he rolled onto his side and grabbed his jaw. My chest was heaving, and all I saw was red. Zach looked at me with sheer hate, launching himself up off the ground, and rushed me.

I was ready, and we locked together as he tried to knock me down.

I wasn't falling. I outweighed him by fifty pounds easily and I was a head taller. He reared back his arm and took a cheap shot in my kidney. It was enough for me to let him go, but it didn't help his cause.

He threw his fist at me, and I caught it. Holding his arm suspended in midair, I brought my free arm around and caught him in the face again.

He went down and didn't move.

I turned back to Rimmel, who had a horrified, stricken look on her face. I snatched the car keys out of my pocket and put them in her hand. "Take the Hellcat and go to my place. I'll meet you there."

"But—" She began.

"Go," I growled as commotion erupted behind me.

Someone rammed into me from behind, and I stumbled. I reached around and pulled Jack off me and tossed him into a couple of his buddies.

"Now!" I shouted, and she jumped.

"Romeo…" Braeden warned me, and I turned away from her.

Zach was on his feet and approaching me once again. He threw out his fist and I dodged it, but he kept lunging. His lower lip was busted and bleeding and his jaw was already bruising.

I wasn't proud of myself, but I sure as hell wasn't sorry.

"Enough!" Trent yelled, and a bunch of Omegas swarmed through the crowd. Zach and I were both restrained and yanked apart.

I shook them all off and straightened my shirt.

"What the fuck, man?" Trent said, turning to me.

"Ask your president," I spat. "I might be just a pledge…" I snarled, not caring that I wasn't supposed to announce it. "But I will not roll over and take his shit anymore. He crossed the line."

Everyone looked at Zach, who was standing there bleeding all over himself.

"I want him out of here!" he yelled, his voice slightly thick from his fat lip.

I held up my hands. "Oh, I'm gone. Omega can kiss my ass."

Trent glanced at me sharply. I saw the warning in his eyes, the reminder that we were going to get rid of Zach together. I shook my head. "I'm out."

He frowned slightly but nodded his understanding.

Braeden clapped me on the back. "I think we should go."

After giving Zach another long, measured look, I turned to leave.

"This party is lame!" Braeden said loudly. "WOLVES, party at my dorm!" he yelled.

People cheered.

"Dude, how the fuck are you gonna fit all these people in your tiny-ass room?"

He grinned. "Sure as hell will be fun to try."

Out in front of the Omega house, there was hardly anyone around; they were all too busy in the back, checking out the drama. We were silent a moment. Then Braeden said, "You don't need them. You got more than enough talent to bring in the NFL on your own."

"Fuck," I muttered. "When did everything get so damn complicated?"

"When your life became about more than just football."

"You sound like Yoda." I grinned.

"It's the beer."

We both laughed and headed out to the parking lot.

I joked and was laughing, but really, he was right. For so long, my life had been nothing but football…

But now there was something more.

CHAPTER TWENTY-NINE

#BuzzBrawl
Fists were flying Friday night at Omega. Word is the war isn't over. Who's your money on?

... Alpha BuzzFeed

RIMMEL

I felt stupid standing out here.

I hadn't wanted to leave Romeo.

But it seemed my presence only made things worse.

So I took the keys and walked out. I hoped it would put an end to the fight. Clearly, there was a lot of tension there, and I really wanted to know the whole story.

And what was with that Zach guy? What a douche.

Up until that point, the party had been pretty fun. It was kind of cool to see how the other side lived. It was a lot more interesting over here.

I glanced at the house and wondered about Romeo. Where was he? What if he got hurt? Should I go back in and find him?

I pulled out my cell. I'd text Ivy.

Just then I heard gravel crunching under foot and a couple male voices floated my way. One of them was very familiar.

"Romeo?" I called out.

The footsteps increased and he came around one of the SUVs parked nearby. His eyes were wide and he let out a string of cuss words. Braeden was close behind and gave me a smile.

"Rimmel?" Romeo said. "I told you to leave."

I looked him over, trying to see if he was hurt. He didn't look to be, and some of the tension left my shoulders.

I shrugged and held up the keys to the Hellcat. "I can't drive a stick."

Braeden laughed. "Damn, girl. You gotta learn." He glanced at Romeo. "You better teach your girl."

Romeo scrubbed a hand down his face. "We're out of here."

Braeden nodded. "I'll take Missy and Ivy home."

"You promise?" I said.

He made a big X over his heart and nodded. I texted Ivy quickly to let her know Braeden was their new ride. "Thanks."

Romeo plucked the keys out of my hand, guiding me around to the passenger side and opening the door. He leaned in and fastened the seat belt around me, and I couldn't help but study his strong profile in the dark. I felt bad he'd gotten in a fight tonight because of me.

"You didn't correct him," I said when he pulled out onto the road.

He glanced at me quickly before turning back to the road. "Correct him for what?"

"He called me your girl."

He paused. "Maybe I want you to be."

Something inside me ached. "Surely after tonight you know we won't ever work."

He nodded slowly and the ache intensified. "Yeah. I know." He turned the Hellcat onto the main road that led away from campus.

"Where are we going?" I asked.

"My place."

"But you just said…" My voice faded away as confusion took over. Confusion and ache did not mix well.

"I know what I said," Romeo replied, keeping his eyes trained on the road. "I don't care."

A little bit of that ache went away, but I didn't allow myself to hope. "Tonight was just the beginning. The past few days were just a glimpse at what's to come if you don't take me home."

The car swerved abruptly as Romeo pulled to the side of the road. It was barely in park when he surged across the seat and took my face in his hands.

"I can't take you home right now." His voice was thick and husky. "Please don't ask me to do that."

"Romeo," I whispered.

I can't even explain the kind of emotion that erupted in the air and encircled us at that moment. He kissed me like I was the breath in his body, like I was the blood in his veins. I kissed him back just as fiercely, as if his lips were the cure to the ache in my chest.

I grabbed onto his wrists and squeezed, holding him close as our lips melded together. My heart thudded in my chest and everything between my thighs throbbed with need. Romeo's fingers bit into the back of my neck, but it didn't hurt, and I urged him closer.

When we broke apart, he rested his forehead against mine as we both pulled in heavy gasps of air. "Baby," he murmured, his voice breaking on the word. "You're making me crazy."

"What happened back there?" I asked.

"Don't bring him into this moment," he whispered. "This moment belongs to me and you."

I reached up to cup his face and he tilted his cheek into my palm.

"Stay with me tonight."

I didn't really have to think about it. I already knew. My body wanted him so badly I almost hurt. The need, the want, the feelings swimming around inside me all eclipsed that little bit of fear I felt at giving myself to him.

I brushed the backs of my fingers across his cheek. "Yes," I whispered.

His eyes lifted to mine, staring at me through the dark, looking for confirmation of what I just said.

He saw it.

He kissed me again.

And then he put the car in drive.

By the time he parked near his house, my knees were shaking. It wasn't because I was having second thoughts, but I was nervous. I was about to have sex with Romeo. I was going to do something that would make him a part of me forever.

Most college girls probably didn't think about it like that, but I did. I knew I was the kind of person that couldn't do something like this without it altering me at least in some way forever.

When the car was off, he turned and looked at me through the dark. "If you changed your mind, I'll take you home right now."

"I didn't."

He came around to my side of the car when I was climbing out. His body was a good shield against the cold air as he wrapped his arm around my waist and walked us inside. The only light he turned on was in the hall leading back to his bedroom.

It filtered into the large space, giving the room a soft glow. In the center was a gigantic bed. It made my bed at the dorm seem like it belonged in a dollhouse. The comforter was white and flung up like it was a last-minute effort to make the bed. Up near the dark wooden headboard, there were pillows lining the mattress, making the top of the blankets look lumpy.

There was a set of windows off to my right, but they were covered with curtains. There were a few more traditional pieces of furniture, like dressers and nightstands. Hanging on the wall directly across from the bed was a large flat-screen TV and below it was a fireplace. I smiled when I saw it because I could imagine Romeo watching football games in bed.

But it didn't really matter what was in the room.

What mattered was *who* was in here with me.

His hand lightly pressed to the small of my back, and I turned. His arm slid around me and I was brought up against him. "You're shaking," he said, a frown lacing his tone.

"I know."

"We don't have to," he said. "I'm a patient man."

"Are you really?" I asked, my tone slightly rueful.

His white teeth flashed. "For you I would be." The sincerity in his voice was my undoing.

"No more talking," I whispered.

He groaned and lifted me off my feet. My legs wound around his waist, and I sighed when my center came into contact with his muscled body. He didn't take me to the bed as I suspected he would.

Instead, he carried me across the room and sat in a leather chair I hadn't even noticed. My feet were pinned between his back and the cushion, and I rocked a little in his lap to get closer.

A low growl filled the room and he reached up to strip the blazer off my body and peel it down my arms. When it was gone, he leaned up and kissed me, splaying his hands out over my ribs.

He kissed like he wasn't in a hurry, even though I felt the persistent need between his legs. I couldn't help but rock against it every few minutes and then gasp at the sensations the movement sent through me.

His hands were all over me. Across my stomach, down my back, and he filled his hands with my breasts more than once.

Eventually he stripped off my T-shirt and reached for the necklace. "That's important," I whispered and he nodded. He placed the necklace gently on the small table beside the chair and then reached around me for the clasp on my bra. It gave way easily, and the fabric sprang open in the back.

Before he pulled it away he looked up at me, just to make sure it was okay.

I held his gaze as I reached up and pulled each strap down one by one and then tossed the entire thing off into the darkness.

His lips fastened on one of my nipples immediately. I arched into him and cried out. It felt so damn good. My fingers dug into his back, and I realized he was still wearing his shirt.

I pulled at it, wanting it gone, wanting to feel his skin beneath my fingers.

He left my breast to pull it off and toss it aside and then came back, lavishing even more attention on my needy flesh.

I let my head fall back, and he reached behind me to tangle his fingers in the long strands of my hair. I closed my eyes and gave myself up to the sensations rocking my body, and he sucked and pulled at each breast.

When I started moving restlessly against him, he pulled back and I crashed my lips to his. I dragged my nails down the sides of his spine and kissed him with every ounce of passion I had inside me.

Without breaking the kiss, he got up with me still in his arms and carried me across the room to the bed. Instead of laying me across it, he let me slide down his body until my feet touched the floor.

I kicked out of my boots and he did the same. My eyes were presented with the wide expanse of his chest. He was so sculpted and smooth. The ridges of each muscle in his body were incredibly defined. Without thought, I traced those lines with my tongue.

His hand found its way into my hair and held me to him as I kissed his chest and abs. When I leaned up to kiss across his shoulders, my fingers found the waistband of his jeans and dipped inside.

He muttered my name, which sounded more like a prayer, and I reveled in the power I seemed to hold over him. In that moment, he seemed as vulnerable as I was, and it made us totally equal.

I was no longer the #nerd with no friends. He was no longer the popular jock with a million conquests under his belt.

I was just a girl.

He was just a guy.

And there were just a million different emotions spiraling around the room with us.

I reached for the button on his jeans and let it free. Then I kissed along that V-shaped muscle that always drew my eye. He groaned and pulled me up to crash his mouth over mine and delved his tongue deep into my mouth.

The way my silky hair brushed against my bare back only heightened my senses, and I pushed against him farther, loving the feel of our bare chests meeting.

Romeo scooped me up into his arms and kissed me again, then laid me across the bed. He left me long enough to shuck his jeans, and then he reached for the waistband of my leggings. They joined his jeans in seconds flat.

"Fuck," he cursed as he dragged his fingers up the insides of my legs. I was shaking so much now that I couldn't make it stop. When he got to my center, he curved his hands out to slide up over my hip and then up to my breasts once more.

He kneeled on the bed between my legs to stare down at me before pressing me into the mattress with his body. He was so warm and delicious feeling that I licked my lips.

We kissed some more, our hands roaming over one another, learning everything we could. His hips rocked into me steadily, and eventually my body joined in the rhythm. Soon we were swaying together, the movements growing more desperate with every thrust.

"Romeo," I whimpered when I felt like I couldn't take any more.

"I got you," he whispered and slid down my body, trailing kisses as he went. He hooked two thumbs in the waistband of my panties and tugged the fabric free. He smoothed his hands over my shaven area and sucked in a breath.

Two fingers dipped down to my center and met with silky juices. "Shit, Rimmel," he groaned. "You're so fucking wet."

I was beyond talking. In fact, I barely heard what he said. I was so far gone on the cusp of passion that nothing else mattered.

One of his fingers slipped into my opening and slid in and out. My moan filled the darkness. Another finger joined it, and for long, blissful moments, he pumped his fingers in and out, stretching my walls and making me pant.

"I can't take it anymore," he finally groaned and pulled out.

I gasped at the loss of his hands, and he chuckled. I heard a drawer being opened and the distinct rip of a foil packet. Romeo was back on the bed between my legs in a matter of moments.

Using his hands, he spread my thighs wide and settled between them.

I tensed slightly, ready for him to push inside me, but he didn't.

Instead, he rested his arms on either side of my head and cupped my face. "You're so beautiful," he whispered. "You're fucking perfect."

He kissed me the exact moment he plunged into my body. I cried out, and he swallowed the sound. I was tight and he felt large. My body burned a little as it stretched around his girth, and he held himself still, trying not to hurt me.

It didn't take long for my body to adjust to his size, and I stirred against him. He kissed me again and started moving.

I couldn't keep my eyes open; they rolled into the back of my head. Every single thrust felt like pure bliss, like my body might break apart from sheer joy.

His body filled my sight when I opened my eyes, the strong lines of his shoulders, and the solid width of his chest. He was in me, around me, over me.

His thrusts became faster and harder, until I was gripping his hips and matching him speed for speed. I was right there on the cusp of orgasm, and I knew from the tension in his body that he was too.

He looked down at me as we moved, and our eyes locked. With one great, hard thrust, he buried himself all the way inside me. My eyes flew open and I cried out yet made no sound. Light burst behind my eyes as the most intense feeling I'd ever known ripped through me. Wave after wave of ecstasy rolled over me.

Vaguely I heard his shout and I felt his cock pumping inside me. I knew he was going as well, but I couldn't think beyond my own insane pleasure.

When it was done, he collapsed on the bed beside me and pulled me into his chest.

Every so often, my body would jerk with the aftershocks of his expert lovemaking. My entire body was boneless and satisfied. I prayed he felt the same.

Neither of us said a word; we couldn't speak. Instead, we lay there in the dark and he drew lazy circles over my lower back as my cheek pillowed on his chest.

Eventually, he got up and went into the adjoining bathroom. I still couldn't move. When he came back, the mattress dipped under his weight as he tucked the soft comforter up around me and pulled me back into his arms. He kissed my forehead and my cheek, then my lips.

* * *

If I could've stayed wrapped up like this with him forever, I absolutely would.

CHAPTER THIRTY

ALPHA U 101:
~~Stick to your circle.~~
Date whoever the hell you want.
#NewRules #RomeoSaysSo
... Alpha BuzzFeed

ROMEO

The war inside me was over.

The tension that plagued me was gone.

Rimmel was curled up beside me. Her small body fit against mine like she was the missing piece to the puzzle that was Roman Anderson. Her breathing was steady and her body was so relaxed I knew she was asleep. Over and over, I dragged my fingers through the length of her hair, loving the way she felt in my arms.

Usually once I slept with a girl, I ushered them out of my bed. Very rarely did one stay, unless I was drunk and passed out before I could tell them to leave.

I didn't want her to go. I wanted her again. My body craved her like some illicit drug. Being inside Rimmel was all it took.

I knew where I fell between her, the frat, and my NFL dreams. Something Braeden said before reverberated through my head like a mantra.

You don't need them. You got more than enough talent to bring in the NFL on your own.

He was totally right. I did. I'd been playing football for more than half my life. I trained hard and I played harder. I hadn't become starting quarterback by my sophomore year at Alpha U because I had a nice smile.

The Omegas were shady. Zach was a turd. Becoming one of them was almost a step down. Yeah, they carried a prestigious reputation and they definitely wielded power on campus. But it just wasn't enough anymore. I'd been on the inside. I saw the way they treated each other, the competition between them.

I thought frats were supposed to be like an extended family, a team.

They weren't.

And I already had a team. The Wolves were my family. We watched each other's backs and we didn't try to break down one of our over petty jealousy shit.

That shit was for women.

Rimmel sighed against me and pressed a little closer. I turned my head and touched my lips to her forehead. Maybe if she hadn't come along, I would have put up with the shit and waltzed right into Omega. I would have enjoyed overthrowing Zach.

But I couldn't have everything, and I wanted Rimmel.

There was no way in hell I would subject her to the Omegas.

My thoughts were interrupted when a small hand worked its way across my abdominals and curved around my side. My hand tightened on her hip, and I felt her smile. Her hand moved back across my stomach and the muscles tightened in response. She lingered on them before slowly traveling lower, dipping her fingertips into the muscles that led down to my package.

My hips rotated of their own accord, and I let out a low moan. Her hand continued lower, her silky skin causing goose bumps to trail along behind her touch. When she met the short, wiry hair just above my cock, she paused. I didn't say anything or urge her forward. I wanted her to move at her own pace.

My heart was thumping so hard I knew she could probably hear it against her ear, and my breathing turned shallow. She started moving again, pushing into the nest of curls and sliding down to where I was already achingly hard.

Her touch was cautious at first, and it drove me mad with desire. Her palm cupped my sack, testing the weight and exploring the fine skin that stretched across it. Fingertips grazed across my inner thighs until I clenched my jaw muscles against the urge to order her for more.

Slowly she became bolder, and then she wrapped her hand around the base of my rod. My chest rumbled with pleasure as she stroked up the length. Her fingers encircled my swollen head and she rocked it back and forth. I sucked in a deep breath as she continued to feel and stroke me.

Her glasses were on the mattress beside us, so when she lifted her head and stared up at me, all I saw was her round, brown eyes. It was too dark to see what color the center was tonight, but it didn't matter.

Her tongue darted out and wet her bottom lip as she looked at, still stroking me beneath the blanket. "Can I taste you?" she whispered.

"Baby, you can do whatever the hell you want," I rumbled.

She slid herself down my body, her dark head disappearing beneath the covers as she settled between my thighs.

The anticipation of what she was about to do was so intense I fisted the sheets in my hands.

Her hand slid down to the base of my cock and it jutted upward, likely pointing right at her. The slightly rough, wet texture of her tongue glided across my head, and all the muscles in my body tightened.

She hesitated a little at the jerking movement of my body, but when I didn't say anything, she wrapped her lips around me and sucked me into her mouth.

My eyes rolled back in my head and I let out a moan. She started dipping with rhythmic movements, sliding up and down, and her fingers caressed my inner thighs.

It was almost sensation overload. I'd received a lot of blowjobs over the last few years, and they were all basically the same.

But this one was different.

Everything in my world condensed down to her mouth and her hands. The little sounds she made as she tasted me made me even harder. Rimmel licked and teased until my cock started jerking and I knew I was going to blow. I reached beneath the covers and tangled my fingers in her hair.

"Come here," I said, my voice so deep and thick I didn't even recognize it.

When her face cleared the comforter, I could see the need in her eyes as well. I flung a hand out to the dresser and grabbed a condom.

"Wanna help?" I asked.

Her eyes went to the packet and she nodded. She was still sitting on her knees between my thighs as I ripped it open and smoothed it over my head. I took her hand and guided it down as we both rolled the latex over my length.

I hooked my hands beneath her arms and lifted her so she was straddling my waist. I could feel the slick heat of her core and I knew she was already ready for me.

"I've never…" Her voice fell away when my cock rocked against her center.

"I know," I whispered. "Trust me."

She nodded and lifted a little as I positioned myself at her entrance. I palmed her tiny waist and slowly guided her down, inch by inch.

"Ohh," she purred.

Smug satisfaction burst in my chest when I caught the blissful look on her face. She started rocking without any kind of instruction. Her hips rolled and moved in perfect cadence with mine. Her body above me was on full display, and I ran my hands over her curves and kneaded her breasts as she rode me.

"Romeo," she whispered, her hair falling over her shoulders and her lips swollen from my kisses.

I jerked up into a sitting position and wrapped my arms around her waist. Her legs automatically went around me, and the angle of my cock inside her changed and deepened.

Her breasts pressed against my chest and her forehead fell against my shoulder. Her fingernails cut into my back as we rocked together. I held her as tight as I could. I wanted as close to her as possible.

Tension built up inside me until my movements almost became desperate.

She moaned and made a sound, rubbing against me. I rolled, pinning her beneath me, and thrust deep. She splintered apart in that second, her cry filling the room. I followed right behind her as I spilled my seed.

Once I could think again, my arms were shaking with the effort to not crush her, so I rolled off and onto my back. "*Fuck*, Rimmel."

She was silent a moment, and I turned my head.

She was chewing on her bottom lip. "Did I do something wrong?"

A groan ripped out of me, and I rolled onto my side and tossed my arm across her waist. "Not one damn thing. I just hope this wasn't too much for your first time."

The air around us changed. Something intruded on our moment. Something dark. Something I didn't like.

"Rimmel?"

She looked away. "This wasn't my first time."

I felt like I was kicked in the gut, and tightness gripped my chest. I pushed it away because of the regret I heard in her voice. Maybe she thought I wouldn't want her as much if I knew someone else had her first.

It drove me insane to think of anyone else touching her, but I wasn't about to throw stones. It would be the pot calling the kettle black.

"Hey, it's okay," I said softly, pulling her against me. I kissed the top of her head without even thinking about it. "I'm not upset."

She buried her face in my chest and that feeling in the air pressed in on us. It seemed a little odd that this wasn't her first time. I had her pegged for a virgin almost since the moment we met. She was so damn shy and innocent at times. She hid herself in way too large clothes, she barely ever looked at people, and animals were her preferred company.

When I slid into her body, she was tight, so tight and small I didn't think twice about her being inexperienced. And when I pulled her on top of me, she said she'd never…

A sick feeling twisted me up inside.

My hand on her hip fisted and my breathing became a little labored.

She must have felt the sickness and anger radiating from my pores, because she looked up. I reached over and snagged her glasses off the side of the mattress and gently slid them onto her face. I wanted her to see me clearly. I wanted to see her clearly.

"Rimmel." I began, hating the thoughts in my head, the suspicions that would keep me up at night.

She tried to duck back into the safety of my arms, but I pulled back, unwilling to let her have what she wanted until I knew.

I caught her face in my palms and forced her to look at me. I stared into her eyes, which had turned wary and a little ashamed. "Did someone…?" I began forcing the words past the lump in my throat. "Did someone hurt you?"

Her lashes swept across her cheeks when she closed her eyes.

I made a sound and shook her slightly, and her eyes opened once more. "Did someone rape you?" I burst out, harsh and low.

She stiffened and hers eyes widened. "No!"

My entire body went weak. I sagged against the pillows and blew out a breath. "Fucking shit, Rimmel. I was already planning that scumbag's murder."

"I'm sorry," she whispered, her hand on my chest. I picked it up and kissed her fingers. She glanced away and then back. "I wasn't forced into anything I didn't want to do. But I was taken advantage of, and it hurt me."

I brushed the hair out of her face and swiped the pad of my thumb along her bottom lip. "Tell me."

"It was a long time ago." She hedged.

"Yet I still see the shadows in your eyes right now," I murmured.

She scooted up and laid her head on my chest. It scared me how good it felt to have her against me like this. How complete I felt. I tucked my arms around her and rested my chin on top of her head.

"I told you my mom died when I was eleven," she said.

"Yeah," I replied.

"She drowned." Her voice was quiet. "We had a pool. Everyone in Florida has a pool, it seems. One day when I was at school, she must have been in the backyard doing something and she somehow fell, hit her head, and fell into the pool. No one was home to help her."

And that explained why she skirted around the pool in the yard and looked at it with clear fear and hate.

"When I got off the bus, she wasn't waiting. So I walked home by myself. I searched through the house for her. I was yelling her name and she didn't answer. I thought she was playing some sort of game with me."

I felt her words like a knife to the heart. I pictured her at eleven, smaller than she was even now, with all that dark hair and wide eyes, calling out for her mother.

"I went out in the backyard…" She paused. "She was floating in the pool. The water had turned pink because of all the blood."

"Baby," I murmured, gathering her closer. Her hand curled around my bicep, and this fierce possessive feeling ripped through my chest. It was dangerous how strong the urge was to protect her from everything.

"I don't remember what happened much for a couple weeks after that. There was a funeral and an investigation. My dad had the pool destroyed and filled in with dirt. My grandmother stayed with us for a while, but eventually she had to get back to her job, my grandpa."

"I'm sure it was very hard for your entire family."

"Yeah, and I didn't make it any easier."

"You were a kid." I defended.

"After about a year of nothing but grief, life kind of had to go on. At least that's what it felt like. I was so angry I was expected to just go on and leave Mom in the past. My dad worked full time. He worked a lot to cover the bills and I think because it helped him deal. But it left me sort of on my own. I spent a lot of time with my grandmother on the weekends, but after school, I was alone until he came home."

I didn't know what to say so I just continued to hold her and listen. I never expected any of this. I would have never known by looking at her what kind of pain she'd had to endure.

"I started rebelling. I was only twelve, but I acted a lot older. I started wearing all this makeup and obsessing over my hair. I'd cut my shorts super short." She took a deep breath. I felt her lungs expand against my chest. "My dad didn't know what to do. I mean, I was a teenage girl who was acting out. I had a lot of anger and rage. We fought all the time. He would throw out my skimpy clothes and refused to buy me makeup. I'd find ways to get it anyway, and I'd hide it. I'd wait 'til he left and put it all on."

"You were so young," I murmured.

"Too young to realize what I was doing would affect me for years to come." Rimmel agreed. "I felt incredibly alone. There was this hole where my mom used to be, and my dad just kind of disappeared. I think part of me wanted his attention and that was how I got it. There were these older kids that lived down the block from me… a couple guys and a girl. They used to hang out all the time, so I started hanging out with them too."

My stomach tightened. I knew where this was going.

"One of the guys was interested in me. He gave me a lot of attention. Made me feel good. Less alone."

"You slept with him," I said. I just wanted to get it out there. I wanted to get it over with.

"Yeah, I did. He pressured me, and I gave in. He said he loved me." The hurt in her voice made me pissed all over again. "He didn't force me. I was thirteen and I gave him my virginity."

"How old was he?" I asked. I had to know.

"Seventeen."

I swore under my breath. That kid knew better. He damn well knew better.

"Afterward, he totally ignored me. I was confused and didn't understand why. I mean, they had been my friends and he was my *boyfriend.* Then they all just stopped talking to me. They avoided me and refused to hang out. Basically, he used me. He was nice and friendly. He said the things I wanted to hear so he could sleep with me. Once I gave him that part of myself, he turned his back. He didn't want anything to do with me."

How was I supposed to act here? What was I supposed to say? Because what I really wanted to do was yell and punch something, to pound down a couple of beers to dull the ache I felt for her. But that was selfish. She didn't need that. She'd opened herself up to me, let me in.

"After that, I stopped dressing slutty and wearing makeup. I started covering up and keeping to myself. I was ashamed. Once I stopped acting out, my dad and my relationship got a lot better. He started coming home before dinner, and we settled into a normal life. I studied all the time and spent a lot of time volunteering at the local shelter. I knew I wanted to become a vet, and because I studied so much and had good grades, I got a scholarship to Alpha. My dad didn't want me to move this far away, but this was the only free ride I was offered and I didn't want to saddle him with my college bills. Besides, part of me wanted to leave. I just wanted to get away."

It explained so much about her. Before, I only had half a portrait of her, but her words painted the rest.

Rimmel hit rock bottom at an age no person should. What was even more remarkable was she bounced back, and she did it so well.

"I need to kiss you," I whispered and dragged her up so she was lying across my chest. She yielded to me without the slightest hesitation.

I kissed her slowly and thoroughly until my body began to ache for more. When I looked into her eyes, they were fuzzy and unfocused. I pulled the glasses off her face and brushed another kiss across her lips. "How sore are you?" I rasped.

"Never too sore for you," she replied.

I rolled on top of her, clasped each of her hands in mine, and lifted them above our heads.

Then I made love to her with all the tenderness she deserved.

CHAPTER THIRTY-ONE

Go Wolves!
Show your team spirit by wearing blue and gold today!

...Alpha BuzzFeed

RIMMEL

I found something to like as a result of this cold autumn air. Warm apple cider. A vendor was selling it in the bleachers as the Wolves played down on the field.

A tall paper cup with a plastic lid was snug in my hands, and the sweet, spicy aroma wafted up through the open sipping portion and tickled my nose. I didn't think I would like it, but my fingers and nose were so cold I bought it just for the warmth.

The second the cinnamon sweet liquid burst over my tongue, I was in love. It was sort of like apple juice but better. It was thicker and had more of a bite because of whatever spices they mixed in. I took my time sipping it, enjoying the pleasure of being warmed from the inside out.

Beside me, Ivy was drinking hot chocolate and Missy had cider also. I was wrapped up in Romeo's hoodie, showing my support just like he wanted. Just recalling the way his sapphire eyes deepened when I stepped out with my lone pair of skinny jeans, boots, and his hoodie made my stomach summersault.

I knew it was possessive and probably some form of chauvinism that he wanted his name plastered across my back, but I didn't care. I liked it. I liked being claimed by Romeo.

The full crowd around us cheered and yelled, and I focused back on the field, my eyes going right to number twenty-four as he threw the ball and sent it spiraling down the turf. One of the other guys on his team snatched it out of the air, dodged a defender, and ran all the way to the end zone.

Everyone went crazy and jumped to their feet. People were chanting Romeo's name and the guys on the field celebrated the touchdown.

I stood there in the center of the enthusiastic crowd, holding my cider and wrapped up in his sweatshirt, so full of joy.

Ivy grabbed my arm and shook me. "Did you see that?" she exclaimed.

I grinned and cheered.

I never thought I would be someone to enjoy football. But the energy out here in the crowd, the intensity on the field… it made me see why Romeo loved it so much. This was definitely something I could get used to.

The game continued, and Ivy and Missy both leaned around to give me knowing grins. "Where were you all last night and all day today?" Ivy asked.

I pressed my lips together and smiled.

Ivy's eyes got wide. "I *knew* it!" She looked at Missy. "Didn't I call it?"

"She called it." Missy agreed.

"Called what?" I asked innocently, sipping the drink.

"Go ahead and play coy all you want, Rimmel," Ivy said, elbowing me. "But we all know what you spent all night doing."

I grinned again and felt a blush sweep my cheeks. Ivy giggled. Missy stood and called out for Braeden and gave him a little cheer.

I spent the entire night in Romeo's arms. In his bed. But it was him who was under my skin. I felt consumed by him. My insides were jittery from the thrill of being with him. It was almost like I drank fifty cups of coffee and my body was so keyed up it could run ten miles.

When I admitted to not being a virgin, to the age I was when I lost it, I thought he might look at me differently. I thought maybe it would turn him away. But it didn't. Baring that part of myself to him—*to anyone*—for the first time ever only pulled him closer.

The sheer bliss I felt in his arms and beneath his touch was something I'd never even dreamed about. He made love to me so many times I lost count. In the morning when I reached for him, he was there, and he made love to me again. I dozed in bed while he trained in the other room. He woke me by carrying me into the shower with him because he "needed help washing his back." Then we went for pancakes and he held my hand beneath the table.

When he drove me back to the dorm before he had to go get ready for the game, he made me promise to wear his sweatshirt. And then he asked me to be his.

I said yes of course. There was nothing I wanted more.

And now here I was, tracking his movements down on the field and giggling with my friends on the bleachers. I knew I would see him later and I knew I'd end up in his arms again.

"He really is the best player on the team," Ivy said. I followed her eyes to Romeo running out on the field.

She was right. He looked so at home there. Like the turf was in his blood. The guys all responded to him, looked to him for direction. He was basically the backbone of the team, the glue that held all the pieces together.

He was so many things to so many people.

A small pit of worry formed in the bottom of my stomach. I tried to push it away. I tried to ignore it, but it wasn't to be ignored. Romeo had a very full life, a very demanding life, and just like me, he had dreams of his own.

This weekend had been wonderful…

What if it was too good to be true?

What if he decided he didn't want a girlfriend after all? What if after the glow of a new relationship faded, so did he?

I shook my head against the thoughts. My brain was saying one thing, but my heart was saying something else.

He cares about you. I heard it with every beat of my pulse.

I was going to focus on that, because listening to my head hurt too much.

Almost as if Ivy heard the struggle going on inside me, she leaned over and whispered, "I've never seen him like this before."

I gave her a sideways glance. "Who?"

"Romeo," she replied. "We've been going to the same parties and I've been coming to all the games since freshman year. He's never shown this much interest in anyone before."

"Really?" I asked, truly wanting the truth.

She put her arm around my shoulders and gave me a one-armed hug. "Really."

I blew out an anxious breath as some of my worry went away. We went back to cheering for the Wolves along with the rest of the crowd. A little while later, I stood up to wave to the vendor with the apple cider. Mine was long gone and I desperately wanted another (the start of a new obsession? Possibly).

He waved back and motioned he would be over so I moved to sit back down. A creepy feeling crawled over the back of my neck, and I fidgeted with the glasses resting on my nose.

My wavy hair was in a high ponytail—Ivy said it looked perfect for the game—and I resisted the urge to tug it down and hide.

I looked around, trying to figure out what would cause me to feel so… *off* all of a sudden.

And then I saw him.

Zach was sitting in the bleachers, several rows over and up. I met his stare and something passed between us. Something I didn't like. He really hated Romeo and now by extension he hated me.

He had a large bruise on the side of his jaw and his bottom lip was slightly puffy with a red split on the side.

He didn't do anything really. He didn't mouth any foul words or snarl and show his teeth. He just sat there and stared… his eyes empty and cold.

A chill worked its way up my spine and crawled slowly over the rest of me.

"Everything okay?" Ivy asked, breaking the spell he seemed to cast.

I jerked away and blinked, trying to brush off the horrible sense of foreboding that wrapped around my neck. I faked a smile for Ivy and bobbed my head. "Great."

The vendor stepped up beside me and I paid for another cup of cider, and then he wandered away. The crowd cheered and I yelled along with them, not really sure what went down on the field.

I resisted the urge to turn and look at Zach again. When I couldn't anymore, I peeked over my shoulder where he was sitting.

He was gone.

CHAPTER THIRTY-TWO

Faculty Announcement
Professor Wiggly would like his toupee back. The guilty party should return it immediately to avoid punishment.
#ImNotLaughing #YesIAm
... Alpha BuzzFeed

ROMEO

I was the worst kind of ass there was.

I took her out for pancakes. I held her hand beneath the table. I made love to her. More than once.

None of it was a lie.

But didn't it start out that way?

I didn't seek her out. I was ordered to be tutored by her. Then I was challenged to sleep with her. I didn't think it was that big of a deal. I mean, it was just sex. So I made an effort to get to know her.

And that's when things got complicated.

My world seemed to collide with hers. We were two people with completely different lives, yet she pulled me in anyway. And now here I was, caught. Ensnared by a situation of essentially my own making.

How could I tell her about the initiation? After everything she told me, after everything she endured at such a young age? It made me sick to my stomach that there was any type of similarity between me and that seventeen-year-old punk that took her virginity.

But there didn't have to be. I'd already made up my mind. I chose her. The decision was finite even though I knew it might cost me a lot. I would do right by Rimmel. And I would do right by myself.

Starting now.

I arrived early in the locker room to get ready for the game. No one else was here yet, and I wanted to take advantage of it to have a talk with Coach.

He looked up from whatever he was doing at me hovering in the doorway and motioned at the seat in front of his desk. "Looks like you got something on your mind."

"I'm out of Omega," I said, deciding not to mince words.

His eyes lit with surprise and he tossed aside his pen. "You know your path into the NFL would be a hell of a lot easier if you weren't."

"Yeah," I said. "That's why I'm here."

He waited for me to continue.

"I'm gonna do it without Omega," I said. "I think I'm a good enough player. I want to know if you'll help me get scouts here when the time comes."

He studied me for long, measured moments. I didn't back down, not one inch.

"This about a girl?"

"No," I said. Because in reality it really wasn't. Yes, Rimmel played a factor in me not wanting to be associated with Omega, but this was about more than that.

This was about me blazing a path to what I wanted, to my end goal on my own terms. When I got to the NFL, it wouldn't be because I bent over and kissed some douche bag's ass for a couple years in college so he would make a couple phone calls.

I was better than that.

"What I'm hearing is there might be some cracks in Omega's foundation."

"Yeah," I agreed. "There might be." *And his name is Zach.*

"You keeping your nose clean?" he asked.

"Yes, sir," I said. *For now.*

He grunted like he heard my unspoken thought. "It takes a man with heavy balls to step away from something that could give him everything he wants."

I just sat there unflinching under his gaze. My mind was made up. He wasn't going to change it.

"I'll make the calls. I got a couple favors in my back pocket," he said finally.

I stood and held out my hand to shake with him. "Thanks, Coach. I won't let you down."

"Romeo," he said when I would have stepped out the door.

"Yeah?" I asked, turning back.

"This crack in the foundation, is that something I need to have the university step in and handle?"

"No," I said. "I can handle it."

"The Wolves are behind you, son."

I grinned. I knew they were. It's why I was able to walk away from such a jacked-up frat. I already had a family. And this family would accept Rimmel without a fight.

"And, Romeo!" he yelled after I'd stepped out of his sight. "Don't get caught!"

It was pretty much Coach's blessing to handle my business.

CHAPTER THIRTY-THREE

#TGIF
Don't do anything I wouldn't do.
#WhichISNothing

... Alpha BuzzFeed

RIMMEL

I don't like scary movies. I didn't think it was fun to be scared. Because of this, Halloween was never my favorite holiday. I would much rather stay home and hand out candy while something *not* scary played on the TV in the background.

Here at Alpha U, Halloween was just another reason to party. Every year the frat houses took turns putting together a haunted house, and students would swarm the place for a night of being scared and drinking beer.

I never went last year. I stayed in and studied, which was precisely what I planned to do this year.

Until Romeo showed up at my room.

He smiled that charming smile, kissed me dizzy, and the next thing I knew I was riding shotgun in the Hellcat on the way to the haunted house.

Braeden and Missy were still "having fun" and were currently in the backseat making out. Clearly she didn't have a problem with haunted houses… or PDA.

Romeo reached across the seat and tangled his fingers with mine. His grin was highlighted in the glow of the dash. "It's gonna be fun. You'll see."

I gave him a look that said I knew better, but his smile only got bigger. "You can hold on to me all you want."

I rolled my eyes. "If you wanted me to jump you, you could have just asked," I muttered. "You don't need to make me wanna pee my pants to get me in your arms."

He laughed, yet he still didn't turn around.

I resigned myself to my immediate future. I really hoped I didn't embarrass myself.

The haunted house was hosted by Beta House this year, and we had to pass by the Omega house to get there. I shivered a little thinking about the week before when I saw Zach at the game. I hadn't seen him since, and I never told Romeo about the odd way he made me feel. Romeo already hated the guy enough without me adding more gas to the fire.

The whole week had been drama free. Sure, I still got scathing looks from some jealous girls, but I ignored them. I never cared what people thought before and I wasn't about to start now.

We spent some time studying and even more time making out.

Ivy, Missy, and I had pizza and soda one night while Ivy tried to make sense of my wardrobe and put together some outfits she liked. She gave up after ten minutes and told me we had to go shopping. Up until now, shopping wasn't high on my list of priorities. 'Course, given where Romeo was dragging me off to, I sort of wished I'd made plans to go with her and that we were there tonight.

"I really don't like Halloween," I said, my stomach twisting a little as he parked the Hellcat. Creepy music and high screams pierced the air.

"It'll be fun," Missy said from beside the car. "The scariest thing you'll see in there is someone getting it on in the corner because they think no one can see."

Braeden and Romeo laughed. "Dude," Braeden said. "Do you remember last year when that guy from Phi K was having sex with one of the girls supposedly working the house?"

Everyone snickered but me. "What happened?" I asked.

"Her fake arm fell off and he starting screaming and ran off with his dick flapping in the wind."

I giggled. Missy grinned. "Bet he won't be coming back this year."

Romeo wrapped his arm around me and pulled me into his body. I snuggled closer just because I could. The closer the four of us drew to the house, the more nervous I became.

Braeden and Missy went ahead of us and stepped up to the line, but Romeo drew me back and turned so he was standing in front of me. "We can wait out here. We don't have to go in."

"Isn't that why you wanted to come? To go inside?" I asked.

He smiled. "Yeah, but I really just wanted to be with you. And here you are," he said, leaning down to kiss me.

Inside the house, someone screamed and laughter rang out. I drew back and took a breath. "Let's go in."

He raised his eyebrows. "Really?"

I chewed my lower lip and then nodded. College was supposed to be a time to have fun and do crazy things. Plus, I knew Romeo really wanted to go in. "Yeah. But only if you hold my hand."

"I won't let go." He promised.

Of course, the second Romeo stepped up in line, he got waved to the front. Part of me was really irritated because I wasn't sure I was ready, but the other part was glad because at least I wouldn't have time to stand there and doubt myself.

The first room we stepped into was completely dark with only a strobe light set up off to the side. It went off randomly, lighting up the space with bright, quick strobes of intense light. The way it went off made it nearly impossible to see. The room was filled with cobwebs and silky thread-like material draped around the room, hanging in every nook and cranny. And as we went, the fine, almost hair-like material caught on our hair and clothes and brushed against our skin.

Music full of moans and loud shudders filled my ears, and full-on goose bumps broke out across my arms and legs. My hand tightened around Romeo's and I squealed as I walked right into a thick web.

Romeo laughed and drew me back against his chest. His arms came around me from behind and I felt his warm breath against my ear. "I got you."

We continued into the next room, which was full of zombies that came dangerously close and smelled eerily of rotting flesh. Romeo laughed. I kept my eyes closed.

There was quite a bit of screaming in the rooms ahead of us, and I began to wonder if maybe this was my worst idea ever. As if he knew, Romeo's arms tightened around me and his shoulders hunched down, making me feel protected and secure.

I sighed a little and leaned into him as we passed into the next room. Someone jumped down from overhead, landing with a startling thud. I screeched and stumbled back. The man was dressed in a grim reaper's outfit, and when he lifted his head, his face was covered in a gruesome light-up mask.

He rushed us and I screamed again, turning in Romeo's arms and practically climbing up his chest. He took my weight with ease even as I scrambled. The reaper thingy rushed past us with a high-pitched squeal and rammed into Romeo's shoulder as he went.

Though he teetered on his feet just a bit, he managed to take the hit, my weight, and carry me all at once. I ducked my face into his neck and shuddered.

"That was pretty damn good," he rumbled in my ear.

My fingers curled into the hair at the base of his neck and he pressed a kiss to my head and started walking, carrying me through the next room.

I have no idea what was in it. I didn't dare look.

"One more room," he whispered in my ear as he continued to walk. I pulled my head back and blinked against the neon-green light and rolling fog, which I assumed was the result of some hidden machine.

Weird high-pitched music pierced my ears.

I leaned up and spoke in his ear. "Put me down."

He glanced at me. "I like carrying you."

I was tempted to settle back against him, but instead I shook my head. "No, if Braeden see's this, he'll never let me live it down."

Romeo's white teeth reflected the green of the room. He put me down and we began walking again. I stuck close to his side. The room was some kind of alien autopsy setting. There was blood splattered around everywhere, leaving dark spots in the green. The fog was thick and it made the back of my throat burn. Off to the sides of the room, long hands reached up out of the mist. They were three-fingered and had extremely large knuckles.

Against the wall was a large steel table with a body laid out and mad scientists and doctors standing around with all kinds of vile and tortuous instruments.

My stomach twisted a little because it all looked so sick and so real.

I pressed against Romeo and focused on the neon-orange EXIT just a few steps away. I stumbled and tripped, catching myself before I fell. Romeo reached out to steady me.

"Stupid pants," I muttered. I really did need to go shopping with Ivy. Falling over my clothes was annoying.

I stepped forward, back to Romeo's side, but I felt resistance again. I made a frustrated sound and looked down at my pant leg, thinking the wide hem had gotten stuck on something.

It wasn't stuck on something.

It was stuck on *someone*.

A large deformed-looking hand was wrapped around my ankle. I jerked my leg up, as if to shake it off, but it only grabbed harder. I kicked out and yelled, but it wasn't enough to dislodge its hold.

Panic flooded through my system like ice water, and I reached out for Romeo, who was turning around to help.

Something seemed to materialize out of the heavy fog. Something covered from head to toe in some scary as hell alien costume. It had large black eyes, a bald head, and a scary grinning mouth.

It lunged as I screamed to warn him. He jerked in surprise as it basically leapt on his back. The hand on my ankle yanked, and I fell to the ground. I cried out in pain as my hip hit the floor and took the brunt of my fall.

I scratched at the floor, trying to crawl away. Whatever was in the fog had me by both ankles now.

"Romeo!" I screamed.

"Rimmel," he called back.

I glanced up as I was being dragged away and the fog swallowed me whole.

"No!" I screeched and started kicking and fighting with everything I had. I heard whoever had me grunt in pain, and I struggled even harder. One of the hands dragging me disappeared, and I heard someone yell, "Get her!"

I opened my mouth to scream bloody murder, but something was stuffed between my lips, a rag of some kind.

Hands grabbed me by the wrists and bound them to the floor as more hands did the same with my feet.

Panic was full-fledged now as I was being held down to the ground, lost amid a sea of fog in a dark, loud room.

I used my tongue to try and force the rag out of my mouth, fighting and working my jaw and turning my head to dislodge it.

A dark figure appeared over me, straddled my waist, and leaned down so we were face to face. My eyes widened and my heart about burst when I saw it was the person in the reaper's costume, the one with the scary as shit mask.

He laughed, a high-pitched, evil cackle, and my knees started to shake. He was practically lying across me as I struggled and was held down.

The freaky mask sneered down at me even as he kept his body low, like he was afraid if he moved too much, the fog wouldn't conceal us.

"Ask your boyfriend why he's really with you. Ask him about *initiation*."

I stopped struggling and looked up, not understanding what the hell was happening.

"A guy like him doesn't date a nerd like you unless he has a reason. Maybe you should ask him what that reason is."

I wanted to yell at him, but the stupid rag in my mouth made it impossible.

"Rimmel!" Romeo roared somewhere close by.

My eyes rolled toward the sound of his voice, and the creepy thing on top of me grabbed my hand and squeezed my jaw until I cried out soundlessly.

"Ask him about the initiation. About the rush. He's only using you," the masked person growled.

And then the weight on my chest was gone. The hands that held my ankles and wrists were no longer there.

I shot to my feet and ripped the rag out of my mouth. I gasped and fell to the side, knocking into some decoration next to me. It made a loud sound, but I barely noticed.

I was shaking so badly I could barely stand. My throat was burning and my eyes were watering. My jaw hurt where he squeezed me and my one wrist felt raw.

"Jesus!" Romeo cried and scooped me up against him. I collapsed into his arms and gave him every ounce of my weight. "What the hell happened?" he demanded.

I wrapped my arms around his neck and shuddered.

I was aware of him walking quickly, but I didn't realize we'd left the house until I felt the cold night air against my skin.

I lifted my head and breathed it in gratefully.

Braeden and Missy rushed up to Romeo's side. "What's going on?" Braeden asked, his voice concerned.

"I'm not sure," Romeo said quickly. "We got separated. Some guy jumped me."

"What the fuck?" Braeden burst out.

"Rimmel got pulled into all that fog," he said. Then I felt his head tilt toward me. "Are you hurt? Did you fall?"

I glanced up at him through watery, burning eyes. "I want to go home."

His entire body tensed, but he only nodded. I sank back into him as we went to the car. No one spoke on the way back to the dorms, not a single word. I could feel Romeo's concerned gaze on me as we drove through the darkened streets.

I only gazed out the window, my eyes not seeing anything at all.

But I could still hear that voice telling me to ask Romeo, to ask about initiation.

I had a very bad feeling I wasn't going to like the answer.

CHAPTER THIRTY-FOUR

ALPHA U 101:
Never get between a guy and his girl. Especially if you're an asshole.

... Alpha BuzzFeed

ROMEO

One minute she was plastered to my side and the next she was jerked away. I didn't think much of it at first. I mean, I just figured it was her being adorably clumsy as usual.

But when I turned to help her, I was jumped. Attacked from behind. He almost brought me down out of sheer surprise, but in the end, I held my ground.

He wasn't that big. I must have outweighed him by a lot.

He clung to my back like a stupid spider monkey, and I almost laughed because it was obvious he had no idea he wouldn't be able to take down someone twice his size.

I reached around my back and filled my fist with his costume. With one hard tug, I pulled him over my shoulder and drove him into the floor.

He rolled and moaned, but he didn't get up.

I turned back to get Rimmel, knowing she was probably scared shitless and I'd never get her in one of these damn houses again, but she was gone.

At first I didn't panic. I knew the fog made it hard to see.

But then seconds stretched longer and I still didn't see her. I still didn't hear her.

I'd felt adrenaline pump through my body more times than I could count. I was used to a rush, the fast pace of football… but this was different. I'd not felt this before.

Fear, dark and sticky, wrapped around my chest as I searched and searched and my eyes came up empty.

When she didn't call out for me, I got scared. I punched out a couple guys and threw someone into the wall while searching through the fog for her.

And then suddenly she was there, stumbling around shaken and dazed. When I put my arms around her, she trembled so badly I knew she wouldn't be able to stand.

She'd barely said two words.

That dark and sticky fear still clung to me. It seemed to get harder to shake the quieter she became. I waited until I dropped off Missy and Braeden at his truck near her dorm before I pulled near the back of the lot and shut off the car.

"Hey," I said soft. "They scared you bad, huh?"

She nodded.

"I'm sorry, baby." I reached across the seat and put an arm around her. She stiffened.

Something cold unfurled deep in my chest.

"Rimmel?" I asked.

She turned to me then. The moonlight reflected off her glasses and her eyes were wide behind the lenses.

"Whatever happened with initiation?" she said.

The random question threw me at first. I couldn't understand why she would bring this up. "Initiation?" I asked.

"Yeah. The frat you were rushing. Did you get in?"

"No," I said, caution in my tone. "Why are you asking about this?"

"They dragged me into that fog," she said, her voice breaking. "They pinned me down to the floor."

"*Who?*" I growled as the edges of my eyesight began to tinge with red.

"They were wearing masks," she said. "I couldn't see. He sat on me. The one with the scary mask, the one who tried to knock you over."

"He sat on you?" I repeated. Anger so calm rose up in me that if I'd been thinking straight, I would have been scared.

She nodded. "He told me to ask you about initiation. About rush. About why you're really with me."

What. The. Fuck.

It was all almost too much to process at once. I went from thinking she was the victim of some stupid prank to realizing she was targeted and basically attacked. She was clearly beyond scared, and now she was looking at me like she didn't know me at all.

"Why would he say that?" she asked, her voice small.

Because he wanted to get to me. To take something he knew I wanted. I would bet my Hellcat it was Zach behind that mask tonight. "I don't know." I lied as a new kind of fear came over me.

I still hadn't told her about the initiation and that she was the chosen girl for me to get into bed. After she told me about losing her virginity, after everything she'd been through that made her who she was, I couldn't. I was afraid. Afraid the truth would cost me. Afraid she would realize I was no better than the guy who stole her virginity.

I knew I had to tell her.

I wanted to wait for initiation to pass so I could prove to her that she wasn't just some dare. I figured once she saw I wasn't a member of Omega, she would believe me.

Induction into the frat was tomorrow night.

Zach beat me to the punch.

"Romeo," she said, pulling her knees into her chest and looking so small sitting there in the leather seat. "Was I some kind of initiation for Omega?"

I closed my eyes. It was a direct question.

"Remember when you told me a while ago that I could ask you anything and you would give it to me straight, even if the answer was something I wouldn't like?"

Oh, I remembered. I regretted those words right now.

I opened my eyes and looked at her. "Yes," I whispered.

"Yes, you remember, or yes, I was some kind of initiation?"

"Rimm—"

"The truth," she said, cutting me off.

"Both." I admitted.

Her sharp intake of breath was like a knife to the heart. "So what was it?" Her voice was flat, devoid of emotion. It was the worst sound I'd ever heard. "Were you supposed to date me?"

"It doesn't matter because I dropped out of the frat," I said.

"What was it?" She pressed.

My hand curled around the steering wheel and tightened. "To sleep with you."

Her body jerked like I slapped her.

"You gotta understand. It was before I got to know you. I dropped out. I told them I wouldn't do it."

"But you did." Her voice was so quiet and calm it was chilling. "You did sleep with me."

"Not becau—"

"You used me," she whispered, pain filling her voice. "Did you laugh with your friends behind my back?" she accused. "Did you give them a play-by-play of everything we did? I shared part of myself with you I've never shared with anyone."

"I'm sorry." It was the most pathetic thing to say, but I didn't know what would make what I did okay.

Nothing. Nothing would make this okay.

"Please listen to me, Rimmel," I said, reaching for her hand. She pulled away. "Please."

She just stared at me. I could see the unshed tears shimmering in her eyes.

"I care about you. I dropped out of rush. You're more important to me."

The silence stretched between us. And then she spoke.

"I wish I could believe you." She reached for the handle and pushed open the door.

"Wait," I said. She paused but didn't turn back around. "I swear to God, everything I've ever said I feel about you is real. Please believe me."

Her shoulders slumped like she was carrying a weight so heavy it was crushing her. "I need time to think."

"I can give you that." I promised, even though everything in me was shouting no.

She slipped from the car and ran to the dorm. I sat there for a long time even after she went inside.

I knew I should be angry. I should be full of rage at Zach and what he might have just cost me.

But I couldn't summon the anger.

All I felt was pain.

CHAPTER THIRTY-FIVE

Can anyone else feel the trouble in the air? #SomethingIsGoingDown

... Alpha BuzzFeed

RIMMEL

I cried myself to sleep that night.

He hurt me.

CHAPTER THIRTY-SIX

ROMEO

She wouldn't answer my calls.

Two days without hearing her voice felt like an eternity.

The hollow feeling in my chest was constant, but even so, the anger came. It lit me up from the inside out. Like fireworks exploding in a night sky. I asked around, called in favors. Rumor was it was Zach who attacked Rimmel, but rumors couldn't be proved.

But even if I couldn't prove what he did, he still had to pay.

I wasn't just going to turn my cheek and let him hurt Rimmel and take shots at me.

I'd told Coach I wasn't going to handle the corrupt behavior soiling the name of his very own frat. I'd let it fall to the backburner because I'd been too caught up in Rimmel.

But it was time to end this. It was time to show Zach I wasn't to be fucked with.

Using some of the friends I had in convenient places, I set a plan into motion.

And then I went to the dean.

He was all too willing to listen to the new information that had come to light. He was even extremely disappointed to learn of such stark disrespect coming from those he still considered his brothers.

Not more than an hour later, I found myself on the doorstep of Omega, waiting to be let in.

The shock that registered on Jack's face when he opened the door made me smile smugly. "Can I come in?"

"Members only," he said with a sneer.

I flattened my palm on the door and shoved, swinging it wide. It slammed against the wall, rattling the old window nearby.

Footsteps sounded on the stairs as several members came rushing to see where the sound came from. They all stopped when they saw me.

Zach appeared from the back of the house, and when our eyes locked, he smiled.

I wanted to knock out his teeth so badly that I actually took a threatening step forward.

"What are you doing here?" he spat. "Come to grovel for a place in the house? Sorry for what you gave up?"

The fucking arrogance of this guy was unmatched. I stalked toward him and he slunk against the wall. I shoved myself up against him, pinning him with my hard chest.

"How's it feel to be pinned down and helpless?" I whispered.

His eyes widened and he shook his head.

"I know it was you," I rumbled. "This is your payback."

"You can't prove shit," he tossed out, but his eyes held fear.

"You're right. I can't prove you were the guy in the mask the other night. But I can prove something else."

Confusion filled his face and he curled his lip at me. I raised my fist, desperate to strike him, and the look wiped off his face. "Touch her again and it will make today look like a kindergarten field trip."

I shoved away from him, and he cowered once more into the wall. Members had gathered all around and were watching the unfolding scene in silence.

I looked at the door, and right on time, the dean stepped through.

"Zachary," he said, his voice filled with authority.

"Dean," he said, straightening from the wall. "Romeo burst in here and threatened me."

"I didn't hear any threats," he said and addressed the crowd. "Did anyone else hear Romeo threaten your president?"

No one said a word.

Zach's face turned red with anger.

"I'm here today because of a recent tip that was brought to campus police," Dean continued and then waved for someone outside. Two uniformed officers stepped into the foyer.

"What kind of tip?" Zach said. "I can assure you it's a lie."

"Yes, well, I agree," the dean said. "I mean, it's utterly preposterous that the president of the most prestigious frat at Alpha U would steal something from me, an Omega alumni, of all people."

"Exactly," Zach said, relaxing a little because he thought the dean believed him.

"But I still have to follow up. Campus rules, you understand."

"Of course," Zach said and waved him off. "Do what you need to do."

"Gentleman." The dean motioned for the officers, and the guys on the stairs parted for them as they ascended.

Zach sneered at me when they were gone, pushing off the wall and coming to stand in front of me. "You're going to pay for this."

I smiled. It wasn't a friendly display of teeth. "We'll see."

It didn't take long for the police and the dean to descend the stairs, looking solemn.

"Dean," Zach said and stepped forward. "I'm sorry to have wasted your time today."

The dean sighed and held out the nameplate that had come from his office. He nodded at the officer to his right, and he produced a pair of handcuffs.

"You're under arrest for theft of campus property," he said as he slapped the metal around a very shocked Zach's wrists.

Zach exploded into a flurry of movement. He tried to knock the officer away all the while screaming that he'd been set up.

"It was Romeo!" he roared, kicking and fighting. "He's the one who did it!"

The dean looked at him calmly. "How would you explain how my nameplate got into *your* room, in *your* closet, then?"

Zach's eyes bulged. "He must have put it there!" he screamed.

"How would I have done that?" I asked calmly. "I don't live here. I'm not an Omega. I don't have access to this house."

Zach started screaming about a traitor in the house and betrayal and loyalty. I really didn't know. I stopped listening as the cops hauled him away and shoved him in the back of the cop car.

When he was gone, I faced the dean. "I'm sorry about this, sir. I hoped I wasn't right."

"Yes. Me too. Thank you, Roman, for doing the right thing."

We shook hands and he left, closing the front door behind him.

The stunned silence in the room was like music to my ears. But it didn't last very long.

Everyone started clapping.

After a few moments, I held up my hand and the group quieted. "Omega used to be the best frat on this campus. It was exclusive and cool. Bring it back. The trash has been taken out." I saw a bunch of people nodding in agreement.

Trent was standing nearby, watching the unfolding scene.

"I think a good place to start is with a new president. Someone who would actually bring a good rep to this house."

Everyone was listening so I pointed to Trent. "I know I'm not a member, but if I was, I would nominate Trent Mask. Who better to lead this frat into a new beginning but one of our own Wolves?"

Trent looked surprised but quickly recovered and smiled. He stepped forward and held out his hand. I shook it. "I don't think anyone would object to you being inducted into Omega," he said.

Everyone cheered.

I smiled. "Thanks, but I think I'll pass."

"I figured you'd say that." He nodded.

I said my good-byes and pounded a couple fists on my way out the door.

It was a good day.

Zach got his.

Now all I needed was to get what was mine.

CHAPTER THIRTY-SEVEN

#PoliceReport
Oh how the mighty have fallen.
#OmegaNeedsaNewPresident
#Karma #Handcuffs

... Alpha BuzzFeed

RIMMEL

Four days. I'd been existing for four days.

Romeo called. He texted. He left messages. I ignored them all.

I went to class. I hid in my dorm.

I went back to not combing my hair and pants that made me trip every time I took a step.

Ivy tried to cheer me up, she tried to talk to me, but I pushed her away too. I was beyond miserable. I just wanted him back.

But I was scared. Scared to get hurt again. Scared to love someone so much that it gave them power over me.

On the fourth day, Michelle called. She was worried I hadn't been by. It wasn't like me to just not show up. Instantly, I felt guilty. It wasn't Murphy or any of the animals' fault that I was a hot mess. I lied and told her I'd been sick. Then I promised I'd stop by later in the day.

I'd been reluctant to go, but once I was standing on the sidewalk, looking at the familiar building, something inside me eased. Murphy would make me feel better. Murphy always made me feel better. I was going to owe him extra scratches to make up for not being here lately.

I walked into the cat room, intent on seeing Murphy and just being with someone that didn't have some hidden agenda. As soon as I walked in, some of the cats came to the door of their shelters and I stopped to scratch behind their ears.

Tears pricked the backs of my eyes because sometimes it hurt to see all these innocent souls all caged up. Most of the time I was able to focus on the fact these cats had a dry, warm place to live with plenty of food to eat. And honestly, most of them never spent more than a month here before being adopted out into loving homes.

Maybe that was why I felt so connected to Murphy. He never got adopted out. Once he got close, but they decided to bring home another cat. That's how I felt.

I'd been so close to having something with Romeo. Something real.

Or so I thought.

I went to the corner and leaned down to Murphy's shelter, peering in. "Murphy," I said softly.

The cage was empty.

He wasn't curled in the back like always.

I fell back onto my butt as I blinked and stared into the bare space. After a moment, I scrambled up and checked the other cages, thinking someone accidentally put him in the wrong one.

He wasn't anywhere in this room.

Michelle walked in and smiled. "Hey, Rimmel. So glad to see you today."

"Where's Murphy?" I said, not bothering with pleasantries.

She frowned.

The bottom of my stomach hollowed out and an ache began in my chest.

"I thought you knew…" She trailed off when it became painfully obvious by the look on my face that I had *no* idea.

"Murphy," I said again.

"He got adopted."

I swayed a little on my feet and reached out to steady myself against the wall.

"Rimmel." Michelle came forward.

I held out my hand, palm out, to stop her. "When?"

"Just the other day." She seemed distressed.

She should be. Someone should have told me. Someone should have said something. He was *my* cat.

And now he was gone.

* * *

"Rimmel, honey, I thought you knew when a good home found him, he would go. We couldn't keep him here until you graduated."

I knew that. I did. It was logical.

I wasn't feeling very logical right now.

Tears burned my eyes and my throat hurt from the effort to swallow. "I understand," I said, my voice hoarse. I looked up at her. "He went to a good home?"

"Oh yes, he did."

I nodded. "I just remembered something I have to do on campus. I can't stay." I didn't wait for her to say anything. Once I was out in the main room by myself. I rushed toward the door and threw it open.

The cold air wrapped around me, but I ignored it. For once, I didn't feel its sting. Everything had been fine before. Life was good… It was steady.

And then I met Romeo.

I fell for his sparkling eyes and easy smile.

I made a couple friends and I started to build a life, a life I wanted. A life I liked.

And then it all changed. I let it all be ripped away.

Yes, I still had Ivy and Missy, but if I were honest with myself, I would admit I was afraid once they realized Romeo wasn't coming back, they wouldn't want to be my friend anymore.

Romeo was gone.

Murphy was gone.

I leaned against the brick of the building and lowered my head until it almost touched my chest. Silent, fat tears dripped from my eyes and fell against my shirt.

It hurt. It hurt more than I remembered it could, more than I ever thought it would. This wasn't the first time I'd been used. At least this time I was older, wiser, and I had my life together. So why, why did it feel so much worse?

Because I loved him.

Because he hadn't used me. Not really. Maybe at first he set out to, but then it changed. We both changed.

And now we were both being punished.

I cried harder, deep, low sobs ripping from my throat. I sagged against the building because I didn't know where else to go.

Familiar strong arms found their way around me and eased me away from the wall. I was pulled against a wide, solid chest that radiated warmth. I knew who it was. I would know the feel of him anywhere.

I stiffened and my tears paused.

He put his hand against the back of my head and tucked my face farther into his chest. Something broke inside me.

I started crying again, harder this time, as my arms wound around his waist. He was the only one I could show how vulnerable I felt right now. He was the only one I wanted. He was the reason I was crying, but he was here. He'd come here because maybe he knew just how bad I hurt.

I pulled back and his thumbs brushed the tears off my face. I sniffled and he tilted my head up, gripping it firmly between his palms.

His sapphire eyes burned into mine.

I saw.

I saw he really did know. He knew exactly how I felt because it was mirrored back at me in his gaze.

Still holding my face, he claimed my mouth. He kissed me slowly, keeping his lips firmly on mine. Emotion so intense swirled around us that more tears leaked from my eyes and mixed with our kiss.

"Please," he said, hoarse, his lips still against mine. "Just talk to me. Please."

I was too weak in that moment to tell him no. I nodded. He kissed me again before tucking me into his side and depositing me into his car parked at the curb.

We drove in silence to his place. I stared out the window and didn't look at him once. I wanted so desperately to reach out and touch him. To link our fingers together, to feel his heat. I denied myself because I didn't know what was to come. He already owned too much of me. How could I give him more?

I waited behind him as he unlocked the door. When it was open, he gestured for me to go in first. I walked past him stiffly, avoiding any kind of accidental touch.

Sunlight poured through the blinds. It was bright and inviting and it made me hurt more. I bypassed the living room and went toward the kitchen, hoping it wouldn't be so damn sunny and cheerful.

When I passed by the couch, my eyes went ahead of me to the kitchen island.

My feet stuttered.

I stopped and stared.

I blinked and stared again.

Romeo was standing just behind me, and I glanced around with a question in my eyes. He smiled.

Fresh tears welled as I surged forward toward the black, one-eyed cat sitting on the island, swishing his tail back and forth. "Murphy." I choked and scooped him up and against my chest. I buried my face in his silky fur as he started to purr.

I carried him to the couch and sat down. He curled up in my lap like he knew that was where he belonged.

"You adopted him," I said when Romeo sat on the coffee table in front of me.

"You love him," he said simply. Like that was all he needed to know.

"But you'll have to take care of him. Feed him. Give him water. Change the litter box."

"Thought maybe you'd want to help."

I looked up. Our eyes locked.

"What if I say no?" I asked. "What happens to Murphy then?"

He shrugged. "He's a cool cat. I'll keep him. He can watch football with me on Sundays."

I couldn't help but smile at the image that cast in my head.

"You'd really do that?" I whispered.

He leaned forward, resting his elbows on his knees. "Yes." Then his stoic eyes turned playful and his smile came out. "You wanna watch football with me on Sundays too?"

I sighed heavily and sat Murphy aside. "It's not that simple," I said, getting up and pacing the room.

"Why?"

I faltered.

"Because I used you?" he said, standing. "I didn't. Not really. The second I got to know you, the second I started having real feelings for you, I made a choice. It might have taken me a while to really admit that choice and to act on it, but it was made."

I stared at him, at the way his muscles moved when he talked.

"I'm not in the frat, Rimmel. I told them to shove it. I never took a picture of us in bed together, which they wanted. Hell, as far as everyone knows, we've never had sex. I've been loyal to *you*. I still want *you*."

I sucked in a breath. I hadn't expected this. The cat. *The fight.*

He was fighting to keep me.

"You know what I think?" he asked, shoving a frustrated hand through his hair. "I think you're scared. I think you're terrified to love me."

I winced. His words hit their mark.

"You're scared I'm going to disappear. Like your mom, like assholes in your past, hell, even your dad." He surged forward and grabbed me by the shoulders. "I'm not going anywhere. You can push me away all you want, but it won't stop me from loving you."

I sucked in a breath.

His voice gentled and his touch became more like a caress. "I love you," he whispered.

"Romeo…"

"I love your glasses, your clumsiness, your wild hair, even the way you snort when you laugh." He smiled. "I love you in spite of yourself, Rim. Can't you love me in spite of myself?"

I couldn't help it. I smiled.

"You do come with a lot of baggage." I sighed. "You're impossibly good-looking, terrible at math, and you like to drink that swill you call beer." I mock shuddered.

He smiled, but I saw the relief in his eyes.

"Me being good-looking is a bad thing?" he teased.

"You have a lot of options," I said seriously. "I'm not the best one."

"No." He agreed. "You're not."

Geez, he could have said it a little nicer.

"You're the *only* one."

Oh, well, that was much better.

"I'm sorry for not telling you about rush right away. I'm sorry for everything I did to hurt you. Now please put me out of my misery, Rim. Tell me you'll be mine. For keeps."

"For keeps?" I whispered.

He nodded once. "No take backs."

I slipped my arms up around his neck and smiled. "No take backs."

He groaned, scooped me off my feet, and carried me into the bedroom.

He was every #nerd's fantasy.

But he wasn't a fantasy.

He was mine.

#TheEnd

... Alpha BuzzFeed

#Nerd
Slow- cooker Apple cider

Ingredients
1 bottle of apple cider (64 ounce)
3 cinnamon sticks
1 tsp whole allspice
1 tsp whole cloves
1/3 cup brown sugar

Rimmel Approved!

Directions
Combine cider, cinnamon sticks and sugar in slow cooker. Wrap cloves and allspice in cheesecloth and place inside. Bring to a boil then reduce heat and simmer on low for one hour.

Garnish with apple slices, cinnamon sticks & whipped cream!

Want more of
Romeo & Rimmel?

Their story continues with

#HATER

Winter 2015

Turn the page for a tease!

The Hashtag Series

#HATER

The Hashtag Series #2

It started with unspoken animosity. The bitter bite of jealousy. And now it's full-blown hate.

It was during my first football game that I first felt the chill of hate. I looked it right in the eyes and felt its sticky tentacles reach out for me. I'd never experienced something so cold and empty before.

The effect of that look lingered, like an unspoken promise, long after it was gone.

Becoming a couple, becoming the other half of a campus celebrity, wasn't easy. I let down walls that were guarding my heart, and he looked past my glasses and accident-prone tendencies. Romeo and I are an unlikely match, a #nerd and a jock. But we made it.

And we're happy.

Zach doesn't want us to be happy. He wants Romeo to pay for getting him kicked out of Omega and for the night he spent in jail. He's going to use anything and everything he can to get his revenge.

Including me.

As the weather on campus grows cold and the days darken, revenge becomes the center of someone's life, and the happiness Romeo and I have worked so hard for is threatened.

I can't help but worry that our love is going to be overshadowed by hate.

AUTHOR'S NOTE

I don't even know where to start with this book. Ha-ha. #*Nerd* was/is truly a #LaborOfLove. The book idea for this series came out of nowhere. It was unexpected and unplanned (at first), but I think maybe all the best things are.

It started really with an image. An outtake photo meant, I think, really as a joke. Regina Wamba (my cover designer and owner of Mae I Design) posted the photo on the front cover of this book on her Facebook page for fun one day. I felt like I was starring in one of those vegetable juice commercials. You know, the one where someone gets smacked in the head and then they say: "Someone should've had their V-8!"

Yep. That was me.

The second I saw that picture, I smiled. Like a genuine smile. And I wanted to tell that girl's story so badly that it basically took over my brain. I mean, she is so adorably nerdy. What was her story? And who would be able to appreciate her?

Also, when I looked at that photo, I got the feeling of cool nights, fall leaves, football, apple cider… basically college.

And so the entire world of #Nerd was born.

I was intimidated as much as I was excited. Most of you know I've been writing the *Take It Off* series for a year now and it is contemporary romance, but I don't think I quite realized how suspense driven those books are. I love suspense. I love the way it drives the plot and keeps the reader on the edge of their seat. But #Nerd wasn't to be suspense. It was basically straight new adult contemporary romance. I found myself asking, *What will drive the plot?* It took a lot of thought, but the answer came. It was the characters' turn to drive the plot, and I think Romeo and Rimmel did that. At least I hope so.

I planned a lot for this one, more so than some of my most recent others. I built an entire fictional world because I wanted the freedom to do what I wanted. I came up with the college name, the frat names, the mascot. I decided to set it in Maryland because that's where I grew up and I thought it would be a great setting for the book. As I started writing, I felt like it needed something, something more… something that would be fun and fresh but also maybe add just a touch to the story. That's where the Alpha App notifications came in. The #BuzzBoss was created, and I decided to post Alpha BuzzFeed notifications at the beginning of every chapter. Some honestly just made me laugh out loud. There are thirty-eight notifications in this book, so it took some time and effort to create them all and decide where to place them. I think they turned out great. I hope they gave you a laugh.

#FunFact: this series was originally supposed to be a series of standalones all set in the college world. But the more I wrote, the more I fell in love. The more I couldn't let Romeo and Rimmel go. And so I decided I would do *#Hater* and *#Player* about them as well. *#Selfie* will still be part of the series, and I'm sure Romeo and Rimmel will be around, but I'm toying with the idea of making that a book for Braeden. I'd love to hear reader thoughts on that.

Bascially, #IFellInLove, #RomeoGivesMeButterflies, and #RimmelRocks. For lack of a better way to put it: #IWantToGoToAlphaU!

I've existed in this story for weeks now. I go to sleep with it on the brain and wake up with it being my first thought. I know it's sort of a departure from some of my other work, but that's also what makes it special.

I'm honestly not sure why this one grabbed me so completely, but it did. I sincerely hope you love this book as much as I do.

I'd like to #Thank the people who worked with me tirelessly to get this book ready for release. I did NOT do this alone. Regina Wamba created the cover and did such a good job. We had the same vision for this book. Fresh, new, and fun. Cassie McCown, my book doctor, stepped up to the plate to make this book read as good as it could. She put a lot of her time and energy into the edits, and for that I couldn't be more grateful. My #WritingBesties Amber Garza and Cameo Renae listened to me talk almost daily about this book, plot this book, and let me bounce ideas off them. #LoveYouLadies. Stephanie Garza, another fellow #WritingBuddy, totally tossed ideas around with me, helped me work out plot points, and inspired me to make this book the best it could be. When I would fall off track, she would be there to remind me I had work to do.

And finally, I'd like to acknowledge my husband Shawn, who also got on board and totally supported me on this one. He's always supportive of my writing, but he took a special interest in this project. He read it as I was writing it. I would send him chapters as I finished. He isn't much of a reader so it was really cool to see him sitting and reading. He says Rimmel is his #BookGirlfriend and that he wanted Romeo to break up with her so I could write him into the story so he could have her.

Not sure if I should be offended or charmed by that?

#I'llGoWithCharmed.

Thank YOU for reading this book, for being part of Romeo & Rimmel's world, and for all the incredible support you (the readers) have shown me along the way. This one is going to stick with me long after I close the cover.

#HappyReading!

XOXO ~ CAMBRIA

Cambria Hebert is a bestselling novelist of more than twenty books. She went to college for a bachelor's degree, couldn't pick a major, and ended up with a degree in cosmetology. So rest assured her characters will always have good hair. She currently resides in North Carolina with her children (human and furry) and her husband, who is a United States Marine.

Besides writing, Cambria loves a caramel latte, staying up late, sleeping in, and watching movies. She considers math human torture and has an irrational fear of chickens (yes, chickens). You can often find her running on the treadmill (she'd rather be eating a donut), painting her toenails (because she bites her fingernails), or walking her chorkie (the real boss of the house).

Cambria has written within the young adult and new adult genres, penning many paranormal and contemporary titles. Her favorite genre to read and write is romantic suspense. A few of her most recognized titles are: *Text*, *Torch*, *Tryst*, *Masquerade*, and *Recalled*.

Cambria Hebert owns and operates Cambria Hebert Books, LLC.

You can find out more about Cambria and her titles by visiting her website: http://www.cambriahebert.com.

Lightning Source UK Ltd.
Milton Keynes UK
UKOW01f0824230916

283653UK00004B/161/P